Cleansed

True Tree Press
TrueTreePress@gmail.com

Cleansed by G. S. Scott
The True Tree Chronicles: Book One

Cover by Colleen Nye
Editing by Gidget Jordan
Formatting by Colleen Nye

Published by: True Tree Press
PO BOX 81168 Lansing, MI 48908
TrueTreePress@gmail.com

This is a work of fiction. All characters and situations appearing in this work are fictitious. Any resemblance to real persons, living or dead, or personal situations is purely coincidental.

For Sarah

Chapters

The True Tree Chronicles:

I am the True Tree.

The Mother of all.

I am the wellspring from which all life flows.

From my branches and roots,

come the seeds and pods of all forms of life.

Wherever there is life, I am there.

Wherever there is death, I am there.

Life and death are one.

What is returned to me in death

shall be brought forth once more into life.

I am the mighty.

I am the meek.

I am the one.

I, am singular.

I, am True.

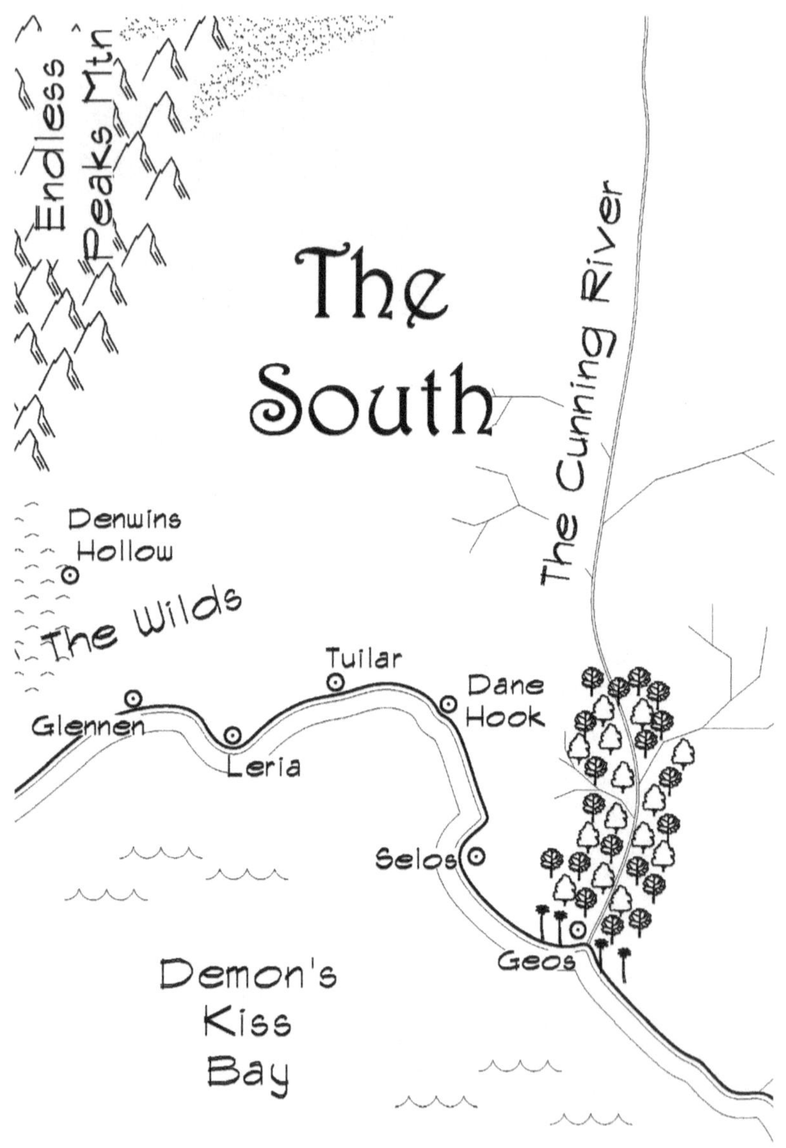
Endless Peaks Mtn
The Cunning River
The South
Denwins Hollow
The Wilds
Tuilar
Dane Hook
Glennen
Leria
Selos
Demon's Kiss Bay
Geos

Chapter 1
Abandoned

(505 years after the start of the Reign of
Chaos -R.C.-)

Dirge lay on the ground, dazed. Above, tumultuous, roiling clouds of gray, red, and black stretched to the horizon. Black lightning crackled from cloud to cloud, like a dreadful spider's web, before coalescing and stabbing into the earth. The ground shook and exploded, vomiting out dirt and rock, hurling bodies in all directions. Long, thin funnel clouds stretched out like grotesque, gnarled fingers tearing the land asunder. The funnel clouds drew in all lying near: soil, trees, animals… men. What little they spat back out was difficult to look upon.

The ringing in his ears muffled the sound, but he could still make it all out: the clash of steel, the crackle of the lightning, and the screams of his dying comrades. The worst were the screeches, growls, or snarls of the Grunkin that prowled the battlefield; those hideous, twisted beasts that embodied Edis,

1

the God of Chaos. They killed anything within reach, including each other.

Dirge struggled into a sitting position, pain wracking his entire body, and gently grasped his jaw, the metallic tang of blood on his tongue. His surroundings came into focus. His once resplendent armor lay about him in ruins. His sword, a gift from his master, lay at his side, a twisted hunk of dross. And worst of all, the mutilated bodies of his friends and comrades littering the field. The stink of burnt ozone mixed with charred flesh, offal, and shit, twisted his stomach.

It wasn't supposed to be like this. An hour before, the sky shone a perfect blue as the victorious cheers of the Army of the Righteous out to rid the world of Chaos filled the air. How could this have happened? Why did Ukase, his god, abandoned them? This was not what he'd been promised.

Chapter 2
The Slums of Juilar
(492 -R.C.-)

Dirge sat alone on a bench next to the fire in the common room of the Angelic Inn as sprinkles of icy rain tapped the windows. He wore only his nightshirt, and his dark curly hair looked to be a rat's nest. He had awoken a short time before in the room he shared with his mother. Life on the streets in the slums of any city proved difficult to any adult let alone a child.

"Good morning, my dear," Katlyn, the owner of the inn, greeted the boy with a twinkle in her dark brown eyes. Her tall, slim form towered over him, her wiry dark red hair, and pleasant smile putting him at ease. Not known as an overly gracious woman, Katlyn doted on Dirge. "Will your mum be joining you for breakfast?"

Lowering his head, Dirge mumbled, "Momma went out."

She shook her head. "I do wish she wouldn't do her business in the alleys and streets. The Slaag is too dangerous."

"Momma likes the room," Dirge said absently. "She wouldn't want to dirty the bed."

Lindsey, one of the serving girls, brought over a large bowl of porridge. The innkeeper took the bowl and handed it to Dirge. "I know she does, dearie."

She stood and spoke to Lindsey. "I've told Sesqua time and again to just bring them back here. I'd only charge her a pittance and it would be far safer."

"She has too much pride," Lindsey said with a shake of her head, her long blonde curls sparkling in the lamplight. "She doesn't like having to give a cut to any house."

"I'd happily give her the back room to use." Katlyn knuckled her back. "As beautiful as she is, she'd have more than enough customers to afford it."

"It would certainly bring in more customers," Lindsey said as she looked at the few folks scattered about the common room.

"Oh, I don't care about that. She deserves better than this, is all, both her and the boy." Katlyn sighed and patted Lindsey on the shoulder while eyeing a group of men who had just entered the inn. "Be a dear and keep an eye on the lad until his mum gets back."

Dirge didn't know exactly what they were talking about but people had said the like before. He and his mother had been staying at the inn on and off for as long as he could remember. People in the neighborhood liked Sesqua. She always kept upbeat even though many said she shouldn't.

Dirge woodenly ate his porridge while staring into the hearth's flames. He enjoyed the heat on his dark skin but it didn't show on his face. Everyone called him "sullen." He didn't know what it meant, but he had an idea. He couldn't help how he felt.

"Are you going to finish that?"

On the opposite bench, a smiling child sat forward. Looking only a couple of years older, and scratching at dingy blonde hair, the boy's bright blue eyes matched his smile. In tattered and dirty shirt and breeches, his bare feet dangled just above the floor. In fact, everything about the boy was filthy, so much so his skin looked almost as dark as Dirge's. Still, through all that dirt the boy smiled. "I said are you going to finish that?"

Without saying a word, Dirge passed the half-empty bowl to the boy who quickly took it, and proceeded to wolf down the remaining meal.

"I'm Jacob," he said between spoonfuls. "What's your name?"

"Dirge," he replied halfheartedly while looking into the flames.

"That's a funny name."

Dirge shrugged. "Momma said I reminded her of music. The kind they play at the funeral marches."

"I like that." The boy cocked his head. "Do you stay here? I don't remember seeing you before."

"Sometimes. Momma says I need to stay out of sight."

"Why?"

Dirge had no reply.

"Well," Jacob said sitting taller, "you don't have to worry about anything happening to you. Me and my brothers will look out for you."

"What's all this, then?" Katlyn yelled from across the room. "Who let that ruffian in here?" She stormed across the room.

With a yelp, Jacob dropped the now empty bowl and made a dash for the door.

The innkeeper cut him off and grabbed him by the arm. "What do you think you're doing in here?"

"I was just talking to my friend," the boy squealed.

"You've got no friends around here." She gave him a quick shake. "I know your Pop. He's got no friends around here neither!"

Standing, Dirge shouted, "Leave him be. We was just talkin."

It was the first time Katlyn heard him speak above a whisper. Her eys wide, she released the boy. Jacob dashed out the front door and into the streets.

With the shake of her head, the innkeeper walked over to Dirge. "Listen, son. You don't want to be mixing with the likes of him." She picked the bowl up from the floor, giving it a quick look over to see if it had broken.

"Why?" Dirge asked, his voice still strong and firm.

"Because his type's always up to no good." She took a seat on the bench and placed her hand upon his shoulder. "I know his father. I know his clan. They moved into the Slaag recently and they'd cut your throat as soon as look at you."

"That doesn't mean Jacob is the same," Dirge said angrily. He'd spent many a night on the street when his mum couldn't afford to get them a room. There, he'd seen children like Jacob dead in the gutter. Besides, there was something about Jacob he liked. He was the first kid that had wanted to talk to him instead of just look at him funny. He told Katlyn as much.

"Oh, dearie. You just had something he wanted. That's all." She sighed. "Okay, fine. *Maybe* he liked you. But, I can't afford to go around feeding the entire Slaag." She hesitated. "If you want to go and give your food to that boy, then fine, but don't expect me to give you more."

She then ruffled the hair on his head. "Why don't you go and get dressed. You're welcome to stay by the fire, but if you do go out, be sure to stay close. I don't want you to wander off and get yourself killed. Your mum would have my hide."

Dirge jumped off the bench and sprinted to his room to change. He didn't want to just sit there and wait for his mum all day—he had no idea when she would be back. So, the idea of going out and exploring sounded like fun. He might even catch up to Jacob if he ran quickly enough.

Once he had on his gray shirt and well-worn breeches, he ran for the front door, his bare feet slapping on the wooden floor. He didn't have shoes or sandals. He was growing so fast that his mum didn't have the extra coin.

Flinging open the front door of the inn, he tore outside. Two steps out the door he ran headlong into a roughly dressed man making his way to the inn. Dirge bounced off the man but kept his feet. He turned and headed for the nearest alley, ignoring the man's curses.

The rain had stopped, and the alley was slick with mud and refuse. He did his best to dodge the stinky puddles and the slick muddy patches. As much fun as jumping into a mud puddle happened to be, every child knew not to do that in the alleys. When you don't have shoes, you might get cut on whatever lay at the bottom of those rancid pools.

Turning the nearest corner and heading away from the inn, a screech and a hiss came from a pile of refuse as two cats confronted one another over a hard-fought meal. The sheer number of feral cats in the city was almost impossible to count. There were likely as many cats and rats as there were people in Tuilar—and the only things outnumbering those were the flies and mosquitoes.

After he turned his third corner, Dirge finally slowed to a walk as he neared the edge of the block. He'd never been beyond it—his mother forbade him leaving their block of the Slaag. She told him that the world beyond was far too dangerous for someone so small.

Nearing the final corner, hushed voices came from the next street, so he stopped and peeked around the corner. About two-thirds of the way down the alley, a small group of young men knelt in the mud, quietly arguing.

Dirge yelped when something grabbed him by the back of his shirt and yanked him backward. He landed with a splat on his behind. Above him, stood a scowling young man he didn't recognize.

"Well, who the fuck do we have here?" the young man said in hushed tones before giving a low whistle and waving his hand around the corner.

Dirge lay there, fear mingling with anger, and refusing to say anything.

"Who in the hells is that?" asked the eldest of the boys who had been in the alley's mouth.

"Don't know, Jack," said the young man who had grabbed him. "Never seen him before. You think he's working for Doomers?"

"We can't take the chance," Jack replied as he pulled a long, wicked knife from his belt.

Dirge did his best not to cry, but tears ran down his cheeks, nonetheless. He tried to crab-walk away through the muck and filth as fast as he could but the first boy stepped heavily on his chest.

"Where the fuck do you think you're going?" he said with a snarling smile.

A young voice piped up from the back of the group, "No, wait!" Jacob squeezed his way through the others and tried pushing the young man's foot off Dirge, to little avail. "He's my friend, Connor. Get off him!"

Connor laughed. "You ain't got no friends."

"You know this kid?" Jack asked.

"Yes." Jacob turned to the one with his foot on Dirge. "I said get off him, Connor!"

"And what if I don't?"

Jacob pulled a small dagger from his belt. "I'll stick you."

Connor guffawed, but Jack hushed him with a low growl, "Keep it down, damn it! You want the mark to hear us? Jacob, put that thing away. Connor, get off him."

Connor reluctantly removed his boot and Jack pulled Dirge to his feet. "You're a tough little one, ain'tcha? Connor would've been bawling if it happened to him at your still your age."

Connor started to protest, but Jack spoke over him, "I said shut it." He then turned back to Dirge. "What's your name, kid?"

"Dirge," he said while wiping his cheeks.

"How do you know my little brother?"

"I gave him half my breakfast this morning."

"You *gave* it, or he *took* it?"

"I gave it to him." Dirge shrugged. "He asked if I was done and I didn't feel like eating anymore, so I gave it to him."

"Where was this?" Jack asked Jacob.

Lowering his head, Jacob replied apprehensively, "At the Angelic."

"Hmmm, nice place. The owner's a bit of a bitch according to Pop but she's got no connection to Doomers that I know of." Jack took a long look at Dirge then turned to Jacob. "You two go take off. But keep a low profile, would ya?"

"But Pop said he was to join us?" one of the others said.

"Shut up, Axe. I don't care what Pop says. Jacob's too young to do us any good and he might end up dead if something goes wrong." Jack then stabbed his finger at Axe. "And I don't want Ma on my ass over it. She'd have my balls if anything happened to him."

"Come on, let's go." Jacob pulled Dirge deeper into the alleyway.

Dirge slowly walked with Jacob while glancing over his shoulder at the now squabbling group of young toughs. Their argument ended when Jack punched Axe in the face, sending him to the ground.

"Come on, let's get out of here," Jacob said. "Don't worry about them. They do that all the time."

As they started down the alley, Dirge wondered what had been going on in the first place. "What were you all doing back there?"

"We were waitin' for folks leaving Doomers' place," Jacob replied with a cocky air.

"Who is Doomers?"

"He runs a hall." Jacob turned left at the next corner. "Some folks leave there with a full purse and a head full of liquor. We're supposed to 'alleviate them of their burden,' according to my pop."

"What does that mean?"

Jacob shrugged. "I don't know. This was supposed to be my first time helping them. Ma wanted Jack to do something too, but I never heard what. Come on, let's go."

The two boys took off at a run. Jacob led Dirge through the winding alleyways, seemingly taking turns at random, until they came to a broad street choked with people and cart traffic.

"This is 'Chunker Way,' it's the main street into the Slaag from Merchant district," Jacob said. "We used to live only a couple of blocks down on the other side."

"Why did you move?" Dirge warily eyed the busy road.

"A bunch of buildings fell down. The first one fell all to pieces, and that knocked down the ones next to it, and they knocked down more." Jacob scanned the street up and down. "We was lucky we was on the edge of it all. None of us died. Most weren't so lucky. And when a pack of dogs came in and started eating the dead people—and the not so dead people—Pa said it was time to go." Jacob finally appeared satisfied at what he saw and headed out onto the busy street.

"Where are you going?" Dirge yelled.

"Just down the street. I want to show you what I'm talking about."

"I can't," Dirge said, shrinking in on himself. "My Mum said I can't cross the streets."

"And do you do everything you Mum tells you?"

"Yes," Dirge replied with a forthright nod.

"Oh, come on. Just this once. It won't kill ya. I know every inch of that place. Besides, if we're lucky we might even find something in all that mess." Jacob turned and continued down the road without looking back.

Filled with uncertainty, Dirge chewed at his lip, and then dashed down the road to catch up to Jacob. Within in three steps, a man pushing a cart nearly ran him over. He dodged the cart but in doing so ran into a big man in a yellow coat who hollered and tried to kick him. Dirge easily evaded that as well and sped off after his new friend.

Reaching Jacob's side, they zigzagged their way through the heavy traffic, being careful not to trip in the ruts. Dirge's head swiveled to and fro at all the people. He didn't want his mum to spot him. She told him, time and again, that he must listen and do as told. She'd said bad things happened to disobedient children: a ghost might snatch him up and carry him to the Lands of the Dead, a Chaos Storm might suck him into the sky, or worst of all, a grunkin could gobble him up.

The very idea that a monster out of the stories might eat him, terrified Dirge. Yet he so wanted to explore, to see something other than the alleyways around the Angelic. He yearned to know what lay beyond his limited world.

Finding the alleyway, Jacob ducked down it. It seemed no different at first, but it didn't take long for that to change. Halfway down, the rear half of the left building had collapsed upon its neighbor, blocking the passage. Not that Jacob seemed to care. His new friend ducked down and crawled through a small opening near the bottom of the rubble. Dirge followed without a second thought. They scampered over piles of shifting wood and brick as rats stopped and watched them pass. Dirge bumped a timber at the end and the pile emitted a low groan as he crawled into the clear.

"Is this where you used to live?" Dirge asked as they ran down the muck-filled alley.

"No," Jacob replied. "That's been there for as long as I can remember. Come on, we're almost there."

The alley twisted and turned so much that Dirge quickly became lost. With each step, the buildings looked older and older—one in three being nothing more than an empty carcass. That's not to say those ruins were lifeless. People dug into the ground, within many of the skeletal timbers. Covered in little more than rags, they hacked and coughed, staring with sunken eyes at their fire pits. Some watched as the boys ran past, but most seemed to see nothing, not even the fire before them.

People weren't the only denizens of those alleys. Lizards and snakes scurried away as the boys ran while feral cats and small packs of dogs eyed them cautiously. Several times, Dirge frantically waved his hands before his face as they ran through masses of swarming insects.

"Are we there yet?" Dirge spat out some insects that found their way into his mouth.

Jacob just kept running.

How could anyone live like this? Dirge wondered. *Why don't they just go to an inn?*

A short distance ahead, the alleyway came to a T where Jacob dashed around the corner to the right. When Dirge rounded the corner, he ran smack into Jacob's back and the two of them tumbled to the muddy ground.

"What's this then?" asked a man in a cold voice.

Dirge looked up while trying to untangle himself from his friend. Less than halfway down the alleyway stood three young men in dark, stained clothes. They stood over the body of a fourth, blood oozing from a wound in his neck.

"Ain't that one of Hoke's imps?" the man on the left asked.

"Sure is," replied the one who first spoke. Using a bloody dagger in his right hand, he pointed at Dirge. "But who's the other one?"

"Never seen him before, Rico," answered the third man. "But by the looks of him, he might have a little coin on him."

Eyes wide, Dirge scrambled away as the men stalked toward him. His hand landed on something hard. Without thought, he clutched it, stood, and hurled it. It was a chunk of brick. The brick struck the man holding the dagger square in the nose. The man let out a scream, dropped the dagger, and fell to his knees, his hands going to his bloody face.

"Come on," Jacob yelled, grabbing at Dirge's collar and tugging hard.

They ran. Dirge, blood hammering in his ears, stuck tight to Jacob's heels as his friend dashed down the alley opposite the one they came. The screams of the man he'd struck, bellowing at his fellows to chase them down, urged Dirge on. They dashed down the twisting alleys, the slick mud making their footing dicey as the sloshing stomps of the men grew closer. Dirge tried to will his companion to run faster.

Jacob never looked back to see how close their pursuers were, but Dirge couldn't help himself. He took a quick glance back at their charging pursuers. With faces like snarling beasts, one grasped a cudgel in his fist, while the other clutched a dagger. Dirge turned back to Jacob ahead of him just in time to watch his friend dodge to the left around a tight corner. Dirge missed the turn. He tried to skid to a halt and turn back but lost his feet and fell hard, sliding several feet in the mud.

Their hunters howled triumphantly.

Glimpsing an opening in the base of the building next to him, Dirge scrambled on hands and knees, into the dark hole. As he crawled into the darkness, the men cursed, quickly followed by the sound of one of them falling in the mud.

One of them stuck his head into the hole. "Get back here, you little fuck!"

Dirge crawled faster.

Choked with dust, and cobwebs covering his face, he continued into the gloom until slamming into something hard. With a yelp, he clasped his head, his eyes squeezed tight against the pain. He lay there for a moment, his breath heaving as his heart beat a rapid crescendo.

After a time, the pain faded, and he opened his eyes. Light pouring through small slits in the floor above, lit the crawl space, allowing him to see that he'd slammed into a large wooden post. He twisted about as things rustled in the darker corners, and bugs skittered about. He saw two more openings into the crawlspace besides the one he'd entered. A glint of light caught his attention—something shiny lay half buried beneath one of the illuminated slits. Reaching over, he pulled out a small pendant from the dirt—a seven-pointed star, nearly the size of his hand, and most importantly, appeared to be silver.

This might get us a few more nights at the Angelic, he thought. *Momma might not even have to work for a while if we get enough.*

Stuffing the pendant into his pouch, he looked back at the hole he'd entered. The man was gone. Dirge needed to get out of there, but not the way he'd entered. Just because he couldn't see then men didn't mean they weren't still there.

He crawled through the dim, shaking away the cobwebs and shying away from the darkest areas. He started to worry about what his mum would say when she saw him, covered in grime with no way to explain it away. His only hope was getting back home before she did.

Maybe Mistress Katlyn will help me clean up. But there was very little hope in that. Mistress Katlyn would likely be even crosser than his mum.

The timbers creaked and groaned above him as he crawled toward the furthest light source, coughing and sputtering as he went. Once he reached the opening in the far wall, he realized it was smaller than he'd thought and wasn't sure he could make it through. He looked back but could only make out the hole he'd come in through. Sighing, he stuck an arm through the hole, followed by his head. It was a very tight fit. He pulled, kicked, and twisted. Finally, after getting his other arm through, he pushed on the wall with both hands and dragged the rest of his body out from under the building.

Panting, he lay on his back, scraped, and bruised, his shirt and pants with new holes and tears as light clouds drifted on high in a sea of blue. He was alive! He was lost, but at least he was alive. His mum was likely to smack him when he got home, but he didn't care. He just stared at the sun and the clouds in the bright blue sky.

A shadow fell across his face.

Emitting a panicked squeak, he scrambled back for the hole, but he knew it was too late. He yelled as a hand covered his mouth. They'd found him. He'd never see his mum again.

"Quiet," Jacob whispered.

Dirge cried in relief as his friend quickly looked about.

"Where did you go?" Jacob helped Dirge to his feet. "How d'you get ahead of me?"

Dirge told him how he had missed the turn and crawled through the hole.

"Really? I'll have to remember that. I never like to go under the buildings. Jack says there're rats as big as dogs under there. Shows how much he knows." He tugged Dirge's arm. "Come on. The way out is just ahead."

The alleyway opened out onto a busy, broad street and Dirge had no idea where he was. With another tug, Jacob urged Dirge to follow him through the heavy traffic, and to the other side where his friend then turned and ran along the side of the road. They passed several more buildings until they came to yet another alley.

This one looked quite familiar to Dirge. "I think I know where we are." He ran through the light debris of burlap, broken crates, and cloth that choked the alley's mouth. "Home is just around—"

Something under the debris tripped Dirge, sending him tumbling—something firm, yet also soft.

Snow began to fall as he pulled away the crate and burlap, exposing what lay beneath: a woman. Pure-white flakes of snow fell upon the dark naked skin of the woman's bruised and broken body. The snow that lit into her coal black hair and lifeless gray eyes contrasted sharply with the red blood pooling about her throat.

Dirge's mouth fell agape, his stomach clenched, and tears burned his eyes. "Momma?"

Chapter 3
Unyielding
(494 -R.C.-)

Dirge was six when Sesqua died. The news of her death spread quickly, and everyone said the same thing, "She should have stayed at a brothel, it was safe there—somewhat, anyway." Some claimed her death had been in retribution for spurning a housemaster. Others whispered that it had been the work of a demon. Some even said it had been a grunkin, but those folks were quickly hushed.

None of that mattered to Dirge.

"He's growing fast," Talic Sern said to Katlyn. The tall, slim, dark-skinned man stood in the corner of the common room next to the innkeeper. He'd been head bouncer at the inn for longer than Dirge could remember.

"Aye, that he has," Katlyn replied as she wiped down the bar. "I can hardly believe it's been two years. But I worry about him."

"How so?"

"Well, the boy was always dour, but since that day, he's become downright emotionless." She tsked. "He doesn't laugh or cry. It's like something snapped in him."

Following his mother's death, the innkeeper had taken it on herself to watch over Dirge. She'd set up a small bed in one of the back storerooms. She also had him doing odd jobs around the inn, having him help out wherever he could—something unusual in the Slaag, where life was anything but precious. Yet, most people deemed the Angelic itself unusual. With rarely a full common room, it always had empty rooms upstairs. But strangest of all, it was clean—Mistress Katlyn hated a mess.

Talic watched Dirge as the boy swept the common room. The bouncer's keen, dark eyes kept a watch on the handful of customers while still following the boy. Dirge didn't know how he did it. The man could spot trouble brewing out of the corner of his eyes, and with a signal of his hand, one of the other bouncers would take handle it.

"What's your interest in him, anyway?" Katlyn asked.

"Who said I'm interested?"

"All right, fine." Katlyn laughed and started for the back of the inn. "Just make sure no one burns down my inn while I'm gone."

Dirge had his doubts. For as long as he could recall Talic was there. When he was three, Dirge had run out of the inn, chasing after his Mum, begging her not to leave. Talic sprinted after and snatched him out of the way of a speeding carriage. Then there was the time his mum had been out during a riot. Dirge had been wracked with fear, but Talic was there, comforting him, telling him that his mum would be fine, while ordering two of the other bouncers to find her. And lastly, Talic had been there the day he'd found his mum's body. The man covered her with the burlap, and gently picked her up in his strong, dark arms. Keeping an eye on

Dirge, they made their way back to the inn, ushering Dirge along with soft, consoling words.

Dirge shook his head, stifled a yawn, and continued his sweeping. He'd not gotten much sleep the previous night. Nightmares plagued his dreams. The most common dream found him staggering down dark, mist-filled alleyways with the angry voices of strangers chasing him. They never caught him, but he got the feeling he never got away, either.

When Dirge finished his sweeping, he looked up at Talic. The bouncer was eyeing him with a slight grin upon his face. Dirge didn't return the smile, but he didn't frown either. Most people seemed to fear the large, dark skinned man, calling him dangerous. But Dirge remembered that his mum had liked Talic, so he decided that he did as well.

Dirge placed the broom in the corner of the room, where it belonged, and moved on to wiping down the tables. He was half way done when a short, dirty, gruff faced man entered the inn. Talic eyed the fellow as he shuffled over and greeted a man sitting at one of the few tables that sported customers.

"Did you hear the news?" the newcomer said with a voice as gruff as his face. "A Chaos Storm struck the town of His-tone—nearly wiped the place out."

"Gods, man, that's just down the coast," exclaimed the man already seated.

The dirty man took a seat. "That it is. Hear tell it nearly tore the place apart with its wind, rain, and snow. Hells, I even heard it rained fire for a time!"

The other man scoffed.

"Tis true I tells ya! Kelly seen it wit his own eyes!"

"Kelly?" The second man seemed to ponder for a moment. "Hmm, well, if you say so. Did it sprout any grunkins?"

"Not so's I know." The first man waved his hand. "That'd be a sight to see though, wouldn't it? Something actually touched by the Great Lord?"

Mistress Katlyn marched to their table. "That's enough out of you two. I'll have no talk of grunkin in my establishment. You hear me?" She sniffed and walked back to the bar.

The two men's eyes grew wide. The newcomer huffed. "What's wrong wit talkin' 'bout grunkin? You got sometin' against Chaos?"

"That's it," the innkeeper snapped. "Talic, get them out of here."

The head bouncer nodded and waved his hand toward the men at the table. Dennis and Dobbs strode over, picked the men up by their shirts, and threw them out into the street where they landed face first in the mud.

"Thank you, Talic," mistress Katlyn said, and the bouncer nodded in return.

Talic's eyes quickly swung to the door again as another man entered from the front street, this one short and bow legged. Bowed legs were common in the Slaag where the rickets ran rampant in its children.

The stranger stood by the door a moment, his gaze swinging across the room until it landed on Talic. He stared at the bouncer a moment, licking his lips and shuffling his feet, before approaching the big man.

"Might you be the one they call, Talic?" he asked in a soft, shaky voice.

"I am."

"Well, um…" The man snatched a dirty hat from atop his head. He cleared his throat lowered his eyes and clenched his hat in both hands, twisting it. "Well, you see, um, not sure what to say, um, you see there's this man I'd like—"

Talic cut him off. "Let's go up to my room where we can talk." He put his large hand around the shoulders of the stranger who was now shaking, and started them toward the back stairs.

"Dobbs!" Talic called out.

Another of the bouncers stuck his head out from the back kitchen. "Yea, Boss?"

"You've got the front."

Dobbs nodded. Before taking his place at the end of the bar, he called back into the kitchen, "Hake, you got the back."

Dirge watched Talic take the jittery man upstairs to his room. All five of the bouncers had rooms upstairs. Four of them shared two rooms on the second floor while Talic had one all to himself up on the third. Everyone else who worked there either lived elsewhere or had a small room on the main floor.

Dirge wondered what was going on but then decided that he didn't care. His next task was taking out the refuse, so he got on with it.

He walked into the back kitchen and took up the small open topped keg used for accumulating the scraps and garbage. The built-in handles made the job easier and far less messy. Mistress Katlyn didn't like mess, she didn't like the rubbish and feculence thrown out the inn's windows, and doors like most folk did with their homes and businesses. She wanted to keep it clean and smelling pleasant. Well, as pleasant as one can in the Slaag where the stink was an ever-existing haze that covered the district.

He opened the back door and walked down the small series of steps to the alleyway. He took the alley, walked a good block away, and upended the cask into the gutter on the main street, downhill from the Angelic. It wouldn't do to put it on the upside because as soon as it rained it would all end up right in the front where he'd have to clean it out.

On his way back, he saw Jacob talking to Connor, along with three other boys Dirge didn't recognize. The look in his friend's eyes was one of uncertainty. Most folk wouldn't have noticed it, as Jacob was a great one for putting on faces, but Dirge knew him too well. All the other boys, including Connor, were sneering and lightly pushing his friend.

Dirge decided he didn't like it, so he walked up to Jacob. "Is everything all right?"

"Well, if it isn't my little brother's beau. What do you want, Deadeyes?" Connor sneered.

"Are you looking for trouble, freak?" one boy barked, jabbing his chin out at Dirge.

"No, everything's fine," Jacob said with a laugh. "We's just swappin' stories. I's just tellin' Thom bout that time I got ole' man Winters to hit himself in his stones with his own cudgel."

"Shut up, runt." One of the others shoved Jacob in the back.

"What? I's just sayin'? Come on, you seen it! His face 'bout turned plum." Jacob laughed. Before long, the rest of the boys laughed as well.

"Yea, I think he shit himself," another of the boys said.

Connor wasn't laughing. He just stared at Dirge, his hand creeping down to the dagger at his belt.

"What in all the hells is going on here?" a man bellowed from the end of the alleyway. It was Jacob's father, Hoke. For a small man, he had a big voice.

He marched up and clapped Connor across the back of the head. "You little shits have got a job to do, so go do it! And you," he pointed at Jacob, "I'll have none of your smart mouth here. Go use it on 'ole lady Guthrie and see if you can get some more coin from her."

The man paused, his eyes peering at Dirge a moment. "Give my regards to Talic." He then cuffed Connor once more and ushered the boys away.

"I'll talk to you later." Jacob winked to Dirge and followed his father.

Jacob's a wizard at talking himself out of trouble, Dirge thought. *Nearly as good as he is at talking himself into it.*

Dirge turned and headed back to the Inn, his thoughts on the way Connor had eyed him with his hand on his dagger.

Jacob's brother didn't like him. No one did, no one but Jacob. Again, not that he cared. He had work to do.

He shook his head and returned to the inn. As he approached the door, he felt as though someone was watching him. He stopped and looked around but saw nothing. He glanced up at the upper floors of the inn. Three windows from the inn's hallway opened out to the alley, one from each floor. They all stood empty. He looked closer at the one on the third floor. For a moment, he thought he'd seen movement, but the window stood empty, so he shrugged it off.

His next task, somewhat akin to his last, was far more foul; the chamber pots. This required a different cask, one with a lid to prevent spillage. He retrieved the cask from its place under the alleyway stairs and entered. He marched up to the second floor and knocked on doors. If someone answered he asked if their needed their chamber pot emptied and if no one answered he peeked in so as not to disturb anyone.

Once he finished the second floor, his cask was more than half-full. He decided that rather than overfilling it and causing a spill; he'd make two trips. He made his way back into the alley, but this time he followed it to its furthest point away. Mistress Katlyn wanted to make sure there was no way any of it found its way back to their front door. She'd even had a ditch dug along the front of the inn so that her neighbors' waste wouldn't end up at her door either.

At the alley's mouth, he carefully emptied the cask in front of an empty warehouse. Once finished he stepped back and, for a moment, watched the traffic on the road.

Where do they all come from? he wondered. *Where are they all going in such a hurry?* Shaking his head, he deciding not to care, and headed back to the inn. As he passed the intersection of the alley where he'd found his mum, he swore to himself that if he ever found out who'd killed his mother…

He sighed. It didn't matter.

As he approached the Angelic's back door, a sound behind him caught his attention. He whirled about and there, only ten feet away, stood Connor and his three friends.

"You never answered my question," Connor said, his voice harsh.

"I think the freak was lookin' for trouble," the blond boy on the right said as they slowly approached.

"Is that it?" Connor asked, his voice like a knife. "Or did you come to protect your little sweetie?"

Dirge regarded the boys as they approached him. They were all older and much larger. He didn't care. He quickly took the top of the cask off with his left hand and smashed it into Connor's face. He then swung the cask at the blond boy with his right, striking him in the shoulder. Connor dropped to his knees while the blond tripped and fell to the ground. Dirge then tried to swing the cask at the third but the fourth boy slammed him to the ground.

Dirge tried to stand up but the fourth boy punched him hard in the face, sending him back to the ground. He refused to stay down. As he started to stand, a foot caught him in the stomach. Air exploded from his lungs and he dropped. More kicks followed, as the others joined in, but Dirge refused to give. He did all he could to regain his breath, and his feet.

"Stay down, you little fuck," one of them shouted, and punched him in the head.

It was a glancing blow and Dirge ignored it. He shook his head and stood… then went down in a heap when Connor punched him square in the nose. Dirge saw stars and everything warbled. His mouth held the metallic taste of blood and a whooshing sound filled his ears. The older boys' shouts seeming to come from far off, somewhere full of echoes. When his eyes cleared, Connor stood over him.

"Had enough?" The boy spat.

Dirge began to stand only to be punched in the face once more. He dropped back down and shook his head. Again,

Dirge regained his feet but was kicked in the leg, dropping him to the ground, face first.

"I said stay down!" Connor bellowed.

Dirge spat out the blood and dirt. He didn't care. There were going to kill him, and he didn't care. They could hit him all they wanted. He didn't care. It didn't matter. The only thing that mattered to him was standing. He didn't know why it was important; he just knew he had to. His arms and legs trembling, he forced himself to stand. Once up he wobbled, but that didn't matter, he was standing!

"You stubborn little fuck." Connor's hand drifted to the dagger at his belt. "I think I'll just end you—"

"Take your hand off that hilt, boy." Talic slowly walked from behind Dirge, his hand resting on the hilt of a sword at his belt—a sword Dirge never saw before. The bouncer's voice was like iron. "If you boys want to keep drawing breaths, you'd best get the fuck out of here, lest you want me to send Hoke your heads."

The four boys slowly backed off. Connor's face blazed red, his hands shook, and his eyes burned with anger, yet he retreated away all the same. They were halfway down the alley before they turned and slowly trudged away.

"Arrogant little fucks," Talic said under his breath. He looked down at Dirge. "Come on, let's get you cleaned up." He took Dirge by the shoulders, turned him, and helped him up the stairs.

The door to the main hall opened and Katlyn rushed out. "What happened?"

"He got into a fight." Talic gently walked Dirge toward the door.

"What do you mean, he got into a fight? With whom?"

"It doesn't matter," Talic said as they entered the main hall and headed for the back stairs.

"It does too, matter!"

"No, it doesn't. Sometimes boys just need to get into fights."

"No, sometimes *you* need to get into a fight because it's your job."

"We all have to start somewhere," Talic said as they ascended the stairs. "Anyway, I took care of it so you needn't worry. I'm going to get the boy cleaned up. Dobbs, you're still on watch. I'll come relieve you as soon as I can."

"Yes, sir."

Dirge frowned. *Yes, sir? That's an odd way to say 'all right,'* he thought as he slowly walked at the bouncer's side, each step sending a jolt of pain through his chest. *And since when does a bouncer have a sword? A cudgel, sure, but never a sword. It would make too much of a mess. Mistress Katlyn doesn't like messes.*

Once they entered Talic's room, he led the boy to a large, comfortable chair near the window. "Have a seat, my boy."

A shock of pain jolted into Dirge's mind as the bouncer helped him into the seat. It took a moment for him to regain his breath. Sitting warily in the overstuffed chair that was far too large for him, his back didn't touch the back of the chair and his legs dangling several inches above the floor. He hurt, from head to toe, his body burned with the pain, but he sat erect and as still as he could. All the while doing his best to not let any of it show on his face. He didn't care how he felt, so why would anyone else.

Yet, Talic wanted to look after him all the same. It confused the boy to no end.

Talic brought over the washbasin, placed it on the chair side table, and washed the blood from Dirge's face. "So, what got them all riled up?"

Dirge just shrugged.

"Come now. Hoke's boys are an egotistical bunch of rats, but there had to be something?"

Dirge refused to answer. What did it matter why they did it?

"Did it have something to do with Jacob?"

Dirge looked up at Talic, his eyes growing wide. "How d'you know?"

Talic smiled. "It's not tough to figure. That boy's a quick wit and a smart mouth. Unlike the rest of his family," he added under his breath. "When you have friends like him, you're bound to be dragged into his troubles."

Dirge relented, telling the bouncer all that occurred. He figured the man would understand why he'd started it—trying to protect Jacob. Even if he wasn't sure why he did it himself.

Talic shrugged, finished cleaning Dirge's face, and then went about to checking him for other injuries. "Well, looks like you'll survive. Your ribs don't look broken, most like just bruised. You get to bed. I'll have Katie bring you something for the pain."

Katie was one of the serving girls.

Dirge gingerly got down from the chair, doing his best not to grunt from the exertion, and slowly walked to the door.

As he reached for the handle, Talic spoke up, "You will do well."

Dirge turned and tilted his head. "What?"

"You will do well. You've what it takes to survive—a sharp wit and quick reflexes. More importantly, you're also fearless and tenacious." As Dirge opened the door the bouncer added, "Just remember, my boy. You're not alone."

Dirge shook his head as he walked down the hall. What a silly thing for Talic to say. Of course, he was alone. He had no mother. No father. No one. Well, no one but Jacob.

It took three days before he could go back to all his work. He was back at the sweeping and wiping the next day even though mistress Katlyn said he didn't have to, but the heavy

lifting was impossible. When he picked up the heavy garbage cask that first day he nearly passed out from the pain.

Jacob came to see him almost every day. Mistress Katlyn
didn't want to let him in at first, but she looked at Dirge and
acquiesced, which came as quite a shock to him. Usually
when mistress Katlyn made up her mind, she didn't change
it.

When he asked her why she relented, she told him, "It's
just nice to see a smile on your face, my dear."

What does she mean by that? Dirge wondered.

Chapter 4
A Spark of Recognition
(494 -R.C.-)

Two months passed before he no longer felt discomfort. In that time, he spent only a short while out on the streets with Jacob. Mistress Katlyn didn't want to see him get into another dustup. Dirge doubted such a thing would happen, but he did find it odd that they saw Connor and his friends every time they went out.

One day while sweeping, Talic walked up to him with an odd-looking stick. It looked like a short wooden sword with an even smaller hilt. "It's time you learned to defend yourself, my boy. You've got no quit in you, I like that, but if you don't learn how to fight, they are going to beat you to death one of these days."

"Who, Connor and his friends?"

"Yes, them, along with the rest of Hoke's brood, and everyone else out there as well. It's a dangerous world, Dirge, and if you want to survive, you need to be just as dangerous."

Dirge stared at the stick a moment. He reached for it but Talic pulled it away. Dirge looked at the bouncer, his brows furrowed.

"Not just yet. This is for later." Talic placed the stick upon his bed. "First you learn to fight with your hands and feet, and most importantly, your head," he said, poking Dirge in the forehead. He then placed his hand on Dirge's shoulder. "We're going to go up to my room and begin with some simple exercises."

Dirge entered Talic's room. It was only the second time he'd ever been there, but he immediately noticed a difference. His first time there the room had been quite Spartan, with only the bed and chair. Now, along with those furnishings, he saw several things hanging upon the walls as well as a small table. On the wall next to the window, hung the sword he'd worn earlier, along with a small, black shield and four black daggers. Next to his bed, hung a piece of square black cloth with a strange white symbol upon it. Below the cloth sat the small table, and upon it, at either end, stood a pair of lit, white candles in black holders. Next to each candle stood a long smoldering stick placed directly into the table, and at the table's center sat a jet black, human skull.

Dirge had never seen its like, yet something seemed almost... familiar. The smoke from the smoldering sticks filled his nostrils; its sharp and earthy scent seemed to fog his senses. The world around him shrunk, his vision blurred at the edges, and all he could see was the skull.

"Don't touch it." Talic's voice snapped Dirge out of his fog. He was completely across the room, his hand just inches from the skull. Dirge didn't remember moving. He snatched his hand back and quickly backed away.

"What is it?" he asked, his voice trembling.

"It is an altar to my God," Talic replied.

"Chaos?" Dirge didn't know the bouncer was religious, but he'd never seen anything like it. He knew many people who wore symbols to the God of Chaos, and none of them looked exactly the same. But this? This was new.

"No, boy. I'm no worshiper of that anathema. This is to Aza'zel, the God of Death." The bouncer chuckled when Dirge's eyes went wide. "Yes, Death. There are more gods out there than Chaos. Most are not worshiped openly, but they're worshiped, nonetheless. It was said that in the early days one could worship as they pleased. The minions of Chaos would laugh and deride you but let you do as you wished. Those days are gone." Talic knelt in front of Dirge, putting a hand upon his shoulder. "Chaos has changed. You are far too young to know such things and many are blind to it, but as of late Chaos has become… dark, and cruel."

Dirge looked at the bouncer, still not quite understanding. Yet it made sense for some reason. He glanced at the weapons upon the other wall. "Where did you get those?"

"I wasn't always a bouncer." Talic smiled, stood, and walked to the center of the room. "Now then, I want you to stand opposite me and do as I do."

Dirge did as asked and stood in front of the older man.

Talic stood stock straight, with his palms pressed together before him, and slowly breathed in and out, ten times, before holding it. He then jutted his hands into the air directly over his head, expelling his breath in the process.

Dirge did his best to mimic the bouncer.

They did this several times before Dirge finally asked, "Why are we doing this?"

"It is a simple exercise that calms you and allows you to find your center."

"Center of what?"

"Just do it."

After a time, the breathing exercises gave way to one of smooth movements, and flowing arms with legs in varying positions. They spent the rest of the afternoon together, going through various lessons.

At the end of the day, Talic retrieved the stick, along with a pair of small wooden blocks, and presented them to Dirge in both hands and with a slight bow. "It's called a bokken, a training sword, and it's for another day. For now, I want you to use these," he held up the blocks, "and hang it in a place of prominence in your room. Now it's late. Off to bed with you."

The light from the setting sun shone through the window, illuminating the bouncer's altar. Dirge hadn't realized it had gotten so late. "Mistress Katlyn will be sore that I missed so much of my chores."

"I'll explain it to her. She'll understand. From this day forth, half of your day will be doing your chores and the rest you will be practicing with either me or one of my men."

"Are you sure Mistress Katlyn will be okay with this?"

Talic placed a hand upon his shoulder. "It'll be fine. I assure you."

Dirge still had his doubts as he walked to his room. He luckily found a pair of nails in his wall, nails he'd not noticed before, and affixed the blocks upon them. He then hung his bokken upon the pegs, crawled under his sheets, and quickly drifted off to sleep.

He walked the alleys around the Angelic in nothing but his small clothes, his breath visible in the chilled air, and his skin pimpling in the cold as he stepped through puddles of black water. At one point, he realized he held his bokken in both hands. The usual screams of his pursuers faded away as he gripped the practice sword tighter.

He squinted his eyes in the mist and saw the end of the alley just ahead. As he neared the end, he saw something upon the ground. He slowly walked toward it, he didn't want to, but he had no choice. There, lay Talic's shrine to the God of

Death. The black skull again called to him. He knelt and reached out to it. It was ice cold, as cold as death itself.

A voice came floating in upon the wind. "Where are you? I can't find you."

Dirge looked about but could not see who spoke. He looked back at the black skull, which now had hair as black as a raven's. The skull stared back at him with the most beautiful blue eyes he'd ever seen.

"I told you to not leave the inn," his mother's voice called out from the ether. "Why did you do this to me?"

Dirge woke, drenched in sweat. "That was new," he croaked. His nightmares about his mother were getting worse. There had been nights that he feared going to sleep.

He dragged himself out of bed, and cleaned himself from the washbasin next to his bed, something for which Mistress Katlyn was adamant. As he was drying his face, Mistress Katlyn came to him in his room. She looked about the dark accommodations at the back of the storeroom, the only light coming from a small candle on the same table as his washbasin, and shook her head.

"All right, my boy, pack up your things."

Dirge stared at her in disbelief and then frowned. *I should have known better,* he thought. *First the nightmare and now this.*

He should have seen it coming. Of course, she was kicking him out. He was a penniless orphan that no one cared about. It was something that should have happened long ago. Nevertheless, it hurt. Refusing to let his feelings show upon his face, he placed his largest shirt upon the bed, intending to use it as a would-be sack, and started piling his clothes on top.

"Don't do that, boy," she said with a shake of her head. "You'll wrinkle them. Use your soils basket."

Dirge glanced up at her, then quickly away. *Why does cleanliness matter?*

Carefully placing his clothes in his soiled-clothes basket, he then added his odds and ends: the lucky stone he'd found in the alley, the pristine black feather he found atop a refuse pile, and the piece of green, polished glass Jacob gave him. Atop it all, he placed his most prized possession, the seven-pointed star silver pendant he'd found the day his mother had died.

He reached for the bokken but hesitated. How was he to learn now that he was getting kicked out? He chose to take it, anyway. Talic gave it to him, and just because the bouncer and the Mistress had a falling out over him, it didn't mean it still wasn't his. Whatever it took, he intended to keep up with his training.

He picked up the basket and looked Mistress Katlyn in the eye. "Mistress, what have I done? Why are you kicking me out?" He couldn't help the small catch in his voice.

She knelt and cupped his chin. "Oh, sweetheart, I would never do such a thing. You're our lucky charm and I wouldn't dare part with you."

She straightened and held out her hands, a smile upon her beautiful face. "Come with me, my dear."

She led a perplexed Dirge through the inn and up the stairs up to the second floor. She stopped at the room next to one shared by Cal and Dennis—the two youngest bouncers—and ushered Dirge inside.

He felt more confused than ever as he looked about the room. The large bed across from the window with a view of the street as already made. The padded chair next to the window was clean and brushed and the writing desk next to it shined with polish. The floor was swept and the window washed.

"Do you need me to clean the room?" Dirge asked, his eyebrow raised.

"Yes, my dear. From now on it will be your duty to keep this room nice and neat." She pointed to the wardrobe in the corner. "That is for your clothing, and the small trunk under the bed is for your other personal items.

"Talic has convinced me you need to spend time with Jacob as well," she went on. "He says you need your friends. I still say that boy is nothing but trouble, but I must admit, that boy is far better than the rest of his damned clan. And who knows, he might even learn something from you."

Dirge, having stopped halfway into the room, barely heard her comments about Jacob. "My clothes?" He turned to her, his eyes blurring from unshed tears. "*My* items? You mean to say this is… *my* room?"

When she nodded, he flung himself at her, wrapping his arms about her as tight as he could. Years' worth of unshed tears fell. His throat closed in on itself and he dared not say another word for fear of his voice warbling. He shook and hugged her with all his might.

Mistress Katlyn might have looked after him since his mother's death as a favor to her, but this… this was something you only did for family.

Chapter 5
The Paladin
(497 -R.C.-)

Over the next three years, Dirge trained with Talic and the others. They schooled him on how to fight, not just fisticuffs, but with his hands, his feet, and with every other part of his body. They taught him how to grapple and entangle an opponent, how to get them in close where you could use your elbow or knees or even head. He also learned the use of daggers—both large and small—as well as how to fright with clubs, sticks, or whatever was handy. "You never know when you'll end up in a scrape," Dennis once told him. "So, you need to use everything you can to your advantage."

One morning, Dirge awoke, following another of his nightmares, and started his ritual of daily exercises. Climbing out of bed, he slipped on his loosest pair of pants, and stood in the center of his room. Out his window, the rising sun touched the rooftops of the Slaag, bathing them in its light. It was one of the few times the place didn't look ugly.

Taking several deep, measured breaths, he raised his hands above him, palms out, and then slowly swept them to his sides. He did this for several minutes, before adding his legs into the movements. His arms and legs flowed from one position to another, one stance to another, all in harmony. He loved these exercises; they centered him and gave him a sense of balance. He craved both their structure and their discipline.

A knock upon his door broke his concentration.

He bowed upon answering the door. "Good morning, Master Talic." The man had not asked for the title, but Dirge felt right in giving it.

"How are you today, my boy?" the bouncer asked, attired in his own loose fitting black pants and shirt. But unlike usual, that morning he held a bokken in his hand.

Dirge's eyes went right to the practice sword before returning to his face. "I am well. Thank you, Master. Would you like to come in?"

The man glided in and cast his eyes about the room. He walked about, running his finger along several different surfaces, checking for dust, and smiled upon not seeing any. "Retrieve your bokken and stand before me," he said as he took up position in front of the window.

His heart fluttering, Dirge had difficulty in keeping his composure. He'd waiting a long time for this. Sword practice! Ever since he hung the bokken in its place of reverence, he'd dreamt of using it.

He bowed again. "Yes, Master." He had difficulty in keeping his hands steady as he took it down from the wall. He strode in front of Master Talic, set his feet shoulder width, and held the bokken with two hands before him at a slight angle.

"What made you choose that stance?"

Dirge shrugged. "I don't know. It just felt comfortable."

"Excellent."

His Master's smile sent a thrill through Dirge. The thing felt…right…in his hands. He was made for this.

With a blinding whirl, Talic brought his sword across his body, knocking Dirge's to the side, and with the return, he smashed it into Dirge's side just below the ribcage with a loud CLACK!

"Don't get cocky, boy."

Dirge grunted and dropped his right elbow to his side for a moment, but brought his sword back into a defensive position in front of him. He did so just in time to catch another of his Master's strikes from the other direction. It knocked his sword off to the side so he jumped back and raised his arms over his head.

The move caused his Master's return strike to catch nothing but air, but the man rushed forward and brought his sword down upon the side of Dirge's left thigh with another *thwack*!

Dirge stumbled to the floor in shock. The strike had come so fast he'd not even seen it. His eyes went with with surprise to see his Master smiling rather than frowning in disgust. He reached out and took Talic's offering hand to help him to his feet. The training continued.

The next hour was much of the same, and by the end, welts covered Dirge's body.

"I am sorry to disappoint you, Master Talic," Dirge said as he rubbed a particularly hard hit to his left forearm. "I guess I'm not meant for the sword."

"Hardly, son," Talic said to him. "You did quite well. It is a skill that takes a great deal of time to master, just like anything else." He put has hand upon Dirge's shoulder. "Truth be told, you're far more advanced than you should be. By the end, we were doing moves an advanced novice would be learning. You are a natural and you have it in you to be great. Perhaps one of the best." He then smiled. "Just don't let that go to your head until *after* you're the best. You hear me?"

Jacob burst through the door. "Wake up, lazy bones!" The boy stopped cold and looked between Dirge and Master Talic as they stared at him. "What?" he asked, "Have I got poop on me or something?" He checked his pants and shirt with a broad grin.

"I am training," Dirge said.

"That's all right," Master Talic interrupted. "That's enough for today. You two run along. I'll explain it to Katlyn. A boy needs to find time to play and enjoy himself as well, and frankly, it's something you need. You're far too somber, especially for one for your age." He then grinned at Jacob. "And this one's always good for a laugh."

Jacob put on his best cheesy smile.

Noticing Jacob's eye looking red and puffy, Dirge slipped on a gray, loose-fitting shirt. "What happened to your face?"

Bringing his hand up towards his face, Jacob frowned, but dropped it and smiled once more. "Oh, I just said something I shouldn't of."

"There's a surprise," Master Talic quipped.

"What did you say?" Dirge asked. He always worried over his friend. He didn't want to lose him.

"Well, Pops just opened his own hop house and was tryin' to woo some fella into going to his place instead of Doomers. He was tellin' him that ain't no one gonna touch him; that he's safe."

The drug was common in the Slaag, whether drunk as poppy milk or smoked as opium. It was also dangerous. Aside from people dying from taking too much, if one took it out on the street they were likely to be robbed or killed while in their stupor.

"That's not very smart of Hoke," Master Talic said. "Doomers is very touchy over people trying to take away his custom."

"Eh, Pops don't care."

"What did you say," Dirge urged.

"Well, as I said, Pops was tellin' this fella that no one would touch him. So's I said 'unless Connor likes the sight of his bum.' I guess the fella didn't like my joke and he left." Jacob lowered his head and shook it a moment. "Pops was pretty sore 'bout that and cuffed me good."

"You're lucky he didn't do worse," Dirge said with a shake of his head.

"Oh Connor took out his knife and said he was gonna gut me but Pops cuffed him too. So I took off out'a there and figured I'd lay low for a bit."

"Well, you two just steer clear of him," Master Talic said to Jacob before turning to Dirge. "I'm going to take over for Dennis, downstairs. You two go have fun." He pointed his finger at Dirge. "I mean it. Have *fun*."

After the bouncer left, Dirge turned to Jacob. "So, what were you thinking?"

Jacob beamed. "Word is that a Chaos paladin went into Doomers' place and half the folk there hightailed it out with their britches full of poop. Want to go see? If we're lucky, he might still be there and we could see him."

Dirge thought about it. Chaos paladins were the right arm of the church, roaming the lands, doing as they wanted, and upholding the will of Chaos. Incredibly dangerous, they were both powerful and highly unstable. Word was, if one even looked at you, you might burst into flames. Dirge doubted last bit, but knew it was stupid to tempt anything dealing with the Lord of Chaos.

And yet, he wanted to know what a paladin looked like.

Dirge nodded and the boys dashed down the stairs, through the common room and out of the inn. Mistress Katlyn gave Jacob the evil eye as they ran by, to which the boy grinned even bigger. Once out onto the busy street, the boys turned north toward Doomer's, at the edge of the Slaag. Word was, Doomers opened it there to get customers from the ghetto as well as the northern, more commercial, parts of the city.

They ran along the edge of the muddy street, weaving through traffic. When they came close to the large brick building, Jacob ducked behind a pile of crates that sat in front of the warehouse that sat next to the alleyway and opposite the brothel. Dirge took a quick glance down the alley, out of habit, to see if it was empty. Never put your back to an alley in the Slaag without checking it first, and even then, keep an eye on it.

They hid behind the crates for some time to no avail. Dirge wondered if the entire thing was a hoax until a man, who'd just entered, came running back out. He was in such distress he ran into the street right in front of a speeding horse and wagon team. He bounced off the horse, and fell to the ground in front of the over-laden wagon. His scream lasted only a moment as the wheel crushed his ribcage, causing blood to vomit from his mouth and burst from his chest. People screamed, some vomited, and the horse team whinnied and pawed at the air in distress.

"That'll ruin your day," Jacob quipped.

Disgusted, Dirge felt sorry for the man. He was about to say so when someone exited from the brothel, causing Dirge to catch his breath.

The man was of average height and weight, with a rather unremarkable face, and bright green hair. Yet his eyes, which had a wild, wicked look to them, spoke volumes. As the man moved, his mail shirt of overlapping scales glittered in the sun, causing a rainbow of cascading and changing colors, shades, and shapes. The fluctuations were both subtle and stark. His metal arm and leg greaves, along with the metal backing on his gauntlets changed just as did his mail. Even the air about him seemed to twist and contort.

"Paladin," Dirge whispered, his hand going to his belt pouch where he kept his lucky seven-stared pendant. He grasped the pouch with an unsteady hand.

All eyes now gazed upon the Chaos paladin. Many of the surrounding folk screamed and fled. Yet just as many stayed and knelt in open worship. The devout filled the city of Tuilar, the Lord of Chaos held in the highest regard. It was even said one of the largest temples to Edis in the entire region lie at the center of the city.

Dirge bristled in disgust and anger. His hand clutching his pouch, he stood from behind the crates and scowled at the paladin. Jacob hissed at his side, but he ignored his friend. His mind clouded and his vision tunneled; the only thing that mattered, the only thing he could see, was the monster across the street. Dirge felt when the creature of Chaos locked eyes with him, and a slight shiver ran down his spine. The shiver only made him angrier and his hand gripped his pouch so hard it seemed to burn.

The paladin smirked and stepped out into the street. "Aren't you a cocky one," he said, his pipping voice had an odd warble to it.

"Ukase take you," Dirge spat back at him. He didn't know where the term came from, let along what it meant, but it felt right.

The smirk fell from the paladin's lips and his brows furrowed. "What did you say?" he spat.

"Dirge, let's get out of here," Jacob insisted. "Run," he yelled and ran down the alley.

He pulled Dirge as he ran, causing Dirge to catch himself to keep from falling. When Dirge turned back up at the paladin, his anger and revulsion evaporated. Whatever spell he'd been under had dissipated, and he now felt only fear. He staggered a moment before regaining his feet and sprinted after his friend.

"That's it, run little rabbits." Dirge heard the paladin say behind him. "I do so love a good hunt."

Dirge did not understand what had come over him. He'd taunted a paladin of the Lord of Chaos! Had he gone mad?

What the hells was he thinking?! Jacob dashed down a side alley ahead and Dirge followed. When a crash came from behind him, he glanced back. The top half of the wall collapsed but not enough to block the way.

"Where are you going, little rabbits," he heard the paladin call behind him. "Or maybe I should call you rats?"

They sped through the twisting alleyway, the mud slick beneath his boots. He knew if he fell he'd die. Jacob pulled away the farther they went. It reminded him of the day they'd run from Doomers' henchmen all those years ago, until a brick fell from far above, almost hitting him. He sped on when another nearly struck him, then another, and another. The walls undulated and wobbled, sending more bricks to the ground. That's when Dirge realized the first few bricks weren't happenstance.

"You can't hide from me, rats," came the call from behind him.

The paladin was getting closer.

A multihued orb, the size of Dirge's head, sailed past his left side. It struck the building ahead of him, splattering across the brick wall like a ball of mud. The stain upon the wall—looking much like the paladin's armor, a myriad of colors, tones, and shapes—expanded. It bubbled and hissed, and slowly ate away at the brick until the wall above gave way.

Dirge was abreast with the wall as it tumbled down. He veered sharply to the right to avoid large chunks of masonry, bounced against the wall on the right, and fell. His training kicked in without thought, making his fall became a forward roll and a dive to avoid the collapsing wall. Dust clouded his vision and caused him to cough, as debris fall across his back and legs. He lay there for a moment, surprised to be still alive. Coughing, he smiled as Jacob ran toward him.

"Are you all right?" Jacob asked, bending over to help Dirge. "I figured you was gone for sure!"

"I'm fine," Dirge replied as Jacob helped untangle him from the timber and plaster. He got to his feet and tested his legs. Nothing felt broken but he would sport several bruises in the near future. He turned and examined the wreckage behind him. The entire building had collapsed, completely blocking the alleyway.

"Well, at least we don't have to worry about him anymore," Jacob said with a chortle.

"Oh, but you *do* have to worry," the paladin said from beyond the rubble. He laughed maniacally as the rubble shook and shuttered. To Dirges horror, the debris parted like drapes.

The boys turned and ran in a full flown panic. Dirge's only thought was getting to the Angelic. Nothing else mattered. They made several more twists and turns before Dirge felt a moment of elation. Ahead of them, the alley ended at a T, and one hundred feet down the alley to the right lay the Angelic.

As they reached the corner and started the turn, Dirge felt something slam him in the back, hard. The blow sent him flying forward into Jacob. They both went tumbling to the ground and into the wall, with Jacob taking the brunt of the blow. Dirge lay upon the ground, dazed. The world spun and his ears rung, but it didn't prevent him from hearing the laughter of the Chaos paladin. Through blurred vision, Dirge watched the man approach, step after agonizing step. He turned to Jacob and his eyes went wide. His friend's head lie against the wall, blood covering his face.

"No," Dirge mumbled. Jacob couldn't be dead. He just couldn't!

"Aww, did I kill you little friend, Rat? Don't worry, you'll join him soon enough."

Dirge's fear vanished. He felt only rage. He reached down, grabbed the dagger at his friend's belt, and stood to face the paladin.

"Oh, still have a little fight in you, do you?"

Dirge charged the paladin.

The paladin smirked. "That's it, give me some sport."

The paladin didn't even bother to draw a weapon. Dirge slammed into the man, attempting to drive the dagger through the interlocking scales of his mail shirt. The dagger skimmed along the armor and broke. Undeterred, Dirge continued to drive the remainder of the weapon—the hilt and about an inch of steel—up toward the man's face. The ragged end of the blade struck the paladin in the cheek, tearing open a large gouge that fountained blood.

The paladin screamed in rage and pain, backhanding Dirge, and sending the boy hurtling through the air. "You rotten little rat!" The paladin put a hand to his ruined face. "How dare you!"

The paladin held out his blood soaked hand and a gelatinous ball of color filled it, the same type that struck the wall during their chase. A dark shadow formed behind the man, like a black cloud of dread. "I was going to take it easy on you. But now I'll make it nice and slow."

The horrific shadow behind the paladin shivered, and a dark hand, clutching a black dagger, emerged from it. The hand plunged the dagger into the paladin's ear, and withdrew it. Blood fountained from the paladin head as he dropped to the ground, lifeless.

Chapter 6
An Invitation
(497 -R.C.-)

Dirge stared, his eyes wide and his jaw slack. *What just happened?*

The shadow quaked once more. He steeled himself. This thing, this demon, had just killed a paladin of the Lord of Chaos, and he was next.

The dreadful shadow split open and Talic stepped into the light.

Dirge's jaw dropped open. "Master?"

"Are you all right, son?" Talic asked, looking majestic, covered head to toe in black leather armor. Pulling out a small cloth, he wiped the blood from his dagger and returned the blade to its sheath. He then knelt to Dirge. "Are you hurt, son?"

Dirge looked down at his aching hand where it had slammed into the paladin. He'd noticed the pain at first but thought it was just from the blow, but blisters covered it as though burned.

Talic pulled out a pouch and gently applied some kind of salve to Dirge's hand, then wrapped it with a clean cloth. "Their armor is infused with Chaos," his Master explained while tying off the bandage. "It corrupts anything that touches it. Well, anything that's not warded against it," he added with a smile as he tapped his dagger.

"Who are you, Master?" Dirge asked. "You're not mercenaries like they say, are you?"

"No," Talic replied. "Most think that, and we let them. We are members of the Brotherhood of Assassins. We are the right hand of Aza'zel. People come to us with contracts, asking for the deaths of certain people, and if Aza'zel finds it worthy, we carry out those contracts."

Talic went to Jacob and checked his head. "He's alive."

Dirge felt a pang of guilt. In all the excitement, he'd forgotten his friend.

Talic added a powder to the boy's head and then wrapped it in another bandage. "Head wounds tend to bleed a lot, so it looks worse than it actually is. He should be fine in a few days with rest."

Dirge simply nodded his head. "So, did someone pay you to kill the paladin?"

"No, my son. I killed him to keep him from taking your life."

Dirge shook his head. "But wouldn't that upset Aza'zel, keeping me from dying?"

"Son," Talic said softly, placing his hand upon Dirge's shoulder. "Unlike what most think, Aza'zel does not revel in the taking of all life. He accepts all those that come to him, but he knows life is as important as death."

Hake and Cal came running out the back door to the inn. They gathered up the body of the dead paladin while Talic picked Jacob up in his arms and they all started for the inn. Dirge expected them to burn themselves on the paladin's armor, but the moment the man died his armor lost its coloring.

"Aza'zel decides when the taking a certain life fits into the greater balance of the world," Talic continued.

When they all reached the back stairs, Dirge got another surprise when Cal reached down under the left side of the steps, caused something to click, and raised the steps, revealing a trap door leading into the cellar.

Dirge stared at Talic, his eyes wide.

His Master chuckled. "We wouldn't want to drag bodies through Katlyn's kitchen, now would we?"

Dirge, still a bit dazed, followed Cal and Hake as they descended the stairs into a portion of the cellar he'd not seen before. He looked about the gloomy room; what little light there was, came from a single lantern hanging on the far wall. A single table lay along one wall next to a rain barrel. Butchers implements hung on the wall above the table.

"She'd hate the mess," Dirge mumbled.

Talic laughed. "That she would, my boy. That she would."

After Hake and Cal placed the body on a table, Talic handed Jacob off to Hake. "Here, take him to Katlyn and have her look after him for a bit. Cal, you deal with this one. I'll take Dirge up to his room and have a word with him."

Cal stripped the body, throwing the items into different crates lining the wall next to the table. Hake carried Jacob to the wall opposite the stairs. Pressing a seemingly random brick something clicked. He then pushed on the wall, opening a hidden door leading to the rest of the cellar.

"Come, my boy." Talic placed a hand on Dirge's shoulder and guided him to a small stairway along the wall opposite the table. It was nearly pitch black but Talic made his way up the stairs with ease while keeping a steady hand upon Dirge. At the second landing, Dirge heard yet another click as Talic opened another hidden door opening to the hallway near Dirge's room.

Once inside the room, Talic sat Dirge down on his bed and took the comfortable chair. The man eyed Dirge for several moments. "Tell me exactly what happened to cause a paladin of Chaos to want to kill you."

Dirge fidgeted a moment, cleared his throat, and told his Master all that transpired, paying special attention to what he'd said to the paladin.

Talic smiled. "I'm very proud of you, Dirge."

Dirge dropped his head, blushing with embarrassment. "What's to be proud of? We almost died because of me."

"You did well. You stood up to him when most would simply lay down and die." He tilted his head a moment. "I'm thinking you've been touched by one of the gods, one long forgotten." There was a hint of awe in his voice. "No one's heard of, let alone spoken of, the god Ukase in hundreds of years. The only way you could have said and acted as you did, is if he—or one of his lesser's—reached out to you. Hells boy, you shouldn't have been able to touch that paladin with a simple dagger, let alone cut him. He was protected by Chaos."

"But the dagger broke."

"Yes, the dagger broke. But you didn't." The man's eyes burned with excitement. "The veil is thinning and Chaos is losing his hold. His time is nearing its end."

Some forgotten god is touching me? It made no sense. No one cared about him. *Well, that's not true. Jacob cares. At least I think he does.* He shook his head. "What are you saying?"

"I'm saying you are special, son." Talic grasped Dirge's shoulder. "And I'm asking if you want to join us."

Chapter 7
Covered in Blood
(498 -R.C.-)

The booming lightning accentuated the clack of Dirge's sword against Talic's. The older man breathed easily as he slid to the side and blocked another of Dirge's attacks. They circled each other in a dance of death. Stripped to the waist, with sweat covering them both, Dirge's ebony chest matched Talic's in everything but size. The only illumination came from a pair of lamps in the dank, dark basement. That darkness might seem oppressive to most, but to Dirge, it was like a lover's embrace.

Dirge had not been sure about joining the Brotherhood at first. He supposed some people deserved to die, but he wasn't sure he had what it took to take a life. Even though he grew up around death, as had everyone who lived in the Slaag, the paladin's death had been the first he'd witnessed. Seeing life leave the man's eyes had been a sobering experience.

Talic gave him time to decide, for which Dirge was grateful for. And once he agreed to join, Talic doubled his training, choosing to focus on the sword. In a year's time, Dirge had grown in both size and skill.

"You've a natural affinity with the long blade," Talic told him as he blocked another blow and stepped to the side. "It's your calling from the Gods."

They'd been sparring with blunted blades for over a month yet Dirge hadn't struck his master even once. But then, Talic had yet to strike Dirge either. His master might have been holding back, but Dirge doubted it. One did not improve at this stage by holding back.

Dirge danced to his right, then ducked left, his sword driving toward Talic's leg. His master deflected the blow at the last second and followed up with a strike at Dirge's head, but Dirge tumbled out of the way.

"Don't get ahead of yourself, my boy," Talic said as he slowly advanced. "You want a fight to be over as quickly as possible, but don't lose your head over rushing." He smiled and added, "Your mother would be cross with me if I brained you."

Dirge slowly stood—his entire focus on the elder swordsman. It was apparent to Dirge that Talic wanted to be some kind of father figure to him. He found it admirable, but pointless. Dirge had no father, and to pretend otherwise would simply be a lie. He appreciated Mistress Katlyn never trying to do the same regarding his mother.

They sparred for another ten minutes before Talic called an end to it. "You did well today, my boy. Go get yourself cleaned up and then something to eat. Then report to Cal for your letters."

Cal was easily the most rounded member of the Brotherhood. Not only a skilled assassin, he'd seen more of the world than any of them. He'd been teaching Dirge to read and write from the moment Dirge joined. The man even played several instruments and had a more than fair voice. Mistress Katlyn had been pressing him for some time to perform before the customers, but he always refused. "That part of my life is over," he told her one time with a smile. "Besides, I'd end up breaking far too many hearts."

With a bow, Dirge sheathed his sword, toweled himself off, and put his shirt back on before heading upstairs.

Later that evening, Dirge sat cross-legged before his own shrine to Aza'zel, opening himself up to his new god—he'd been doing so for several months. The rituals and training soothed him. He loved it. It helped fill a small portion of the void left in his heart with his mother's passing.

Upon finishing his meditations, he stood facing the shrine, bowed in reverence, and kissed his pendant to Aza'zel. Yet, as usual, something about his prayers didn't seem quite right. It felt… off, somehow.

With a shrug, he changed out of his black practice garb and headed down to the common room. For the sake of appearances, they also trained him as a bouncer, and that evening was to be his first working the common room with only Talic. His stomach fluttered and his palms itched. It didn't exactly bother him that the job required him to not wear any weapons, he simply felt more centered when he had either his bokken or his blunted blade at hand.

Once in the common room he approached Talic and bowed. "Good evening, Master."

Talic cast his gaze around the room. "None of that here, you understand me? Here I'm just your boss. No 'Master' and no bowing. It calls undue attention."

Dirge resisted the urge to bow again, but it wasn't easy. He took up position across the room from Talic as instructed and tried to gauge the room. It was busier than usual with over half the tables filled, and the night hadn't even begun. He looked back at his master who gave him the sign to stand vigil, with a slight raising of the hand followed by a small spin of his finger.

Talic had dozens of signals, of which Dirge only knew a few. It frustrated him. But Talic said not to worry. "You're a quick student, a natural. You'll do fine."

As the hours passed, the inn filled, it grew more difficult to monitor everyone. Dozens of people filed into the warm common room to escape the cool evening. People traded simple conversation, jokes, and wild stories, each one more incredible than the next filled the air.

"I'm telling you I saw one," a black-bearded man in leather armor said, his voice slurring. "Me and Hank was guarding a wagon train when the most ungodly stench you ever heard hit me."

"You heard a stench?" the man on his right said with a smile as he knuckled his chin-long mustache.

The bearded man waved him off and continued. "You know what I mean. Anyway, here we was doin' our job when I smelt it. It burned the hairs out my nose, t'was so bad. Then I heard it. It was like… well… it was like someone got booted in their rocks, you know. The scream was so high, almost like a woman. But it twern't no woman. Twern't no man, neither. Cause this thing grunted and snorted at the same time. All the horses started makin such a fuss they was likely to tear apart their bridles." He stopped for a moment and took a long pull on his ale.

"Well, what happened next," the blond man across from him urged.

"That's when I seen it." The bearded man stared into nothing. "It was bluer than the sky and half covered in green hair, with five arms and three legs, all of um with claws. It had a mouth full of fangs and no eyes. I tell you it had no eyes!"

"Grunkin," the blond man said in a hushed tone.

"Oh, piss off," mustache-man said. "Next you'll be tellin' us you seen a spook from the Lands of the Dead."

"It's true," the bearded man said. "The thing grunted and slammed into the wagon just behind of us. It tore the horses to shreds and then the driver, even after he put a crossbow bolt into its chest. T'was like it didn't even notice. That fool, Hank, then ran at it with his spear. He stuck the think square in the chest. Hells he hit it so hard the spear when through it and stuck in the wagon. It didn't care. I'm tellin' you it didn't care! It tore the spear apart with its hands and jumped on poor Hank… there was so much blood."

"Whad'ya do?"

"I ran. Whad'ya think!? I wasn't about to let it do that to me."

"What happened to it?" asked the man on his right, enthralled.

"I don't know," he replied. "I heard so much screamin' I just kept runnin' till I hit the nearest town." He took another long pull on his ale, emptying it.

"When'd this happen?" asked the blond man.

"Two weeks ago," he replied, his eyes still glazed. "Just outside Brampton."

"Hells man, that just over a day's ride from here!"

They all went quiet.

It wasn't the first time Dirge had heard stories of grunkins. He'd once asked Master Talic if they were real.

His master nodded. "They are the spawn of the Lord of Chaos. They come out of Chaos storms; as terrible and wicked as their master. They're damned hard to put down too. They don't eat or sleep. All they do is kill."

Dirge shook his head to clear the thought. He needed to keep his eye on the crowd, not stand there, and listen to people and their stories.

As the night wore on more and more people came to the inn, and as usual, with more people came more unrest. Dirge did his best to keep an eye on everything. He was tall for his age, standing just over five feet, but he still needed to stand upon a corner table to see the entire room. He kept expecting Master Talic to fetch one of the others to help, but he didn't. The man stood stock still with his arms across his chest surveying the room as Lindsey and Hanna ran ragged trying to keep up with the crowd.

Lindsey set a cup of water on the ledge lining the wall behind Dirge. "You'd think Talic would at least get one of the other boys to help manage the crowd," the brown-eyed blonde said as she rubbed her bum. "I'm going to be black and blue from all the pinches they're dealing out."

Dirge's hackles rose and his brows furrowed. He'd known her all his life and hated to see the way many of the men groped her. *She deserves better,* he thought as she walked away, her brown skirt hugging her bottom, showing everyone in the bar just how perfect she was.

He saw motion across the room and looked up. Talic was staring at him. His master shook his head, pointed at his eyes then at the rest of the room. Dirge blushed and dropped his gaze before going back to surveying the crowd. He should have known better. Just because he liked Lindsey, it didn't alleviate his responsibility of keeping watch.

A crash of pottery to his right brought his head around, sharp. Having dropped her tray, Hanna struggled as a man with bright red hair pulled her down onto his lap. Her brown hair flailed as she squealed at him to let her go.

Dirge looked to Talic, but the man simply nodded at him, then at the door. Dirge's stomach filled with butterflies as he jumped down and quickly made his way to the table. "Let her go, and get out," he said in a stern voice.

The men at the table laughed.

Dirge tried to stand taller and repeated himself, adding, "You are no longer welcome here."

"Get a load of this little shit," one of them said.

"Aw, come on, little tuff. I'm just wanting a quick go at her. I promise you can have her back to wipe your ass as soon as I'm finished." The red-haired man said. His friends laughed harder.

Hanna took advantage of the man's momentary distraction. She stomped on his foot and jumped away as he let go with a yelp.

"You miserable bitch!" The red-haired man grabbed her back.

Dirge acted without thinking. He rushed forward and grabbed the man's arm. Using the man's own momentum, Dirge pulled him out of his seat and slammed him to the floor face first, where he groaned and went still.

Dirge quickly reset his feet and eyed the rest of the men. Half laughed even harder at what happened to their friend, but the rest stared at him, their eyes burning with rage.

"Insolent little fuck," a blond man said. He started to stand, but one of his compatriots—a dark-haired man with a grizzled beard—grabbed him by the arm, and nodded toward Talic. The blond man eyed Talic and then turned back to Dirge. "You're not worth it." He huffed and gestured to the others. "Let's get out of here."

The rest of the men stood, picked up their unconscious friend, and headed toward the door. The man with the beard nodded respectfully at Talic as he left.

As Dirge made his way back to his corner, several of the regulars patted him on the back, while others throughout the room, laughed, whooped, and hollered. Dirge ignored it, his heart hammering as he tried not to shake from the adrenaline. Once he stood back atop the table, he took a deep breath and calmed himself with one of his mental exercises. As he scanned the room, he didn't feel elated at doing his job—there was nothing heroic in saving Hanna. Neither did he feel pride in seeing Talic smile and nod toward him. He felt... unresolved.

After that, several customers glanced at him from time to time. Some smiled, but many held uncertainty in their eyes.

"He's a cold one, isn't he?" people said.

It was late in the evening when Talic came to him. "That's enough for tonight, son. Dennis will take over from here. You head up to bed." He clasped Dirge on the back once the boy jumped down from the table. "You did well tonight."

"I did?"

"Certainly! Hells, boy, you handled that ass perfectly."

Dirge shook his head. "I'm not so sure."

"Why do you say that?"

"Well, what's stopping him from doing it again? What if he attacks an innocent because I embarrassed him?"

"Nothing," Talic replied. He took a long look at Dirge. "Do you think you should have done more?"

Dirge considered the question. "No, for me to do more to him for that offense would've been wrong. But I can't help but think he'll do worse."

"And if he does?"

"Then he should pay for it." Dirge held his head high.

"What if he killed someone? Does he deserve to die?"

"Yes."

"Would *you* be the one to carry out that judgment?"

That gave Dirge pause. "I don't know." He shrugged. "I don't know if I could kill anyone."

"Our way is not to kill because we think they deserve it, but only if it sanctioned and agreed upon by God. It is not for everyone." He patted Dirge on the back and gave him a gentle push. "Go, off to bed with you. In the morning, I want you to think about what I told you."

Dirge thought about what his master said regarding the Brotherhood. One day he'd have to kill in cold blood, not during a fight where the people could defend themselves, but to kill with stealth and intent. It was not a new thought to him. What if the person were innocent? Could he still take their life?

In the following weeks, he contemplated the heart of what it meant to be part of the Brotherhood. It didn't feel quite right. He said as much to his master one morning during sword training.

"Do you dislike the training you are receiving?" Talic asked.

"No, Master."

"Do you feel you're in the wrong place?"

Dirge thought a moment. "No. No, this part feels right."

Master Talic smiled. "Then I wouldn't worry about it. God will show you the way, and until he does, we shall continue as we have."

Dirge wasn't sure which god his master was referring to, but he nodded and they continued the drills. He threw himself into the training that day forward, forgoing all other things, including Jacob.

Two months passed and the only times Dirge went outside was when Master Talic or Hake taught him the art of stealth. He wasn't great at it. He had the self-discipline for an ambush—standing silently, without moving, for long periods until your quarry came within reach—but he found it difficult stalking someone. Nor was he believable at feigning a casual stance. "You're simply too deliberate in your approach," Talic told him. "That's all right, though. You're quick, and you'll use that to your advantage. Believe me, one of the best ways to catch someone by surprise is to approach them head-on."

Dirge didn't understand how that could be so, but he wasn't going to question his master. The man knew more about stealth than anyone.

One early afternoon, Talic followed Dirge as he slunk through the shadows of the alleys, trying to creep up on Dennis who lay somewhere ahead. Dirge placed each footstep with calculation—one allowing good footing and free of debris. It took ten minutes to reach the nearest corner, and Dirge found every moment ponderous.

Ahead, darkness clung to the alley like a beast ready to pounce causing a thought to pop into Dirge's head. "Master Talic, I've a question." He kept his voice soft and low so it wouldn't carry. "The day you saved me from the paladin, a dark shadow formed behind him as he was about to strike. For the longest time, I thought the shadow was some kind of... I don't know the word for it, essence, I guess, a thing of Chaos. It wasn't though, was it?"

His master smiled. "That, my boy, was the Shroud of Aza'zel. Few can summon it, but those of us blessed to know the true touch of Aza'zel, can pull God's cloak about them, masking them from prey."

"Do you think I'll ever be able to do it?"

Talic pursed his lips. "Let's just work at this one thing at a time. His touch will come or it won't, you cannot force these things."

They continued down the alleyway, Dirge in the lead. Once they reached the corner, he stopped and listened. The sound of someone staggering through the rubbish prevalent in the alleys of the Slaag echoed off the walls. At a nod from Master Talic, Dirge pulled himself up tight against the wall— their mottled outfits of blacks and grays melding with the surrounding shadows. Soon enough, a blood-soaked young man staggered into the intersection. He was dragging an arm along the wall to aid his standing but fell when that aid disappeared. He landed with a grunt and didn't move thereafter.

Through blood covered, tattered clothes Dirge recognized the young man. "Jacob!"

With a glance down the alley, Talic dashed to the boy's side. He gently searched Jacob for his injuries, then rolled him onto his back and put his ear to Jacob's face. "He still breathes, but it's shallow."

Talic gingerly picked up Jacob, and they raced back to the inn. Talic took him to the spare back room, telling Dirge to fetch hot water and some clean cloths. When Dirge returned, his master had already stripped Jacob of his clothes. Blood and dirt covered Jacob, but he appeared to have no gaping wounds—only cuts and scrapes.

Dirge sighed in relief as though he'd been holding his breath the entire time. "Is he going to be all right?"

"Some blood looks to have come from a split in his scalp, but I'm guessing the rest is from others." He placed a small folded cloth to the side of Jacob's head and held it in place. "As to whether he'll live, I cannot say. Blows to the head can be strange. I've seen men refuse to stay down after taking massive strikes to the head, and I've seen folks die from slipping on the ice."

Dirge stared at his one and only friend. *Come on, you've got to be all right. What am I going do without you?*

Dirge jumped at a sudden rap at the door.

"Talic, I've news," Dobbs said, stepping in.

"What is it?"

"Word's come down that Hoke made a move on Doomers. Didn't go well. He, two of his boys, and about half of his tuffs are dead."

"Anything else?" When Dobbs shook his head Talic continued, "All right. Tell the others to keep sharp. They kicked the nest, and it's bound to stir the hornets. Tell Katlyn that I suggest she close the inn for the night and maybe the next day as well. Regardless of her reply, we're on high watch. Anyone comes close to here that we don't know or like, I want them roughed up. Got it?"

Talic's eyes turned to Dirge. "Come here, son. I want you to keep an eye on him for me. Hold this until someone comes with bandages. I need to go."

Dirge trudged to his friend, knelt, and held the bloodstained cloth. "I should have been there for him."

"Nonsense—"

"I should have! I abandoned him, and this is what happened."

Talic left without another word.

"I'll look after you," he said to his unconscious friend. "I promise. You'll never be alone again." Jacob may have had a father, a mother, sisters, and brothers, but Dirge never thought of those people as Jacob's family. "I'll be your family."

He didn't know how much time passed before Mistress Katlyn came with bandages. She checked the wound, washed it, put on a new clean cloth, and wrapped a long strip about Jacob's head to hold it in place.

"Can we take him to my room?" Dirge worried, his friend looked so pale.

"Best not to move him, dear. Least not until he recovers some." She stood and placed a hand upon Dirge's head. "Let's get you something to eat."

"I'm not hungry."

Katlyn sighed and left, only to return a short time later with a hot bowl of stew. "You need to keep your energy."

Dirge sat at Jacob's side for two days. He refused to leave and hardly slept. Every time Jacob groaned or stirred, Dirge popped awake to check on him, but always to no avail. He feared his friend would never recover.

Chapter 8
Truth within a Test
(498 -R.C.-)

"Son, wake up."

Dirge snapped awake and focused on Master Talic, whose face looked grim. "Yes, Master?" Dirge rubbed the sleep from his eyes.

"Come with me."

Dirge glanced at a sleeping Jacob.

"I'll have Lindsey keep an eye on him," Talic added. "We must speak in my room. Come."

Hesitating a moment, he followed Talic out the door. He didn't want to leave his friends side, but Master Talic gave him an order and he had to obey.

Once in Talic's room, he told Dirge to take the chair by the window. Once seated, Master Talic stood in front of him with his arms crossed and a stone-hard face. "Are you sure you want to be a member of the Brotherhood?"

Dirge's eyes went wide at the blunt question. "Yes, Master."

"Are you willing to take the life of another if called upon by Aza'zel?"

"Yes, Master," Dirge said, his voice losing its strength.

"It is time to test that." Talic voice was hard as iron. Turning, he strode to his wardrobe, took something out, and returned. He held a neat stack of black clothes in his left hand and a black hilted sword in an equally black sheath in his right. "Aza'zel has a task for you."

The items filled Dirge with a sense of doom.

"A contract has been brought to us by Doomers, himself. I have consulted with the Great Lord of Death and he will accept the lives that Doomers seeks."

"Who?"

"In retaliation for the assault on his establishment, Doomers wants the lives of the rest of Hoke's family. Hoke's woman, Tessa, is now leading the family, and she wants a war. Doomers wants this over quickly and publicly to remind others of what happens to those who cross him."

Dirge liked his lips. Jacob's family? Master Talic was asking him to kill the rest of his only friend's kin. Jacob hated them—he'd said as much many times. But this went beyond hate, this was family.

"Aza'zel has decreed that these people will die," Talic said. "He also told me they shall die by your hand. Do you accept?"

Dirge's eyes shot up to his master's. "God said I must do this?"

"Will you go against the word of God? If you would truly be one of us, you must do this." Talic placed the objects on the table next to Dirge. "Their lives are in your hands. Remember, Aza'zel's word is as law. If you spurn this, you accept Chaos as your master—for only *He* decrees you can do as you will."

Dirge accepted the objects as thought they were venomous snakes.

Dressed in black, and with his face coated in soot, Dirge knelt in the shadow of the building across for the door to Hoke's hop house. Several rush torches—along with the full moon—illuminated the roughly twenty by twenty courtyard in front the building. At that door, stood Jacob's brothers, Axe and Connor, deep in conversation. Both young men had swords at their belts and Axe held a small crossbow.

Dirge held his own crossbow low to the ground, with a bolt at the ready. He performed deep breathing exercises taught to him by Talic to remain calm. He stayed perfectly still and eyed the alleyways on either side of the courtyard to make certain no one was approaching him unawares.

Dirge knew what to do he just didn't like it. Beyond the fact he'd never taken someone's life, he didn't like the idea of killing someone who didn't have the chance to defend themselves. He found it cowardly.

If you're going to take a man's life, you should at least give him a chance to defend it. Dirge shook off the thought.

He'd hoped that one brother would leave, but luck was not on his side that night. No matter, the job needed doing and Aza'zel demanded that *he* do it.

Dirge slowly raised the crossbow and took aim at Axe. It may be craven to shoot a man from the shadows, but he didn't want to give Axe a chance to shoot back. He took a deep breath and slowly exhaled while squeezing the trigger. The crossbow thumped, and the bolt sailed through the air, striking Axe on the right side of his chest.

Dirge dropped the bow and sprinted toward Connor as Axe fell. Dirge drew his sword while sprinting, bounded up the steps, and slashed at Connor who stared in disbelief at his fallen brother. The black blade's long, slightly curved single edge, bit deep into Connor's neck, and sliced across his rib-cage. Connor grasped his neck, blood pouring through his fingers, gurgled a moment, and rolled down the steps to the ground.

Dirge stood there a moment, shaking. He stared at Connor's motionless form. The blood pooled around his head, glittering black in the moonlight. Dirge couldn't believe he'd done it. He'd taken a life. Sick to his stomach, he did his best not to throw up.

Something thumped, and the right side of Dirge's chest flared in pain as something streaked by his face. He clasped his hand to his side, quickly stepping back. Axe lay on the floor, his crossbow aimed at Dirge. The bolt had only grazed his side, but it hurt like hell.

Dirge slashed awkwardly at Axe with his sword in his left hand. Axe blocked the sword with his bow and swung it at Dirge, catching him in the right leg, and sent him tumbling down the steps. Dirge lost his sword in the fall.

"You miserable little fuck," Axe grunted in obvious pain as he tried to draw his own sword.

Dirge didn't stay down. He sprang to his feet, scrambled up the steps, and slammed into Axe, whose sword was only half drawn. The two of them crashed into the wall next to the door. He pinned Axe's sword hand with his right and grabbed the bolt protruding from Axe's chest with his left. Dirge twisted the bolt. Axe screamed in agony as Dirge pulled the bolt out slightly before jamming it in toward the center of the much larger boy's chest. Axe shuddered and fell to the floor, taking Dirge with him.

Dirge needed to drag himself out from under Axe's corpse, which wasn't easy. Dirge may have matched the young man in height, but Axe outweighed him by a good fifty pounds.

That leaves only Jack... and Tabatha.

His mouth twisted. He wasn't thrilled with having to kill a woman, be it his friend's sister or not. Jacob used to have four sisters but only Tabitha remained. Two had died in childbirth while the other had succumbed to opium only a year before.

Dirge quickly searched for and found his sword. That scream would bring others and Dirge needed to be ready. *So much for stealth.*

The problem was, at that point, Dirge didn't know how many henchmen might still be around. Dobbs had said Hoke died with half of them, but how many had stayed now that Tessa was in charge? For that matter, how many did he have in the first place? Too many questions and Dirge still had a job to do.

With his sword held low, he raced to the door and knelt next to it. He quickly scanned the courtyard to see if anyone approached. Seeing no one, he opened the door and peeked inside. A pair of rough torches at either end, rather than lamps lit the empty, narrow hallway. From the scorch marks on the walls, it was a wonder the building hadn't yet burned down. Torches were perilous when used in rickety wooden structures.

Staying low, Dirge crept down the hall, occasionally checking his rear to see if anyone was coming up behind him. No sound came from any of the doors he passed while heading to the stairs at the end of the hall. *Either no one's here or they're all keeping quiet.* At the foot of the stairs, a door opened behind him. He spun and raised his sword to strike or parry, but stopped.

A young woman staggered into the gloomy hallway, wearing not a stitch. Ribs protruded from her rail thin form and grease matted her dark, stringy hair. Brown, glazed eyes regarded him as she wobbled forward on shaky, bowed legs. "Can I have more?" she slurred, licking her black-stained lips while reaching out with jittery, blackened hands. "Please. I'll do anything you want." Reaching him at the bottom of the stairs, she squinted and shook her head. "Who are you? You're not Jack." Her eyes widened with desperation. "Have you any coin? I'll do anything you want." Her gaze darted over his head and her face lit up. "Jack!"

Dirge spun back around.

Jacob's eldest brother, Jack descended the stair along with a large man Dirge didn't know. Jack stopped short, his eyes going wide. The large man cursed, drew his sword, and charged, his boots thumping on the steps.

Dirge's training kicked in. He raced up the stairs, causing the large man to swing late. He slashed at the man's exposed belly, causing the man to bellow in pain and tumble down the stairs while Jack turned tail and ran.

Dirge desperately wanted to follow Jack but stopped. After what happened outside, he thought it best to not leave an enemy behind him. The large man lay at the foot of the stairs on his side, curled into a fetal position, trying to hold in the blood that poured from his stomach. Dirge hastened down the steps and stabbed the large man in the throat. The man gurgled and fell silent.

"Demon," the woman said, her entire body shaking. "Please don't hurt me." She backed away. "Please don't hurt me. Demon. Demon!" The woman shrieked and ran down the hall to the front door.

Dirge shook his head. If the scream from outside had alerted no one before, those woman's cries would. Feeling he had little time, Dirge raced up the stairs. Stopping short of the top, he peeked over the edge. At the end of the hall stood Tabitha with four large, grimy men, each holding iron wrapped clubs. Her eyes snapped to Dirge. She raised the bow and loosed a bolt at him.

Dirge ducked down. The bolt sailed over his head, ricocheting off the top of the stairway behind him, and clattered down the stairs. He peeked once more, fearing she may have another bow at the ready, but saw her duck into the room instead.

"Kill him," she shouted as she slammed the door.

Three of the tuffs, one with snow-white skin and bright-blue hair, one with coal black skin, and one with tanned skin and a shaved head, raced toward him. Dirge knelt below the top of the stairs. Their boots thundering down the hall and skidded to a halt at the top of the stair, or at least they tried. The front man—the one with the blue hair—was slammed from behind by his fellow tuffs, sending him hurtling down the steps. Dirge hugged the wall as Blue-hair sailed by, crashing headfirst several flights down. Blue-hair's bones snapped and crunched, sounding like a mad child stomping on a pile of sticks.

The second tough, the black, waved his hands back and forth to keep himself from following his comrade. Dirge took the opening. He stabbed his sword forward, slashing the man behind his knee causing it to buckle and dropping the dark man to the floor.

The shaved headed man took an awkward swing at Dirge. Trying not to strike his friend, the swing pulled the shaved headed man off balance. Dirge leapt forward, grabbing the man lying on the ground to pull himself higher. He stabbed the bald man in the gut, pulled back, and chopped down at the neck of the man on the floor, nearly taking the fellow's head off.

The gut-stabbed fellow dropped to his knees with his hands to his belly. Dirge slowly stood and topped the stair. While eyeing the fourth tough who stood guard at the door, Dirge slashed the bald man the throat. Blood sprayed the hallway. Dirge felt his own blood trickle down his side but ignored it. He stalked down the hall with his sword held low.

"I want none of this," the last man said, his long braids waving as he shook his head and dropped his club. He raised his hands, as though to push Dirge away, turned, opened the door behind him. A crossbow bolt slammed into his face and out the back of his skull.

Dirge rushed forward, not wanting to give Tabitha another shot. Keeping low with his sword before him, he slid past the dying guard and ran into the room. His sword sang as he blocked a swing from someone hiding next to the doorway and continued forward at Tabitha who was trying to reload. He slashed at the crossbow, knocking it aside. His return swing caught her in the neck.

Tabitha clasped her hands to her throat, blood spraying around her fingers. Gurgling as more blood vomited out her mouth, she staggered back a step, and flopped to the floor.

Dirge couldn't help staring at her. The dark red blood contrasted with her pale skin, making it all the more perfect. Her long blonde hair fanned out on the floor like an angelic halo, seeming to glow like strands of gold that quickly turned red from the blood pooling about her. Her brilliant blue eyes… turned glassy.

He saw it all in a flash and never realized how beautiful Tabatha was. She was almost as lovely as his mother. *And I just killed her.*

The stomping of boots was Dirge's only warning. He snapped out of his stupor, spun to his right, and raised his sword, but only partially blocked Jack's blow. Jack's blade slid off Dirge's and bit into his left arm.

Dirge stepped back with a yelp… and fell over Tabitha's body. His head hit the floor, dazing him. His right side exploded in pain from his earlier wound, and his sword slipped from his hand.

Jack smiled triumphantly, raised his sword—

"Stop!"

Jack turned back and glared at the woman who'd shouted.

Tessa, Jacob's mother, drifted into Dirge's view.

"I want a better look at him first," she said. She leaned over slightly, her long sandy blonde hair shining in the lamplight. Her blue eyes widened. "I know you. You're Jacob's friend, aren't you? Yes, from that self-righteous inn. You all think you're better than us, don't you?"

Dirge's consciousness began to fade.

"You look just like your stupid, whore, mother," she continued. "She thought she was better than me too." The woman sneered. "But my boys took care of that for me. Didn't you, Jack?"

"Yes, mother," Jack said with a smirk. "We did her up but good. Last thing she felt was my cock up her bum as I slit her throat."

Tessa bent down further and spat at Dirge. "Now it's your turn."

Dirge's pain vanished, his mind went blank, and his vision turned red. With a scream, he kicked Tessa in the crotch with his right leg, causing her to scream. He brought up his other leg and kicked her in the stomach as hard as he could, sending her hurtling backwards into Jack. Dirge grabbed his sword and scrambled to his feet. Turning, Jack and Tessa lie on the floor several feet away with Tessa atop her son.

Dirge leapt on top of the two, driving his blade through Tessa's chest and into Jack's. They wailed and screamed, but Dirge heard none of it. He yanked out his sword and chopped down at the two of them again and again. Blood splattered his face and chest as he hacked, but the only thing he saw was his mother's face, her blue eyes staring blankly into the sky. His vision faded and everything went black.

"Do you think he'll make it?" Dirge heard his mother say in the blackness.

"That remains to be seen," a man's voice replied. "It's up to him. It depends on how much he wants to live."

"He's a strong one," a second male voice said through the din. "Aza'zel has much more for him to do before he takes him, I think."

"Must you invoke Death here?" his mother said.

It can't be Mother. She's dead.

"Katlyn?" he croaked.

He heard a sharp breath. "By the Lord, you're alive," she said.

"I told you he was strong." Pride filled Talic's voice.

"It's a good thing you found him when you did," the other man said. "He'd have bled to death otherwise."

Dirge opened his eyes, his vision hazy. "What happened?"

"Don't you worry about it, son. You just get your rest." Katlyn gently stroked his head until he fell asleep.

Dirge lay abed only two days—amazing everyone but Talic. On the fourth day, Talic entered Dirge's room as the boy was doing his morning meditation and prayers. "Good morning, my boy. How do you feel today?"

"Excellent, Master." Dirge gained his feet and bowed. "And how are you today?"

"I am well. How are your wounds?"

"Nearly gone." Dirge dropped his gaze and shifted his feet. "Surprisingly."

"What is it son?"

"Well, I've just been wondering… who was that other man, the one with you and Mistress Katlyn?"

"He's a good friend to the Brotherhood. A hedge mage and healer by the name of To-kon."

"He used sorcery on me?" Dirge dropped his gaze again and his breath quickened. "Is there any chance he could do that with Jacob?"

His friend had yet to regain consciousness. He remained in the back room—in the dark and on the verge of death—for nearly a week. Dirge felt desperate, and the thought someone might help Jacob got his hopes up.

"No," Talic replied.

Dirge's head snapped up. "Why not?!"

"Jacob is not a member of the Brotherhood," Talic said, somberly. "But more importantly, he is the reason I'm here this morning."

Dirge tilted his head. "What do you mean?"

"You have not yet fulfilled your vow, nor the contract."

Dirge eyes widened. "Yes, I did. You told me you found me on top of Tessa and Jack. And I know I killed Axe and Connor." He lowered his head. "And Tabitha."

"But that's not everyone."

"Who else? Who did I…" He stared hard at Talic. "Jacob? Are you saying I have to kill Jacob?!"

Talic nodded.

Dirge's eyes firmed. He stood as tall as he could and stuck out his chest. "No."

"Are you defying the will of Aza'zel?" Talic asked, sternly.

Dirge hesitated a moment and thought. "No. You said their lives were in my hands; that his life is in my hands."

"So now you choose to mince words." His master's eyes bored into him. "The decision is yours. But just know this: you cannot escape the will of God."

Talic turned and opened the door. "I shall inform Doomers you have chosen to not take Jacob's life. Not yet, anyway. We shall see what he has to say."

It turned out Doomers didn't care about Jacob. "Everyone knows none of them wanted that little shit around anyway," he'd said. "Tell the lad, if he wants a job… I think I can come up with something."

Dirge frowned at the man's wicked grin.

Three days later, Jacob finally awoke—his skin pale and voice weak. "Where am I? What happened?"

"You're with friends. That's what's important," Dirge said. "You just need some rest." He turned to Mistress Katlyn. "Jacob can't stay down here. He needs fresh air and sun."

Katlyn shook her head. "I've no rooms to spare."

Dirge knew it wasn't true, and his stubbornness kicked it. "He can share my room."

Talic nodded. "It would do the boy some good."

"What?" The innkeeper threw up her hands. "Fine!" She pointed a finger at a grinning Jacob. "You'll need to earn your keep. You hear me?"

Talic spoke up. "He's a quick wit and an even quicker tongue. He's also good with his hands. Cal can teach him to play an instrument along with several stories." When Mistress Katlyn raised an eyebrow, he added, "Cal used to run with a troupe Travelers some years ago. The boy can earn his keep by playing the common room."

Jacob's eyes brightened. "I swear to you," he said to Katlyn. "I'll have people flocking here to hear my tales and songs. You'll see."

The innkeeper shook her head, one eye cocked, and her mouth quirked. "We shall see, you little scamp."

Chapter 9
The Cleansing
(501 -R.C.-)

Dirge stood in the center of his room in loose-fitting, yet bulky, black exercise garb. Its extra padding and bulk simulated the weight and encumbrance of armor. Master Talic said he wasn't ready for actual armor yet, but it was best to train for that inevitability. He held his practice sword before him in both hands with his feet set slightly apart, one before the other, and his shoulders squared to the window. The light of the morning sun bathed him, its warmth seeping into his skin and adding to the heat of his morning ritual of stretches, exercises, and sword practice.

"You know you don't have to go through all this just to be a bouncer, right?" Jacob asked, sitting on a small bed lying along the wall opposite Dirge's shrine.

The quip washed over Dirge, having heard it many times over the past three years. He trained nearly nonstop in that time, driving himself to be better. The mistakes he'd made at Hoke's still haunted him. Not his regret at killing Tabitha, nor his dislike of the idea of killing a man from the shadows, both were so ingrained into his being he couldn't separate them no matter how hard he tried. Dirge berated himself daily for his mistakes that night. He'd been sloppy, and it nearly cost him his life. He wouldn't let that happen again.

Dirge went through pose after pose, fluid movements like a dance. His sword and body were one. His body and his surroundings were one. It wasn't something Master Talic had needed to teach him, it came from his soul. He'd found his center over the past three years and he'd fed that with a steady diet of practice, repetition, and discipline.

"Well, it's been fun." Jacob stood. "Watching you make shadow puppets on the wall is great, but I've got a couple of wenches to talk up." He paused, tilted his head to the side, and eyed Dirge. "You know, harlots, slatterns, jades, sluts… whores."

Dirge refused to take the bait. He continued to move, his body a leaf on the wind.

"Maybe I'll bring them back here this time." Jacob sighed. "It's tiresome always having to ride them at their place or in the alley."

Dirge continued to ignore him.

With a grin, Jacob reached down, picked up an apple from his bedside table, and threw it at Dirge. Without missing a beat, Dirge shifted and swatted the apple out of the air, the blunt edge chopping it in half.

"So, you *are* here." Jacob smiled, picking up another apple. It snapped as he bit into it.

Dirge went back his ballet of death, trying to close out the world.

Jacob shrugged and made to leave. As his hand touched the door, Dirge spoke up. "Please, don't."

Jacob pulled his head back. "Don't what?"

"Please don't bring them back here," Dirge replied, his voice barely above a whisper.

"Aww, why not?"

Dirge finally stopped, turning to his friend. He hesitated, knowing the mocking he was about to receive. "It will embarrass me."

Jacob barked out a laugh.

"I mean it." Dirge turned back to the window.

"We'll be quiet, I swear."

Dirge eyed his friend over his shoulder, his brows furrowed, and his face stern.

"Look, just because you're not interested in lying with women doesn't mean I have to give it up."

Dirge turned his head back to the window, his face heating. "I never said I wasn't interested."

"Oh ho!" Jacob laughed once more. "And here I was starting to think you had a crush on me."

Dirge whipped around. "No! I would never do such a thing. It is an abomination to lie with your own."

Jacob regarded Dirge queerly. "Since when?" He raised his hands. "I'm not saying I have, I like women. But I have been with a pair of lasses who were lovers. And let me tell you that was one hell of a good time."

"It's wrong."

"Again, according to who?"

Dirge closed his mouth, and he looked at his feet. "I don't know. I just know it's wrong."

Jacob shrugged. "Hey, to each their own, I say." He took a step out the door and stopped again. "I could always bring back one for you."

"No, thank you." Dirge went back into his routine once more.

"Come on. You've got to lose your maidenhead one of these days." Jacob shook his head and left.

Dirge seethed inside. Jacob knew how to get under his skin and reveled in doing so. Lying with someone of your own sex was abhorrent, but to lie with a woman, simply for the sake of fornication, was also wrong. He couldn't say why, he knew in the bottom of his heart that when the time came for… that, he needed to be Pair-bonded with the woman. It was an ancient ritual, for certain, but a necessary one. He'd first heard of it from Dennis, who had been Pair-bonded before joining the Brotherhood. Dennis never said what happened to his woman, Dirge only knew she'd died.

Dirge was deep into his exercises once more when his master entered the room a short time later. Dirge stopped, faced Talic, and bowed.

Talic returned the bow. "Good morning, my son. How are you this day?"

"I am well, Master."

"That's good. I have something new for you today. It's time you got out of this little room and stretched your legs a bit."

Dirge quickly returned his bokken to its place on the wall above his bed, above his steel, sparring sword. He stripped off his shirt and pants for mundane attire—dark brown trousers and a tan shirt—then followed his master out into the hall, his soft-soled black boots whisking on the floor.

They passed Corrigan and Able, two Brotherhood members who'd come to the city only a few months earlier. Corrigan's long, black hair was tied at the back of his head by a long leather cord that morning. Sometimes it was brown or blue. The color signified the mood he was in that day. Dirge hadn't known the man long enough yet to decipher what color meant what.

The two men talked about the events of the night before. Being the newest members, they were on the night shift. Dirge didn't hear what they said, but it brought a full laugh from Able. Dirge liked Able, with his light skin and bright red hair, the man stood out, and he made the most of it. He was quick with a joke and always seemed to wear a smile.

Both men nodded to Dirge, giving him a smile as they passed.

As Dirge and Talic walked, his master looked at him out of the corner of his eye. "I couldn't help but overhear some of what you and your friend were talking about. Is that truly how you feel regarding who someone lies with?"

"How did you hear?"

"He repeated your conversation to Hanna. I tell you if he hasn't had a tumble with her yet he soon will by the look she gave him."

Dirge wasn't sure what to make of that statement so he answered his master's question. "It is. It is an abomination in the eyes of God."

Talic paused. "There is no such concept in the canon of Aza'zel. He is the Lord of Death. What we do in our brief time in this world regarding who we're with doesn't matter. He doesn't care. It's all the same to him."

Dirge missed a step. How could that be? He knew he was right. *How could it not come from God?*

"Regardless," Talic continued. "That is not why I've come for you. It's time you learn how to scout the enemy."

"Should I change into my stealth clothes?"

"No," Talic said. "For this, what you are wearing is perfect."

"Where are we going?"

"Today, we go to the heart of the city to view the ways of Chaos."

Two hours later, Dirge found himself in the richest quadrant of the city. He and Talic leaned up against a tall, stone building, eating piping hot meat pies. The building stood on the edge of a large open square. All the buildings that edged the square sat on broad, raised foundations anywhere from five to fifteen feet high, with long, broad, stone steps leading up to them.

Directly across from them, stood a massive structure, one hundred and twenty feet of ugly gray stone that ran the length of the square. It had multiple spires, few windows, and a set of thirty feet high, iron-bound doors near its middle. No matter where Dirge looked, his attention returned to it. The building had a darkness to it, like the direct light of the sun couldn't reach it.

Dirge tore his eyes away from the ugly monstrosity and back to the square. He found it impressive. All the roads were cobbled, and all the buildings either stone or brick. There wasn't a wobbly wooden structure in sight, unlike the Slaag. Several-hundred colorful people filled the square, along with dozens of booths where merchants sold their wares.

Nearly everyone overflowed with wealth. Most of the women wore silk or satin dresses of every cut, style, and color, while a few others were in trousers and blouses. Their dresses and skirts were of every length, from dragging upon the ground, to the top of their thighs. Some women's tops were loose and billowy, while others were so tight every bulge shown easily—be they breasts or rolls of fat. To his disgust, some women wore no top at all. They flaunted their nakedness, seeming to beam with pride as people eyed their bosoms—be they ample or not.

The men's garb was just as varied and colorful. Some wearing breeches, both billowy and tight, while others wore trousers, and a few wore knee-length, wool skirts. Some men, as well as some women, wore armor, be it leather or metal, and most of those had weapons at their side. They didn't appear to be part of the city guard or armsmen of the church, but random people. Dirge thought they might be mercenaries or caravan guards—or possibly even be brigands.

What stood out most though, was the number of people who wore hats. Some hats were tall, some wide, while others were long and droopy, and almost all covered in feathers. Each hat was brimming with all kinds and colors of plumage. It was like a feather rainbow from every bird in creation had exploded and rained down upon the crowd.

The only people looking drab were those going about in robes. That's not to say they weren't colorful, they just seemed less so by comparison. Some robes were white, some brown, some blue, some in black, but most were dyed in a multitude of colors.

As he scanned the crowd, Dirge spotted people that gave him a bad feeling, like a spider crawled up his spine and clawed at the nape of his neck.

"Why are we here exactly, Master?" he asked after wiping his mouth of the few remaining crumbs from his delicious pie.

"Look about you and tell me what you see," his master replied.

Dirge shuddered. "An ugly, gaudy, motley that hurts the eyes."

"Anything else?"

"A severe lack of modesty." Dirge sneered as he turned his eyes away from a woman in a translucent, rose-colored dress.

"Is that all?" There was an edge to the man's voice. He then shook his head and continued, "What stands out to you?"

"The ones in robes," Dirge replied after a moment. "Most of them, anyway."

"Only those?"

"No," Dirge said. "Some people in shirts and trousers as well, the ones without weapons."

"What about them stands out to you?"

Dirge snarled. "I don't like them."

"Why?"

Dirge shook his head. "I don't know. They don't feel right. They seem to be... covered in shadow."

Talic smiled. "Those are the priests."

Dirge shot a glance at his master before returning his stare at the crowd. Now that he knew, the priests seemed to stand out to him even more. It was as though a shadow fell upon each one. The itch up his spine became a shudder. "All the people touched by that shadow are priests?"

"Only the darkest. The rest are people devout to the Lord of Chaos, those that have been touched by him."

"Why show me this?" Dirge asked.

"Because we are the only people that can kill a priest without drawing the ire of the clergy," his master said quietly.

Dirge gave Talic a queer look.

"You see, we are known to all who wish to know. That includes the church. From time to time, a priest will have a certain dislike for another. Normally, that one would simply kill the other. The truest adage to Chaos is 'do as thou will,' so if they can get away with killing one of their kind they will do so. But what if the one with the urge to kill is too weak? That's where we come in."

"And they don't care?" Dirge was incredulous.

"Of course, they care," Talic said. "But they're Chaos; each one is an island upon themselves. Each death is likely to cause bedlam within their ranks, and they thrive upon it."

"That's their temple, isn't it?" Dirge nodded to the shadowed building in front. Talic nodded.

Dirge cast his eyes about the crowd, nearly overwhelmed by it all—the shadowy touch of Chaos that lay upon so many people. Some, like the priests, appeared nearly black from Edis's corruption. Others merely appeared bruised, the shade lying upon them ever so lightly. Most people had no shade at all, yet some of them still made him feel odd.

Such was the case with a young woman standing a dozen feet away. She wore an off-white dress that started tight to her neck and hung down to her ankles with little in the way of lace or frills. She stood next to an older man in modest attire of a simple brown coat and black pants. Something about the young woman unnerved him, but he couldn't figure out what. Was it the way she stood, twisting back and forth at the waist, her snow-white hands caressing her long flowing brown hair hanging over her shoulder? Or was it they she held a half smile, while biting her full, pink bottom lip? Or perhaps it was simply because she kept staring at him with large, bright blue eyes... blue, like the sky after a storm?

"What about her, Master?" he nodded toward the lovely—yet unnerving—young woman. "Is she with Chaos?"

Talic swung his eyes in the girl's direction and chuckled. "No, my boy."

"They why do I get this funny feeling from her?" 'Funny' was putting it mildly. The young woman sent a chill running up his spine and caused his cheeks to heat.

His master smiled broadly. "It's likely because she's flirting with you, and you like it."

Dirge's eyes went wide. "Flirting?" he mumbled.

The older man turned and spoke to the young woman, but she didn't appear to hear. The man then glared at Dirge. With a scowl, he grabbed the young woman by the arm, and marched away, pulling her with him.

"Looks like we'll never know," Talic said, clasping Dirge upon the shoulder. "I think it time we head back. Katlyn is making her–"

The doors to the temple swung open and a flood of people poured out, most looked to be soldiers, but many were definitely priests. People scattered out of the way as hundreds of horsemen came from the back of the temple. Again, most were men-at-arms, but dozens of priests were among them.

"What's going on, Master?" A deep foreboding overcame him, like the end was soon to be upon them.

"I've no idea. Let's wait and see." Talic looked at Dirge. "But stay close, regardless. If it turns ugly, I should be able to get us out of here."

Dirge didn't like the hint of doubt in his master's eyes.

One group afoot, headed to the large, red stone building at the far end of the square, the "House of the Masters." The building housed all the City Masters, both political and economic. As the group entered the city's nerve center, the rest of the priests and soldiers separated into groups and went into the city. The people in the square murmured and twitched in a mixture of unease and anticipation.

Agonizing minutes passed and Dirge's spine tingled and his palms sweated. He resisted the urge to shuffle his feet, hoping for any sign of what was to come from his master, but Talic gave up nothing.

Less than half an hour later, the priest and his men exited the House of the Masters. At the priest's side walked a tall man in white. His eyes darted about as he trudged with slouched shoulders.

"This doesn't look good," Talic said.

"Who's the man in white?"

"He's the Herald; he reads the proclamations of the City Masters."

The Herald walked up a large stone pedestal near the center of the square. He pulled forth a scroll, unfurled it, and began to read, but his words were lost in the noise of the crowd. The priest, standing at the foot of the pedestal, waved his hand at the tall man and suddenly the Herald's voice boomed throughout the square, startling everyone including the Herald.

The Herald started again, his voice rich but tight. "By decree of the High Priest. Word has come to him from Lord Heartless, the Champion of the Great Lord of Chaos. Here are the words of Heartless: 'I bring a blessing from the Great Lord. Chaos has decided that he desires a sacrifice be brought on to him so that everyone will be blessed by his touch. He calls for'…" The man sputtered for a moment then raised his head once more. "… 'He calls for the Cleansing of your children.'"

Everyone in the crowd talked at once.

The Herald went on. "The Great Lord of Chaos calls for all children born within the last year, as well as those for the next, to be brought onto him in sacrifice. Their lives will grant you the truest blessings of Chaos from now until the end of time. Their blood shall cleanse you and make you one with the Lord."

The square erupted in pandemonium. People screamed and threw up their hands. Yet to Dirge's dismay and disgust, half of them were screaming out of joy, not terror.

This can't be real?

Dirge turned to his master. "What do we do?"

"We make for the Angelic. I must pray upon this. I must have guidance from Aza'zel."

As they edged the building, heading toward the closest street to take them home, it didn't take long for a full-fledged panic to break out. People pushed and shoved, running this way and that trying to leave the square at once, presumably to go back and protect their children. At least that's what Dirge hoped.

Some in the crowd tried to shove their way through the soldiers that surrounded the priest and the Herald, but those men didn't move. They drew their weapons and attacked. They crushed skulls, hacked off limbs, and disemboweled anyone that came close. Throughout it all, the priest laughed.

Talic grabbed Dirge by the shoulder to get his attention. The press at the roads exiting the square was so overwhelming that folks were getting trampled to death. Talic pointed to the wall next to the road, then up. He meant for them to climb it. Climbing had been part of his training from early on, and the rough-hewn stone held many places for them to catch their fingers and boots in. Since the back alleys often ended unexpectedly, one needed to learn to use the balconies and roofs to get around town. With many of the roofs poorly constructed, potentially giving way when you least expected it, it wasn't the most ideal route, but you made do the best you could.

Bloody bodies littered the narrow street below, crushed, and trampled by the mob three stories. More fell as they fled, tripping in the gore and adding to the mess. Sometimes they got back up, sometimes they didn't.

Dirge followed Talic along the edge of the roof, his soft-soled boots gripping the tiles with ease. They made their way to the next building, a two-story one, jumped down, and continued to the next as the flow of scrambling people below thinned. Dirge thought they could make their way with ease on the road by that time, but Talic remained on the roofs.

Five or six buildings away from the square, a crash of glass followed by a high-pitched scream filled the air. His eyes shot to the street as something fell out of a window below them. He stopped and stared in horror as the thing tumbled through the air then struck the ground with a crunch. It was a child. More high-pitched screams came from within the building only to be sharply silenced. The door to the building across the road opened and five soldiers marched out, splattered with blood.

"They're doing it," Dirge said in whispered horror. "They're actually doing it."

As they slowly continued onward, shadowing the road, Dirge tried not to look; he didn't want to see the depravity. Yet he couldn't help but witness the atrocities taking place. People ran down the streets with crying children in their hands only to have them torn away by soldiers, who would slash the children with swords or club them with maces. If the adult tried to stop them, they died as well.

"How could the soldiers be doing this?" Dirge asked.

"They are not the only ones," Talic said next to him.

He pointed just down the road where a beautiful woman with long, flowing blonde hair walked out into the street. She held a screaming infant in one hand and a knife in the other. The woman sliced the infant's throat, held it high, and let the blood rain down upon her.

Dirge fell to his knees and threw up.

"Come along," Talic urged him, his hand on Dirge's shoulder. "There's nothing we can do here. We must get back."

Dirge shook, slowly stood, and followed his master.

As they ran, more babies, infants, and toddlers were pulled from their homes. People stabbed knives into the children's bellies, or slashing their throats, and watched with glee as the children bled out. They bashed the infant's heads upon the street or against buildings, while others were thrown to the ground and smashed with rocks, boards, clubs, chairs… whatever was handy.

Smoke billowed from a large intersection ahead. A great bonfire sat in the middle of the intersection, and people stood around it, holding wailing children and infants. A man in the garb of the city guard stood at the edge of the flames. His short-cropped black hair shined from the light of the fire, as did a scar that ran from his right ear to his chin. The man laughed uproariously, causing the scar to crinkle. He reached out, took the children given to him, and threw them into the fire. Most of the children were still alive as they were fed to the flames. Their shrieks of pain filled the air.

Dirge looked away. He didn't know how much more he could take.

Talic turned from the intersection, pulling Dirge with him, and headed for the nearest alley where they climbed down and dashed to the alley on the other side. From then on, they made their way by the alleys, from the affluent section of the city, through the more modest ones, and into the Slaag.

Chapter 10
Guardian of the Angelic
(501 -R.C.-)

Dirge had no idea how much time passed when they finally made it to the back door to the Angelic, he only knew he felt numb. Upon reaching the common room, Mistress Katlyn ran up to Talic. "What in all the hells is going on out there? People have been running past, screaming, for the past hour. There's word of killings everywhere. Even children are being put to the sword!"

"It's primarily the children," Talic said, somberly. He went on, telling her about the proclamation, the deaths, all of it. "Riots are sure to break out."

Talic then turned to the Brotherhood members in the room. "Dennis, Able, Corrigan, I want you on the roofs. You see anyone come near the block with a torch I want them put down." A fire in the Slaag could take down an entire block. "Dobbs, get Hake and Cal and go out to spread the word. Garner what help you can. I want this entire block locked down. I also want you to gather what children you can and get them into the basement."

"To what end?" Katlyn asked.

"When things die down, we'll try to get them out of the city."

"But what of the Lord?" Able asked. "What if he sanctions this?"

Dirge's eyes shot to Able. *How could he say such a thing?*

"I go up to ask guidance from the Lord. I highly doubt he approves, but if he does… well, we'll deal with that when the time comes." Talic shook his head. "Go. We've not much time."

Dirge had no idea what to do. He looked about the room. "Where's Jacob?"

"He's not come back yet," Mistress Katlyn said. "He went out before you did and has yet to return."

Dirge headed for the door.

"Wait!" Talic walked up to him. "We've need of you here."

"But—"

"I said no!" Talic took a deep breath. "Come with me, son."

He ushered Dirge up and into his master's room. Once inside, Talic went to his wardrobe and retrieved a large bundle wrapped in black cloth. "This is for you."

"What is it?"

"Your armor. It's time, son."

Pulling back the cloth revealed glittering silver on black. Dirge looked askance at Talic.

"This is not stealth armor. It's for battle. There are times when you need to stand out from the crowd, and today is such a day. What I ask of you is very important. I need you out front—a visible presence at the door to the inn." He then went back into the wardrobe and pulled out a steel, open-faced helm. "Go, now. Put this on. Become what you were meant to be—the Guardian of the Angelic. We'll have need of you in the coming days."

Dirge, at a loss for words, bowed deeply to his master and sprinted for his room to put the armor on. The chest piece was thick, black leather with steel plates sown in. The arm and leg guards thick leather covered with steel plates as were the gauntlets. At first, he feared that the gauntlets would give him difficulty handling his sword. On the contrary, all of it seemed like a second skin to him. For the first time in his life, he felt whole.

He put on the shining steel helm and walked down to the common room. Every eye snapped to him as he walked with pride to the front door. "None shall get past me whilst I still draw breath, Mistress Katlyn. I swear to you." He bowed to her.

Chaos reigned outside the inn. Screams came from every direction, and people ran amok. Smoke filled the air from flames several blocks away. He caught sight of Dobbs off to his left talking with several men that he remembered seeing at the inn before. Whatever it was Dobbs said it didn't take long to convince the men to join in protecting the area.

To Dirge's right, a group of three men hacked and smashed something upon the ground with clubs and knives. They then darted off down an alley on the other side of the street leaving behind a bloody mound of rags. Dirge resisted the urge to examine the body—it might be Jacob.

Shaking his head, he took up position directly in front of the door, resting a hand upon his sword with his back as straight as possible. At well over six feet in height, he'd yet to fill out, so he wanted to be as intimidating as possible. He cast his gaze about, trying to make eye contact with anyone who came near. The best way to intimidate someone was to be aggressive and stern. It was also the best way to instigate something. Not that he cared. He welcomed it. He was doing what was right, standing guard over his home, a shield against the storm of chaos. Blood coursing through his veins, his skin tingled as he smiled. He felt righteous.

"You're all fools. I tell you, that place is protected by the Brotherhood," Alan said, his dark-brown beard seemed to bristle even more than usual.

"I don't care if it's guarded by Death himself. We're blessed by Edis," Aarod said, raising his hands to remind them what covered them. He ran his hands through his bright red beard to clean off his daughter's blood. He'd loved little Cecily, but she sat at God's side now, and with Edis' blessing upon him there was nothing he couldn't do. "Besides, one of those bastards killed Blue, and they're gonna get what's coming to them, along with the rest of the profane bunch that go there."

His brother had liked to go by the name Blue for the way he always dyed his beard. Having worked for Hoke for years, Aarod still cursed himself for falling ill the day before his brother died. "There's no way he could have gotten the drop on both of us," he mumbled.

"If you'd been there, you'd of been just as dead, and you know it," Alan said.

Aarod bristled. Alan had said the same many times before, but it still didn't make it true. "Are you comin' with us or not?"

Alan shook his head.

Aarod's eyes went to Kirk, standing behind Alan, and nodded.

The tall, blond man smiled, drew his dagger, and plunged it into Alan's back. The dark-haired man grunted, dropped to his knees, and fell face first to the floor where he wheezed out his last breath.

"Can you believe that bastard had the nerve to look surprised?" Aarod said with a sneer.

"He's always been too pompous for his own good," Kirk said as he wiped the blood from his dagger and returned it to its sheath. "So, when do you want to do this?"

"We do it now." He walked over and picked up the glass lamp from the table. "You grab that one. We'll light that place up and kill everyone that comes running out." He picked up his iron bound club and smiled. Everyone knew that Chaos wasn't welcome in the Angelic. Well, tonight, Chaos was coming for them.

The eight of them made their way through the twisting alleys with Aarod at their head. The glorious smell of smoke filled the air as did the screams of those dying in the name of the Lord of Chaos. As they made their last turn, a group of three youths entered the alley at a run. Blood covered their clothes and weapons. They ran down the alley, but turned at the intersection before reaching Aarod and his men.

Ah, the excitement of youth, he thought.

Aarod peered out of the alley on to the main street, and there, to the right, stood the Angelic. He'd expected to see the street filled with the people of the Lord running amok. Instead, only a single person stood in the street, wearing gleaming armor like a prized gladiator.

That looks like Talic.

"Hey," Kirk said next to him. "Aint that the runt bouncer that tossed you around the last time we was there? Looks like he's grown some, huh? And where the hells did he get all that shiny armor from?"

Aarod realized that Kirk was right. Rather than Talic, it was the son of that long dead whore that Hoke's boys had killed. "I don't give a shit how big he's gotten, nor do I care how shiny his armor is. You run up and smash him in the knee and I'll crush his skull. Then we'll light that stinking place up."

"You got it, boss," Kirk said with a smile before running out into the street, screaming at the top of his lungs. After three strides, his scream tuned into a gurgle when an arrow burst through the back of his skull. Kirk flopped to the ground, like so much rotten meat, and landed upon the lantern he'd been carrying.

"They've bowmen on the roof," Ansel yelled.

Aarod gave the man a shove toward the street. "Then you best get out there before they reload." He grabbed another of his men by the collar and ran out on the heels of Ansel.

They weren't half way down the street before Ansel took an arrow to the chest. Aarod dodged to the side, sprinted forward, and swung his club at Dirge's exposed knee, but the young man swiftly sidestepped his attack. Aarod didn't think it possible for someone to move that fast. He tried to skid to a halt when his arm holding the lantern exploded in pain. The lantern, and his hand, fell to the ground. Light flashed along the man's blade in its backswing. Aarod's last thought was one of confusion as he lay upon the ground, gazing up at the star-filled the sky. The light of the world winked out moments before his body fell to the ground next to his severed head.

Dirge wiped the blood from his sword after killing the last of the men. Not one came close to touching him; their bodies lay strewn all about in a gory mess. He looked down at the head of the first one he'd killed. The man seemed familiar for some reason. Shaking his head, he turned his eyes back to the street. He didn't have time to gawk at corpses.

In the next hour, he killed three more groups. A fourth group, a dozen men wielding clubs, hammers, and axes, came running up. He took up position, ready to deal with them as well.

They slowed and the lead man threw up his hands. "We're not here to fight you." He shot a glance up at the roof of the inn before returning his gaze to Dirge.

"Until this day, we all thought it impossible for anyone to fight Chaos. We'd intended to flee with our families till we heard what you did here. How could any single man stand up to so many crazed by the touch of Edis?"

The man looked at his compatriots then back at Dirge and knelt. "We did not come to fight you, but to join you." The rest of the men bent knee as well. "We swear on our lives that none shall touch this inn or this block."

Taken aback, Dirge accepted their aid. They stood guard for the remainder of the day and throughout the night. Anyone who came close to their block with malice in their heart died.

By early morning, most of the mayhem had died down. People milled about, some looting the corpses, but most simply assessed the damage. It was in that early dawn when Jacob finally returned looking none the worse for wear. Other than a slightly ruffled shirt, he looked unmolested.

"Dirge, is that you?" he asked as he approached.

Dirge frowned. "Where have you been? I was worried."

"Well, isn't that sweet." Jacob grinned.

Dirge frowned and pointed a finger at his friend. "None of that!" He sighed and shook his head. "What happened to you?"

"Nothing," Jacob replied with a shrug. "I told you, I was meeting a woman." Jacob scanned the carnage, walked forward, and patted Dirge on the shoulder. "What the hell happened? It looks like there was a war." With a shrug and a shake of the head, Jacob trotted into the inn.

Dirge stared at his friend's back with his mouth agape.

Chapter 11
Eyes
(502 -R.C.-)

Dirge stood in the far corner of the common room next to the raised platform that Jacob used for his performances. Even though he was a full-fledged member of the Brotherhood, he still needed to keep up appearances, and appearances were important to him. His dark black pants and light tan shirt—both hugging his muscular frame—were spotless. His black boots were so polished they shined, and his head and facial hair were neat and trimmed.

The evening was early with the room already near capacity. That didn't bode well because with tight crowds came quick tempers. That night was no exception. It didn't take long before a crash to his left caught his attention where two men stood toe to toe, screaming at the tops of their lungs. Dirge calmly made his way over, apologizing to those he jostled in the process.

"How dare you say such a thing," screamed the first man, his long dark red hair flailed about as he shook his head.

"I dare say that and worse," shouted the second. His short-cropped black hair seemed to stand up on edge and his eyes stared murderously out of his coal-black face.

"You were lucky to have the Great Lord bless you that day, and here you—"

"Do not bring up that demon here!" The dark-skinned man drew back his arm, ready to let fly.

"That's enough," Dirge said, his deep voice calm yet sharp. He grasped the dark man's arm, holding it with ease, and placed his other on the chest of the redhead. He towered over the two men.

The red-haired man stepped back. "Take your hands off me!"

"There'll be none of that in here." Dirge eyed them both in turn.

"But he—" The dark man eyes fell on Dirge. His face lit up with recognition, and he bowed his head. "My apologies. It's just that he—"

"It doesn't matter what he said," Dirge interjected.

"Well, if it isn't the Savior of the Slaag," said a short, dirty, dark haired man at the next table. The empty seat next to him made it clear he was a compatriot of the man with the red hair.

"Is that so," said the redhead with a sneer. "You don't look like much to me. By the Great Lord, I bet I could—" He reached for the dagger at his belt.

Dirge was quicker. With his left hand, he pulled the cudgel from his belt and smashed it down on the red-haired man's head, and with his right, he grabbed the now unconscious man by the shirt to keep him from falling.

Out of the corner of his eye, Dirge saw two men—the dirty fellow and a blond next to him—grasp the daggers at their belts. "The Mistress of the house would be cross with me if she'd have to clean up the blood of three dead men." He shoved the redheaded man at his two friends, returned his cudgel to his belt, and placed his hand on his short sword hanging next to it.

The two men scooched back, letting their friend crash to the floor. They both eyed Dirge. The blond man licked his lips and held his now shaking hands out away from his body. The dirty man continued to hold on to his weapon, his eyes filled with contempt, then a pleasant smile blooming on his face. "Let's be on our way, Henry. We're godly men. We've no need to be around these heretics." He stood and walked to the door, not caring about the wellbeing of his unconscious friend.

The blond man slowly stood, his eyes darting from the man on the ground, to Dirge, and to the sword on Dirge's belt. Blond stepped back a few paces, turned, and heading out the door.

The dark-skinned man stood tall. "That's what they get—"

Dirge cut him off. "You'll get the same if I have any more trouble out of you."

The dark man's eyes grew wide and his mouth fell open before closing it and dropping his gaze. "Again, I apologize. You're right, of course. You'll have no more trouble from me or my friends. I swear to you."

Dirge nodded, picked up the unconscious man by his pants and shirt, carried him to the door, and threw him out onto the street. As he walked back to his post, many men in the room nodded their approval. A couple sneered and looked away. He ignored them all. He didn't care what they thought, any of them. He had a job to do. That was all. Once back in his corner, Dirge went back to watching the crowd.

Before long, all eyes turned back to the others at their respective tables, all but one pair. At a far table near the bar, a young woman sat with two men. Her bright blue eyes gazed at him, her pert lips pursed slightly as she caressed her long brown hair hanging over her shoulder. Her cream-colored blouse, buttoned up to her neck, complimented her pale skin that seemed to glow in the lamp light.

Why does she look familiar?

Dirge tore his gaze away and shook his head. He needed to concentrate; now was not the time to gawk. Yet as soon as he went back to inspecting the crowd, his eyes strayed back to her, drawn like iron to a loadstone.

Her eyes sparkled. They seemed to bore into him, seeking out parts he didn't know existed. Her nostrils flared, her cheeks grew flush, and her hands clasping her hair seemed to shake. She smiled and bit at her lower lip.

The older of the two men said something to her, but she seemed not to hear. His face darkened. He placed his hand on her shoulder causing her to jump and turn away from Dirge.

It was as if a spell broke. Dirge blinked hard. *What's wrong with me?*

Movement on the stairs drew his attention. Jacob descended with his lute held lightly in his hands and his head high. He wore a loose fitting, billowy red shirt, tight black breeches, and bright multicolored socks. He had on his silly yellow pointed slippers and worse of all, his long, brown, pointy hat with the long yellow feather. In short, he looked a fool, a popinjay to the core.

All eyes were upon Jacob as he made his way through the crowd. Dirge checked the bar where Mistress Katlyn stood smiling. She still claimed she didn't like Jacob, but she loved to watch him perform. Cal, leaning against the wall at the end of the bar, beamed with pride at his pupil.

"Well, if it isn't my greatest admirer," Jacob said to Dirge with a wink before mounting the dais and striking a pose.

"Good evening, gentle folk. I am Jacob the Divine, singer of songs, teller of tales, and the finest musician you'll see."

Dirge shook his head but couldn't help smiling. There were many things Jacob wasn't, but he knew how to sell himself.

Dirge turned his gaze from his friend and went back to watching the crowd. He still had a job to do after all.

Jacob strummed his lute:

> *"Love*
> *What is love?*
> *Times I want to run away*
> *I run near and far.*
> *But your spirit still haunts me*
> *I cannot go where you are..."*

He sang soft yet strong, seeming to croon to each and every woman in the crowd. They all responded in kind, staring lovingly at Jacob, all but one.

As Dirge scanned the crowd, his eyes once again drifted to the young woman near the bar. She gazed at Dirge like no one else existed. The two men at the table were regarding Dirge as well, now. The eyebrows of the elder man were drawn and his mouth held a distinct frown. Yet the other, much younger man, stared at Dirge with zeal. Like the woman, their clothing appeared clean and new – something unusual in the Slaag.

Dirge tore his eyes from the woman, yet they drifted back as Jacob continued to sing:

> *"... Your lips, they call to me..."*

Dirge remained riveted to the lovely young woman. Her dark hair shone in the lights, her breasts heaved with rapid breaths, and she shakily licked her lips before biting them once more.

> *"... Your arms, I feel the heat..."*

The older man spoke to her but again she didn't respond.

"... In your eyes..."

Dirge tore his gaze away once more. He felt queasy, his stomach, tied in knots. Cursing himself for being distracted once more, he vowed to not let it happen again.

For the rest of the night he watched every other part of the common room. He steadfastly examined every person there, every person but her.

As the night grew late, Dirge stood stock still, refusing to look in her direction. Yet he couldn't help but think about her. "Is she some kind of witch?"

"Who, that little filly that couldn't stop staring at you?" Jacob asked.

Dirge jumped, realizing he'd spoken aloud, nor that his friend had finished for the night. *How did time pass so quickly?*

"Are you well?" Jacob smiled when Dirge eyed the floor. "Ho, ho! So that's the way of it. And here I thought you only had eyes for me."

Dirge stared balefully at him.

"Oh, calm yourself. What is it with you and...? Never mind." Jacob shook his head. "So, you like the looks of her. Can't blame you there. She seems quite scrumptious. I wouldn't mind a go at her myself."

"No!" Dirge barked, then grimaced. "Do as you wish. What care have I?"

He stormed off. There were times when Jacob simply got under his skin. The night wasn't done, but it was Cal's turn to take the late shift. Besides, now that Jacob had finished most of the patrons had left for the night. Most, but not all. The young woman and her two male escorts remained. As Dirge walked up the stairs to his room, he thought he felt their eyes on him with every step.

Chapter 12
Not Alone
(502 -R.C.-)

In the next two weeks, Dirge worked the common room five more times. The beautiful young woman—as well as the two men—returned the first night, but not after. Dirge felt relieved, at first, yet also disheartened. He berated himself for the latter. He had no time for women—even if she was the loveliest thing he'd ever seen. The only thing that mattered was his position in the Brotherhood.

There were times though when he felt doubt. Something wasn't quite right. But that was silly, of course. He was a member of the Brotherhood, and it filled him with pride.

One midday as he took his lunch in his room—a delicious stew whipped up by the new cook, Torrian—Jacob sauntered in with a young, scantily clad woman in tow.

"Don't mind us," his friend said as he sat on his bed, pulling the woman down on top of him.

Dirge scowled. "I asked you not to bring them here."

"It's my room too, you know." Jacob smiled and removed the little clothing the woman wore.

"Is your friend going to join us?" the woman asked, leering at Dirge and licking her bright red lips.

Dirge stood and stormed out; their laughs cut off as he slammed the door behind him. Marching down to the common room—shaking his hand the hot stew burned as it slopped out of the bowl—he took the nearest seat and tried to calm himself. He didn't know what was worse, the woman's lurid question... or the fact that she'd the same color hair as the mystery young woman from days before. He violently shook his head, picked up his spoon, and stared eating once more.

"Something needs to be done, I tell you," a man said at the next table. He wore a dark shirt and pants, and a long black hat. Thankfully, there was no feather in it.

"Aye, but what?" replied the fellow sitting with him, dressed equally somber, though he had a bright gold ring through his nose that Dirge found disturbing.

"I don't know. Something. The Masters of Coin are tired of it, so I hear."

"That may be," said the man with the nose-ring, "but the rest of the City Masters don't care. They call it 'God's will.' Like the Lord of Chaos actually tells these fools to rape and pillage their own people."

"We could fight back," the man in the hat, said.

"Easy for you to say, you've a hammer. Most folks got nothing. Besides, the last group that tried, found a priest with the mob. And he didn't take too kindly to folks fighting back, let me tell you. Hells, he killed half of them in the blink of an eye."

"Half the mob?"

"No," exclaimed nose-ring, "half thems that tried to fight back!"

"I understand they found the priest's head in an alley recently," Talic said as he approached.

"Is that so? Well, good riddance to him," nose-ring said with a smile.

"Indeed," Talic said before turning to Dirge. "I need to speak with you."

"Yes, Master." Dirge jumped to his feet, following Talic through the kitchen, down into the basement, and into their lair.

Once inside, Talic asked, "Have you heard that kind of talk before? I only ask because you seemed surprised by it."

"I've overheard people speaking of such things at night in the common room."

"But never in the middle of the day before?"

"No, Master."

"What's your take on it?"

Dirge thought a moment. "Well, since the Cleansing, some of the devout have gone mad, thinking that Chaos lusts for death."

"And the common folk?"

"The common folk get by as they can, like always. They don't seem to care about the Lord of Chaos. They just do what's needed to survive."

"What about the talk of fighting back?" Talic walked to the far wall, sat upon a stool, and urged Dirge to take the one next to him.

"It is respectable, but foolish," Dirge replied while sitting.

"Why?"

"They have no real weapons, no training."

"Neither does the mob."

"True, but they have conviction. They have a sense of… I don't know, unity. They react without thought and don't care about the outcome." He paused a moment. "The biggest problem the people lack organization and leadership. The mobs have the priests."

"So, you think the priests are behind all this?"

"Some. A small number anyway. It's not in their nature to organize anything. It's most likely just a few individuals who relish the mayhem and blood."

"And what do you think should be done, if anything?"

"May I ask a question, Master?" When Talic nodded, Dirge continued. "Have the Coin Masters approached the Brotherhood?"

"They have."

"To take care of the mobs or the priests?"

"Just the mobs. They're afraid to ruffle the priests. Not that I can blame them."

"Yet we've killed priests, all the same."

Talic frowned. "Aza'zel is still angry over the Cleansing—so many lives taken for no other reason than a god's vanity. He wants a message sent to the priests, but it would appear they're unwilling to listen."

Dirge thought a moment. "Why've you brought me down here, Master?"

"For some time now we've hosted meetings with select members of the community. In particular, those who've grown to resent Chaos."

"What have you talked about at these meetings?"

"You."

Dirge's eyes went wide and his head pulled back. "Me? But I am noth—"

"Don't be so modest. What you did that night is known by more than just those in the Slaag. This place has changed. It's cleaner, safer, and less susceptible to acts of random violence. It's why many came here seeking safety. They sense something in this place, but they also sense it in you, whether or not they know it."

Dirge shook his head. *How could I inspire such a thing from one night?*

"The people talked to me about you and what you did." Talic put his hand on Dirge's shoulder. "You gathered perfect strangers about you that night and they swore on their lives to fight the madness all about them. On a night when Chaos reigned, you brought order."

"What would you have me do, Master?"

"The people need to fight back – or at least know that someone is. Several us are going to patrol the city, and I want you to come with us. We'll hunt out a mob, and when we find them… you will kill them."

"Me, Master, just me?"

"The rest of us shall cover you from the shadows, but you'll likely not need us." Talic sat forward. "Son, these people need hope. They need a symbol, a champion to rally behind. They need to know that they are not alone in this."

Hours later, Dirge strode with purpose down a winding, muddy, cobblestone road in a section of the city nearest the port, called the Gull. His master told him not to wear his armor for their excursion. So instead, he wore a slim chain mail shirt underneath his bright white cotton tunic. Talic didn't want people thinking Dirge to be anything but a common man—albeit one with a clean shirt and a sword at his belt.

Seagulls flittered about as fishmongers sold their wares from carts and huts. The smell of fish, rot, and salt was far worse than the stink in the Slaag. Dirge, along with the others in hiding, had meandered about the city for some time, but it was a quiet day.

"Perhaps Chaos is taking a nap," Able said somewhere behind Dirge.

Screams and crashes erupted ahead. "I think he just woke up," Dirge said as he picked up his pace to a trot.

Rounding the corner, mayhem abounded. A group of fifteen men and women with clubs and chains smashed windows and tore apart fish stands. Several people lay on the ground in pools of blood. A woman screamed to Dirge's left—three men had her pinned against the wall of a shop, two holding her arms while the third tore at her blouse and skirt. Dirge drew his sword and slashed the back of the man tearing at the woman's clothing, sending him shrieking to the ground. The man to Dirge's left let go of the woman and reached for the dagger at his belt. Dirge took off the man's hand at the wrist. The ruffian howled, grasped his stump, and fell to his knees. The third ruffian pulled the woman in front of his chest as a shield. Dirge lunged, stabbing him through the throat, then gave his sword a twist and pulled it out. The man gurgled and dropped.

The woman stared at him with wide eyes, shaking. She crumpled to the ground, trying to pull back the torn remains of her clothes to cover herself.

"You must go," Dirge said. "It is still not safe."

He turned and strode to the center of the mob. A pair of them turned and ran at him with their clubs raised high. Dirge ducked to his left under the man's swing and slashed at his exposed ribcage—the blade digging deep as it slid between the ribs. Blood sprayed as the man collapsed. The follow up strike caught the other thug in the back, whose bones snapped and popped from the force of the blow, sending him sprawling.

The rest of the mob screamed like crazed animals and charged. Dirge ducked and weaved, slashing at arms, legs, necks—whatever was open. Within a matter of moments, they all lay dead or dying, their blood trickling down the road toward the docks. Dirge calmly bent and wiped his sword on the shirt of one of the dead men, doing his best to ignore the women he'd killed.

As he walked away from the circle of corpses, the few remaining city folk came out of the buildings. Some ran up to him but stopped several feet away with their hands before them, showing they'd no weapons. They said nothing and simply stared at him, seemingly at a loss for words.

Dirge wasn't sure what to say himself, so he chose the simplest thing, "You're not alone." He nodded and walked on, leaving the people dumbfounded.

Chapter 13
Prophet
(503 -R.C.-)

In a black leather coat with steel plates woven inside, Dirge strode down the empty street in the Winds district, his boots crunching on the gravel-strewn surface. Rickety buildings swayed and creaked in the ever-present wind gusting through the massive, crumbling breaks in the city's western wall. Sagging, peaked roofs missed shingles, and many sported holes. Crumbling stucco and broken windows on the buildings' upper floors—there were none in the first two— turned the structures into howling specters when the winds tore through them. But regardless of their state, every door was stout, barred on the inside with heavy planks or iron rods, because more than wind made its way over that decomposing outer wall.

Dirge swiveled his head about, his gray eyes peering through the slots in his hull helm. "Where is everyone?" For several blocks, he'd not seen a soul. Even the mongers' carts stood unattended. "Something's not right here." If a Chaos storm had struck, he'd have heard about it.

They'd been out on *patrol* three or four times a week for the past year. The campaign started well. In the first month, they dispersed or slaughtered a dozen chaotic mobs. Yet as time wore on, the number of mobs did not decrease. They increased and spread. The mobs also stopped fighting back when confronted by Dirge's patrol, choosing to flee instead.

As he approached an intersection, shuffles, murmurs, and jingling chains came from all sides, sounding muffled and warbled as though coming from the bottom of a well. He paused and took a step back—the intersection looked distorted, like looking through warped glass.

Taking a deep breath, he drew his sword and stepped into the intersection.

The air shimmered, the warped view disappearing with a pop revealing over two dozen people at each end of the intersecting roads. Their heads swiveled about and then their eyes lit on Dirge. Screaming, their faces twisted in rage and spittle flew from their mouths as they charged, their makeshift weapons rattling in shaking fists.

Not wanting to fight both sides at once, Dirge charged to the right, choosing the biggest man out front to be the focal point of his attack. The big man screamed and raised a large iron bound club over his head. Dirge lunged forward, slashing his blade across the huge man's throat. He danced aside as the large man gurgled and fell, blood spraying from the gash.

Moving into the mob, Dirge ducked, sliced, and stabbed as he went. Shocks and vibrations rippled up his arms as the blade bit into leather, flesh, and bone. Piercing the wall of mad, screaming people, he turned and attacked them from behind. Blood flew, limbs fell to the ground, and shrieks filled the air as he slew anyone near. The stink of sweat, shit, and fear filled the air. It didn't take long for the mob to break, hacking and clawing at each other in their bid to escape.

Dirge let them go, his eyes searching out the real danger. A priest was about, an illusionist. He searched the upper windows, peered into the dark corners all about him, but saw nothing. He considered leaving—it was the safe move. But he refused to leave. He wanted this priest.

As he slowly moved through the dead littering the road, movement to his right brought him around. A body on the ground shifted.

"Should I put you out of your misery?" Dirge wondered aloud.

The body heaved to the side. A club lying beneath it rose into the air, hovered a moment, and flew at Dirge. He knocked it aside with his sword and took up a defensive stance.

"So that's your—"

Something hit him in the back. He turned and at his feet lay a severed head. More movement came from all around as sticks, chains, limbs, and axes levitated into the air. They hovered a moment before hurtling toward him. He ducked, dodged, and knocked them aside as they tumbled through the air, but several still struck home.

Cut, and bleeding from multiple small wounds, he turned to make his escape. Something large hit him in the back, throwing him to the ground hard, knocking some of the air from his lungs. His sword slipped from his grip and tumbled away.

Gasping for breath he tried to crawl, but something pinned him to the ground. When struggled to see what held him, something slammed against his head, dislodging his helmet. Blood poured from his mouth and nose as he sagged to the ground. The small things rose and pummeled him once more. Covering his face and head with gauntleted hands, he grunted and groaned with each strike, until they finally stopped coming.

Laying in a daze, not knowing how much time had passed, he groaned when the weight atop him shifted. A pair of hands grabbed him by the arm and rolled him onto his back. Above him was the smiling face of Able, his bright red hair flowing in the wind.

"You all right, lad?" He helped Dirge into a sitting position.

"I'll be all right. Thank you."

"Sorry 'bout the delay. Took us forever to find them." The grinning redhead pointed to Dirge's other side where Dennis held a pair of heads by their long, black hair. "Looks like they're teaming up. We figure one was an illusionist and the other a telekinetic. The illusionist was a damn good one, had us chasing our tails for quite some time."

Dirge didn't care, he was just happy it was over. "What hit me?"

"The body of the first fella you killed. A big bastard, wasn't he?"

Dirge grunted. "I should have guessed," he said as his Brothers helped him to his feet.

Several days later, he sat in the common room of the Angelic, nursing his wounded pride.

"Do you know what the worst thing is?" he said to Corrigan as they ate their breakfast of sausage and eggs. "The people still aren't fighting back. When are they going to defend themselves?"

"Can you blame them?" the man replied, his black eyes peering at Dirge through a curtain of long black hair. "If it bothers you so, just bring it up at the meeting." He snapped into a piece of bacon.

Dirge frowned. "I don't think so." He wasn't good at talking to a crowd.

"You should speak more at the meetings." Bits of egg and sausage flew from Corrigan mouth as he spoke. "The people respect you. They'll listen to you."

Dirge twisted his mouth at Corrigan's disgusting habit. "What good does talking ever do?"

"Well, for one, it might help you get to know that girl you've been pining over." Smiling, Corrigan nodded over Dirge's shoulder and then stood. "And there's no chance like the present." He bowed his head and spoke to someone behind Dirge, "Good morn, fair maiden. You may sit here if you like. I must be on my way." Chuckling, he strolled into the kitchen.

Dirge froze. *Please, God, tell me he's joking.*

A scent of flowers and freshness drifted over Dirge.

"Is it all right if I sit here? Please say you don't mind." Her voice was soft and musical, yet brisk. "My name's Lynette."

Slowly turning, Dirge raised his gaze. His mind buzzed and his mouth went dry as he drank in the sight. Her dress was a light blue, embroidered with small flowers. Long brown hair hung over her shoulder—her pale hands trembling slightly as she stroked it. With a light nod of his head, the young woman glided to the seat Corrigan had vacated. She sat delicately, straightening and smoothing her dress as she gazed at him. He stared into her eyes—dark blue like the sky before twilight.

"Lynette," he stammered, happy to put a name to the woman he'd seen in his dreams so many nights. "That's a very pretty name."

The girl blushed and lowered her eyes. "Thank you. It's after my grandmother." She lightly licked her sweet, pink lips.

"My name is—" His voice broke, and he cleared his throat. "My name is, Dirge."

Her eyes lit up, seeming to grow as large as the moon. "Yes, I know. Everyone knows. You're the Hero of the Angelic. The Light that Holds Off the Darkness. He Who Fights Chaos." She dropped her gaze once more and cleared her own throat. "I'm sorry. My Da says I talk too much. So does my mum. But I don't talk anywhere near as much as my brother, Eric. He'll talk and talk and talk for hours on end. You can't get a word in edgewise with him about. I—" Her smile slipped. "Um, I'm sorry. I shouldn't have intruded your meal. It was rude of me." She started to stand.

"Stop!" Dirge reached out. "Please don't go." His hand quivered, and he dropped his gaze. "I'm sorry. I shouldn't have raised my voice to you." He looked back up into her amazing eyes. "But please, stay. I am not much with words but know that I dearly wish you to stay." He lowered his voice. "I don't want to lose you again."

"Lose me?"

Dirge shifted in his seat and swallowed. "Yes, lose you. I saw you the first night you came to the Slaag."

"How did you know that was our first night here?"

He smiled. "Because I'd know if I'd seen you before. You're not someone I could ever forget." He dropped his eyes once more, his face burning with embarrassment. *I'm talking like a fool. Jacob's good at this, not me.*

"But you did see me before." She smiled and bit her luscious pink lip.

"What?" He cocked his head to the side a moment. Then it hit him: those eyes… that hair… the biting of the lip… "You were in the Square. That day, the day it all happened. How could I've been such a fool to not remember?"

"I don't think you're a fool," she cooed.

His cheeks heated even more.

"In fact, I think you're the most handsome man I've ever met." Her hand gingerly reached out, shaking slightly. "I thought so, that very day."

He took her hand, his dark skin enveloping her cream colored, silken flesh. Everything about her was clean and fresh… and supple. *Is every part of her this soft?* His heart to raced, spreading throughout his body causing his scalp to tingle, his chest heaved, and his member hardened.

He dropped his eyes in shame—he had no right to think of her in that way. Clearing his throat, he looked back into her perfect eyes. "Where are you from, originally?"

"Well, we used to live just off the Square. That's why you saw us there. Father went there for business and said that I and Eric could come along. But by the time we got back, David… he was my little brother… the soldiers broke down the door and…" Her head fell to her chest and her hand shook.

"I understand." He squeezed her hand, trying to give her strength.

After a while, she lifted her head. Tears filled her blue eyes—now looking like the ocean before a storm—and streamed down her cheeks. "It never gets easier."

She wiped her face with her other hand and cleared her throat. "Anyway. We didn't know what to do at first. Then word got out about what happened here—about what you did. We felt compelled to come. Of all the places in the world Papa knew we'd be safe here." Her face lit up with a smile. "And he was right. They all called him a fool for wanting to come to the Slaag but we showed 'em. From the moment we got here, we felt different."

She tilted her head slightly to the side. "Most don't feel it. Did you know that? For some reason, most people are still afraid of this place. They speak of this area, this very block, as though it were cursed." She reached out with her free hand and touched his cheek. "It's not. It's blessed."

A loud clearing of the throat startled them both. Lynette snatched her hand back as though burned. Dirge looked up into the face of a man who was not happy, the same man that had been with Lynette that first night, her father. A young man, looking remarkably like Lynette, stood behind him, his eyes filled with zeal.

Dirge stood and bowed to the older man. "Sir."

"And just what are your intentions with my daughter?" The elder man's voice was rough, with a sharp edge. When Dirge opened his mouth, the man overrode him. "Never mind that. For now, anyway. I'm here for the meeting. Where is it?"

Dirge hadn't realized how much time had passed. "Sir, this must be your first time." He spoke softly—it was clandestine after all. "Follow me."

Before following, the man pointed a finger at Lynette who'd started to rise. "No! You stay here. Eric, sit with your sister and keep an eye out. You know what to look for."

He turned back to Dirge. "Let's go. I've business to attend to later."

Dirge took one last glance at Lynette then bowed again to her father, led him though the kitchen, and into the basement. The sounds of dozens of people talking at once assailed him as they descended. The stairs hugged the wall then turned into the basement. Upon reaching the landing at the stair's turn, Dirge's eyes went wide at seeing how packed the basement was.

These meetings had always been small, so having them in the basement had never posed a problem. At least they hadn't before. Dirge was embarrassed, so many people had passed by him as he spoke with Lynette and he'd not noticed. His mind went back to her, her lovely eyes, her soft skin… He shook his head. Now was not the time.

"Dirge!" Talic waved to him at the back of the room. "Bring Duncan here and we'll get started."

People turned to see the new comers. They quieted and parted as best they could so the two of them could get by them. People, the ones Dirge knew quite well, regarded him as they passed, their faces a mixture of pride, respect, and above all, adoration. It unnerved him. He understood the respect, but the zeal, the same he'd seen in the eyes of Lynette's brother, he couldn't fathom. He did what needed doing, nothing more, and none of it was worthy of worship.

Once they reached the front of the room, Duncan walked straight up to Talic. "First, I want to know what your apprentice's intentions are regarding my daughter."

Talic's eyes widened a bit and flitted to Dirge. "Your daughter?"

"Yes," Duncan replied. "This young man has been eyeing her for some time. And now I find them holding hands upstairs, in the common room—in front of everyone!"

The corner of Talic's mouth quirked as he glanced at Dirge. "Is this true?"

Dirge eyed the floor, his cheeks hot. "Um, yes Master. She told me what happened to her brother, and I wished to give her strength. She was on the verge of tears."

"You wanted to give her more than strength." Duncan's tone implied something lewd.

Dirge's head shot up, his eyes going directly to Duncan's. "No, sir. I did not— that is to say, I would never do such a thing. It's wrong to… to do… that, with anyone you're not pair-bonded with. I was holding her hand to give her strength. That's all." He realized how strongly he'd been speaking to the man and dropped his head once more. "I am sorry, sir. I should not have spoken so with you. Please, forgive me."

Dirge felt Duncan's eyes bore into him. He started to add something but Talic interrupted.

"As lurid as holding her hand may be," Talic said, his voice laced with the mirth, "I can honestly tell you that Dirge doesn't have a lecherous bone in his body. Hells, until now I wasn't sure he knew what a woman was beyond something to be protected above all else. So, if he does have an interest in your daughter, it is an honorable one."

"We shall talk more on this later." Doubt filled Duncan's.

He turned to the gathered crowd. "For those who don't know me, my name is Duncan Malik. I run several caravans along the coast and into the frontier. Like many of you, I moved my family here to the Slaag because it's the safest part of the city." Duncan paced back and forth, using his hands to emphasize his points. "It didn't use to be that way, I know, but it's the way of it now. The same cannot be said for the rest of Tuilar. Most people in this city live in constant fear of these random bands of marauders, and many of them look to us for protection. Or more succinctly, they look to our champion."

Dirge resisted the urge to drop his head as the crowd cheered. He did not deserve such acclamation, not for simply doing what needed to be done.

Duncan paused, stopped his pacing, turned, and raised his hands to the crowd to quiet them. "I have many connections in the Hall of the Masters, and I'm here to tell you that this has not gone unnoticed by the City Masters… or the priests."

"What are you trying to say?" asked the owner of the local butcher shop.

"I'm saying that someone has grown tired of the patrols, and that they know where they're emanating from."

"What would you have us do?" asked the Baker.

"We need to spread the word, we need to get the priests looking somewhere other than just here," Duncan said.

"There are other meetings," shouted a man from the back.

"I've been at a number of these meetings," said a man who traded in fine goods. "They all lead to nothing but argument. Nothing gets accomplished."

"I too have been to other meetings," added a woman who traded in textiles. "And if not for the support of the Brotherhood, they would all have disbanded long ago."

"Be that as it may," Duncan replied. "We must deflect the gaze of the church. They may respect the Brotherhood; but I can tell you they will not let this go unchecked for much longer."

A man Dirge did not recognize, shouted, "So, we're just supposed to let the mobs return to burn down our homes?"

The crowd burst with angry shouts. Talic stepped forward and did his best to calm them, but the fear and anger was palpable. Dirge took a balanced stance, ready to do what he must if things got out of hand.

Suddenly, the air changed. His skin prickled and his mind cleared. He'd not even realized his mind had been muddied in the first place.

"You must stop the attacks," said a stranger at the turn of the stairs. His strong voice was not loud, but it cut through the uproar as though with a knife.

The stranger descending the stair, surveying the room with sternness and piety, judging them all with each step he took. The man was of only middling height, but his bearing made him seem ten feet tall. His tanned skin appeared to glow in his pristine white robes. Long, curly black hair framed a regal face, and the steel-gray eyes that regarded them all seemed to glow as though a fire burned brightly behind them.

Dirge's eyes widened, for around the stranger's neck hung a seven-pointed star pendant. Dirge reached down and grasped his pouch where he kept one much like it. Heat radiated from his pendant so strongly he thought it mint burn him.

"Who are you and why are you here?" Talic asked, his eyes hooded.

The stranger reached them at the back of the room. "I am Isaac, a prophet of the Lord, sent to place you on the path to Righteousness."

"And just which 'Lord' are you referring to?" Duncan asked, taking a step back and looking at the stranger slightly sideways.

"Ukase," Dirge said, his breath coming short. There wasn't a doubt in his mind that before him stood a servant to the forgotten god.

The man turned to Dirge with a smile, his eyes stern yet knowing. The man's gaze bored into Dirge, into his deepest depths. The gaze fanned embers that lay dormant until a fire burst forth and enlightened his very being. This man, this prophet, delivered the light of God to Dirge's soul, the true word of Ukase, to show him the way.

The Prophet turned his eyes back to the crowd. "The time of Chaos is at an end," his voice boomed. "Ukase, the Lord God of Order, has awakened from his slumber. His flame of Righteousness has been renewed… but is not yet at full strength. We must fan that flame! We must bring it to a roaring inferno before we unleash his punishment upon the wicked! You ask what we should do with the mobs. The answer is we do nothing. We need do nothing. Do the mobs come here? No! And why? Because they fear the Lord God Ukase! Whether or not they know it, they fear the wrath of the Righteous, the touch of the Lord of Law! Let the mob attack where they will, it will only spread more dissent toward the demon that is Chaos! And for those that do not wish to hear the truth of God, let them die, for they are weak! Only the strong can carry the word of God! Only the pure can bask in his greatness! Only the Righteous can carry out this war to destroy Chaos once and for all!"

The people stood enraptured, all eyes filled with wonder and zeal. All except the members of the Brotherhood. Talic's were still hooded as he stood with his arms crossed. He looked about the room, gently shaking his head.

Dirge couldn't understand his master's reluctance. The Prophet spoke the truth. Dirge could feel it. He knew Isaac spoke to the heart of what needed to be done.

I would do anything for this man.

The thought brought him up short. For the first time in his life, Dirge felt true doubt. He could feel a schism in his soul. How could he blindly follow this man, follow Ukase, and still be true to Aza'zel and the Brotherhood?

Isaac and Talic were both staring at him, their eyes measuring. The will of two gods pressed down upon him. "I don't know what to do," he whispered.

"You will in time," Isaac said with a smile.

Chapter 14
Warriors of the Righteous
(504 -R.C.-)

"What does your heart tell you, my love?" Lynette knelt before Dirge, holding his hands in hers.

Her soft touch, as always, thrilled him. His heart raced and his stomach roiled whenever she was near. And when she touched him with such familiarity, he found it nearly impossible to concentrate.

"I'm not sure I can trust my heart," he said, staring at the floor of the common room.

His heart told him many things: to honor his vow to the Brotherhood, to accept the Prophet Isaac as his connection to God, to accept Ukase as his one true god—something he'd never felt about Aza'zel. Above all, though, his heart told him to take Lynette in his arms and kiss her till neither could breathe. As always, his longing filled him with shame.

"Of course, you can trust your heart." She reached out and gently touched his cheek.

His desire flared so bright it challenged the sun. He stomped it down, viciously, and pulled his head back slightly. "Please, don't do that."

"Why?" She drew her hand away.

"We are not pair-bonded. It's not right."

She leaned back, sitting on her feet, her eyes as big as the moon. "Would you have me?"

"Of course. But I must have your father's consent…"

"I'm sure Father—"

"…*which* he will not give," he gently over-road her. "Not until I've proven myself worthy."

"But you have, my dear," she said, her smile soft and sure. "He's seen you stand at the Prophet's side when he speaks to the people. He knows you have the Prophet's favor. The Prophet is the beacon of light spreading God's truth. You are God's sentinel, holding and protecting that light. Father knows this. Everyone knows this."

She got up on her knees once more and took his face in her delicate, alabaster hands. "Dirge, my love, you have his consent. All you need do is ask." Her eyes peered deep into his.

I could get lost in those eyes and never want to be found.

Out of the corner of his eye, Dirge spotted Dennis descending the stair. He took Lynette's hands, and gingerly caressed them a moment while still peering into her angelic eyes. He gently kissed each one upon the back.

"My, how brazen." Her mouth quirked.

"Yes, and I'm sorry." She may have meant it as a joke but his reply was earnest. "I must go. Dennis and I are escorting the Prophet to a meeting deep in the heart of the enemy."

When he stood to join Dennis, he noticed Talic standing in the door to the kitchen. His master's eyes were drawn, and he wore a scowl. Without a word, Talic turned and went back into the kitchen.

"He's upset with us," Dennis said once he stood by Dirge's side.

"He has every right to be," Dirge replied. His soul was still split between his two masters, and his two gods. He knew he could only have one, and with every passing day, the correct one became clearer to him. Talic read it in his eyes.

They exited the inn and marched two doors down to the building owned by Lynette's father. Duncan had offered the Prophet the best room in his home upon completing the first meeting. They held the district meetings there rather than in the basement of the Angelic. Which was fine with both Katlyn and Talic. Mistress Katlyn appreciated the decorum the Prophet brought, but her inn was the home to the Brotherhood and Aza'zel, not Ukase.

They stopped and Dirge knocked twice. Eric promptly opened the door and bowed to them before taking a step back, allowing the Prophet to exit.

The Prophet Isaac peered at them—his steel-gray eyes measuring—before nodding slightly allowing them to take the lead.

The four marched down the busy street, with Eric taking the rear. People eyed them as they passed. Most beamed with pride and reverence while the rest looked on with uncertainty. That look changed to one of distaste and revulsion once they left the Slaag.

"You've not yet reached your decision, Dirge. Why is that?" the Prophet asked as they made their way toward the Square.

Dirge scowled as he surveyed the people passing by. "It's not an easy one to make, Sir. I've made a pledge, and it would be wrong to go back on it."

The Prophet ignored the crowded streets. "Indeed, you have. Yet you hear the Lord's call. I know you do."

Dirge lowered his eyes for a moment. "Yes."

"You gave an oath when you joined the Brotherhood. What if I told you that you'd not made the oath to Aza'zel but to Ukase?"

Dirge stopped and turned to the Prophet. "What do you mean, Great One?"

"I mean that you did not hear Aza'zel's call. What you heard was the call of Ukase. You see, Aza'zel is a vessel for the Lord Ukase. Therefore, when you made your vow to the Brotherhood, in the name of Aza'zel, it was invalid. In your heart, you'd already pledged to Ukase. Am I not right?"

Dirge dropped his gaze once more. "I don't know," he said softly. Shaking his head, he turned, and resumed walking. "I cannot think about that now. I've a job to do and I will see it through."

As passed through the city, Dirge did his best to keep his mind on track, but found it difficult. The Prophet's words clung to him. Had his entire time with the Brotherhood been nothing but a façade? If that were the case, he owed Master Talic an apology… and possibly, his life. Talic told him that the pledge he made to the Brotherhood was for life. So, did that mean his life was now forfeit? It wasn't a pleasant thought.

As they approached the City Square, Dirge turned, leading them down an alley. Compared to most alleyways in the city it was nearly pristine. There was no garbage, no offal, no feculence of any kind, only dirt and mud.

"Order appears to be spreading," Dirge said, keeping his voice low.

"Possibly." The Prophet nodded. "It is also possible that the wealthy simply don't like the smell of garbage."

A short way down the alley, a large man covered with filth and dressed rough with a long shirt and pants filled with holes, stepped out from a doorway recessed into the wall. He held an iron-capped club in one of his heavily muscled arms while his other rested upon his belt – the perfect image of a ruffian.

Dirge, though, saw him for what he was, a well-paid guard. Leather armor was visible through the holes in the man's shirt, and he wore a short sword at his belt.

"What business have you here?" the man growled.

"You know why we are here," the Prophet intoned, his eyes hard as iron.

The guard wilted and dropped his gaze. "Yes, Great one. Follow me."

He ushered them through the recessed door and down into a basement. Over a dozen people, four dressed in silks and satin, occupied the room. Merchants, Dirge wagered to guess. The rest were guards in different types of armor—from the finest leather, to steel mail—all sporting weapons at their belts.

Dirge marched his group to an open area at the far end of the room, and then took up position to the Prophet's right, leaving the left to Dennis. Eric took up position near the doorway so he could keep an eye on their exit.

The Prophet Isaac surveyed the people before him, his steely gaze measuring, as always.

Everyone in the assembled group appeared on edge, eying each other and shuffling their feet, all but one, a woman at the group's center. To Dirge's amazement, she still clung to her beauty for someone her age. She was meticulous, something Dirge respected, but her obvious vanity caused him to shake his head. Her long gray hair matched her silken coat; they both shimmered in the lamp light. Gold rings sparkled on her manicured fingers, and chains of gold and silver hung about her neck. Her bright blue eyes sparkled in the light and her thin lips held a small smile.

"You are the Prophet, I assume." Her voice was as silken as the rest of her.

"I am Isaac, Prophet of the Great Lord Ukase. And you are Allyl, a Master of the Coin and willing disciple of our Lord."

The woman's smile broadened as the other three merchants shuffled their feet, their eyes shifting to each other and then back to the Master of Coin. "I welcome you, Prophet Isaac," she said with a nod. "And I hope our meeting will bear great bounty."

"The only bounty I seek is the eradication of Chaos."

The woman spread her arms wide. "We are people of business, and we understand that the only way for commerce to prosper is through stability." Her arms fell to her sides, and she held her head high. "But unlike my colleagues, I also see Chaos as a blight upon the land; one that must be stomped out at all costs."

"And what are you willing to do to make that happen?"

"What do you need of us?" She once again raised her arms as though to include them all, drawing a scowl from the other merchants.

"We need weapons." The Prophet's voice was hard as an anvil.

"You mean enough weapons to arm all those who would follow you, enough for an entire army." When the Prophet Isaac nodded, she rubbed her chin then gestured toward the Prophet. "It will be difficult. Most on the Masters' Council still hold Chaos in their hearts, even after the abomination that was the Cleansing. The Master at Arms being chief among those. So, believe me when I say that purchasing that many weapons will not go without notice."

"We can acquire weapons from outside," the youngest of the merchants added. "There are many caravans. We can get as many weapons as we need through them." His eyes grew less wary as he spoke and he started to stand taller. The other merchants slowly followed suit.

Dirge had seen it many times. The longer one was in the company of the Prophet Isaac, the stronger they supported him.

"Indeed." The Coin Master nodded. "But it will take time."

"Time is not something we have in abundance." The Prophet's eyes burned with an inner light. "Most of the priests of Chaos are still out in the wilds carrying out the will of the enemy. Many of them will return before long, and with them will come the arms of Chaos. We must strike while Chaos is weak. We must destroy the enemy here and create a bastion of Order. Only then can we move forward. We will cleanse this city of the stink of Chaos. The time of judgment is soon at hand."

Throughout the meeting, and during their way home, Dirge tried to stay on point, to keep his eyes out for any trouble. Yet he found it difficult. His mind kept going back to his conversation with the Prophet. He didn't like that he might not know himself as well as he thought. Moreover, he hated that he may, in the end, let down those that had raised him and stood with him his entire life.

After seeing the Prophet to the Malik house, Dirge went to the Angelic and up to his room. He sat on his bed, gazing out the window, hoping he might find the answer to his question in the oncoming night's sky. It was nearly dark when someone knocked on his door.

"You may enter," he said without taking his eyes off the sky.

Talic stepped in. "We must talk," he said in a somber voice.

"Yes, Master Talic."

The Brotherhood leader took the chair next to the open window. "You've something on your mind. What is it?"

Dirge regarded his Master a moment. He knew what he wanted to say, what his heart told him was right, but he was loath to do so. They were words of betrayal, pure and simple. "I spoke to the Prophet about my vows to the Brotherhood."

Talic's eyebrows furrowed, but he said nothing.

Dirge forged on. "He said that my vow was to Ukase, not Aza'zel."

"Did he now?" Talic's forehead creased even more.

"He did." Dirge shifted in his seat slightly. "He said that Ukase was in my heart long before anything else and that Aza'zel is only a vessel for Ukase."

Talic stared at Dirge with his arms crossed and his scowl fixed.

The silence stretched for minutes and Dirge stared back while trying to keep his composure, but he grew perturbed. He'd explained himself to his master and now Talic owed it to him to pass judgment. Yet as time passed, and the silence lingered, Dirge felt only the weight of his Master's contempt, and Dirge found that contempt unfair.

"You said yourself that I was touched by the Forgotten God, that Ukase had laid claim to me."

"I said he touched you. Nothing more." He paused then slowly stood. "You've made your decision then."

"I have, Master Talic."

"Do not call me 'Master'," Talic said through clenched teeth. "You are forsaking your vow and abandoning your Brothers. I am no longer your Master."

"Yes, Talic," Dirge said, his head against his chest. He couldn't look at Talic, the hurt in the man's eyes struck too close to his heart.

He stripped off his shirt and knelt before his former master with his neck extended. "I await your judgment."

Time passed and Dirge did not move, but Dirge would wait as long as it required.

Finally, Talic spoke, his voice soft, "What are you doing, son?"

"The Brotherhood is for life, and death is what I deserve for this betrayal." Dirge refused to cringe; he'd face his death with eyes open.

"Stand up, son."

Dirge stared up at Talic. "I don't understand."

Talic sighed. "Your life is not mine to take. God will judge you in his own time."

"Perhaps you're right. Ukase's touch has been upon you your entire life. Who am I to question a god?" he said with a shake of his head.

He then stabbed a finger at Dirge. "But that tripe about Aza'zel being a vessel for Ukase, is horse-shit. Death answers to The Mother, the Creator of all, and to no other. You let your *'holy prophet'* know that."

Talic firmed his stance. "Gather your things and go. You are no longer a member of the Brotherhood, so you can no longer stay here."

Dirge nodded and stood. He turned to his bed but stopped. "What of Jacob, Mas–." He compressed his lips. "What about Jacob, Talic? What will become of him?"

"I wouldn't worry about it," he said with a smile. "Katlyn will find him a room in short order, I'm sure. She's taken quite a shine to that rogue, and he more than earns his keep."

Without another word, his former master left him there, in a room that no longer felt like home.

Dirge sighed. *Funny how quickly that happened.*

He gathered up his clothes, what little he had, and put them into his trunk with his bright steel armor. He left the Brotherhood armor. *I no longer have a right to it.*

He hesitated about his sword though. It was something of the Brotherhood as well, but Talic had given it to him long before he'd became a member. He chose to keep it. The decision felt right, and he knew he'd have use of it soon.

As he strode down the hall, Jacob topped the stair. "What are you doing?"

Dirge explained the situation to his friend. He finished with, "So I must leave."

"I've never understood any of this. You know that, right? I just don't understand the allure of gods of Death or Law." He shook his head and smiled. "I find the idea of Order a bit too confining for some reason."

Jacob's smile said far more than his statement. It slipped though as he reached out and took Dirge by the shoulders. "You know I'll back you all the way, whatever you do." He chuckled. "You're the only brother I've got left."

After Jacob went into his room, Dirge regarded the closed door for a moment, then turned and went down the stairs to a nearly empty common room. The only people were a pair of customers in the far corner having their dinner, Mistress Katlyn, Cal, and Dennis.

Cal stood at the door to the kitchen wearing a scowl. Dirge nodded to him but the man. Cal spat upon the floor, turned, and went into the kitchen.

Mistress Katlyn came to him from behind the bar. "I do wish you'd reconsider."

"Does everyone know?"

"Everyone that matters," she replied, wiping her hands upon her white apron. "They've all been wondering for some time whether or not you'd leave, and well... your standing there with your trunk says it all."

"And how do you feel about it?"

"I'm not happy, but it's your decision. You must follow your heart. I don't trust this Isaac fellow, but he's a far sight better than those damned Chaos zealots."

She reached out and cupped his cheek. "I just worry about you. A storm is coming and I fear for your safety." She took her hand back and smiled. "But you'll weather the storm, of that I'm sure. You're a fighter. It's what you were born to do. If anyone can do what needs to be done, it's you."

She kissed him on the cheek. "You are the son I never had. Your mum would be proud of you."

Katlyn's radiant smile turned into a frown and her eyes furrowed. "I need to have a word with Cal." She stalked off saying, "Spit on my floor, will you?"

Mother would be proud of me? He hoped that was true. It was all he'd ever wanted. It didn't matter that she'd not known who his father was—many in the Slaag didn't know their parentage. It also never bothered him what she'd done to make coin. She did what she needed to in order for them to survive. *He* may find the idea of copulation out of pair-bonding wrong, but that didn't matter when it came to his mother. She could do no wrong in his eyes.

As Dirge approached the front door, Dennis strode up, his face unreadable.

"Are you angry at my betrayal as well?" Dirge asked.

"You do what needs to be done," the Brotherhood member said. "I find no fault with that. Unlike the rest, I think that Isaac is right. It's time to end the reign of Chaos. And the only way to do that is by war." He placed his hand upon Dirge's shoulder. "The truth is that I wish I had the courage to join you."

He bowed his head, turned, and strode back to his corner.

A part of Dirge wished the man would join him. He cursed himself for the thought. It was bad enough that *he* was walking out on them. He didn't want any other man to feel the same shame in their heart.

Dirge stepped out into the cool night air. The door closing behind him seemed to echo in his mind, like a hammer of doom striking the anvil. The inn was now closed to him, and he doubted he'd ever return. He marched the short distance to the house of Duncan Malik, set his chest down, and knocked. It was late and the Malik's rarely received visitors at that hour.

Young Eric answered the door, his eyes beaming with zeal. "You have been expected, Great One." His voice nearly quivered with excitement.

Dirge frowned. "Do not call me that, please. I am simply Dirge, nothing more."

"There is nothing simple about you, my friend. Come, I'll show you to the basement. The Prophet Isaac is awaiting you there with the rest." He waved Dirge in.

"What should I do with my—"

"Bring it with you. The Prophet says you'll have need of it."

As he followed Lynette's brother down the hall, he found Eric's statements odd. He asked, "How did the Prophet know I'd be bringing my things? And you said 'others,' what others?"

"The rest of the Righteous." Eric opened a door and headed down the narrow flight of stairs.

The smell wafting up from the basement was unlike anything else he'd experienced. Instead of the usual musty dankness, the air was clean and fresh.

The basement was little more than four walls with intermittent posts holding up the ceiling. The only light emanated from a pair of lanterns hanging below the ceiling at the far end. They burned brightly, illuminating six people. Five men stood along the far wall in matching white tunics and black pants. They stood with backs pillar straight, their eyes sharp and filled with fervor. Each held a sword before them in both hands, its tip resting in the ground. In front of the men stood the Prophet Isaac, his pure white robes glowed in the relative darkness, his eyes seemed afire, and his smile was one of triumph.

He beckoned to Dirge. "You have made your decision."

It was not a question, but Dirge replied all the same. "Yes, Prophet."

As Dirge approached the Prophet, Eric joined the five men along the back wall. It was only then that Dirge realized Lynette's brother wore the same garb as the rest of the men. He took up a sword leaning against the wall and held it before him as the others did.

The Prophet motioned to Dirge. "Kneel."

The Prophet raised his right hand, and as one, the six men behind him lay their swords at their feet, and stripped off their tunics. Upon each man's chest, there were a pair of marks, a seven-pointed star just below their shoulders. The marks glowed red as though alive with fire.

"Behold," the Prophet intoned. "The Warriors of the Righteous. They are the right hand of God, the fist of Ukase made to smite our enemy. They are the sword that takes the lives of the wicked, and the shield that protects the innocent. They are unyielding and without fear, but they need a captain. Would you be that captain?"

Dirge's world rocked. He'd not been expecting any of this. He'd gladly join the Prophet, to be a divine warrior, a sword to smash Chaos in the name of Ukase. It sounded right. It felt right. But to lead, to be the champion of the Prophet and a captain of the Righteous?

The Prophet's eyes stayed locked onto his, compelling. The looks on the faces of the Warriors behind him bristled with pride, their eyes shining brightly, their chests pumped out. The only exception was Eric. He seemed to quiver as he lightly licked his lips. His eyes darted between Dirge and The Prophet. The boy needed this; he needed Dirge to lead him to victory. Something told Dirge that without his help, the boy would likely die in some foolhardy attempt of heroics. He couldn't do that to Lynette.

"I will," Dirge said. "I will lead these men. I will be your champion."

"Would you be a Warrior of the Righteous, the sword to be thrust into the heart of Chaos?"

"I will."

"Would you be the Captain of the Legion of God, and my champion?"

"I will."

"Bare yourself." After Dirge complied, the Prophet reached into his robes and pulled out a pair of round, black iron plates the size of his fist. Embossed upon each plate was a seven-pointed star. The Prophet took hold of one in each hand by grips attached to their backs.

His eyes never left Dirge. "Do you, Dirge, here by swear to uphold the will of Ukase, the Lord of Order?"

"I do."

The black stars glowed. "Do you, Dirge, here by swear to forsake all other gods and demons until your death?"

"I do."

"Do you, Dirge, here by swear to throw down the forces of the God Edis, Lord of Chaos?"

"I do!" Dirge felt the heat coming off the now white-hot iron stars held before him.

"Then by the will of Ukase, the Lord God of Order, I bestow upon you his touch. Let all who see his mark know and fear his might!" The Prophet stabbed the hot iron stars into Dirge's chest right below his shoulders.

Dirge's skin hissed and his mind exploded in pain. His vision when black and he seemed to float in a vast nothingness. Within that void, a light blinked into existence. The light grew as it raced toward him until it enveloped everything, including Dirge. The light was a vast ocean of purity and virtue, of beauty and perfection, of everything that was right in the world... a universe of righteousness.

As he regained consciousness, the pain ebbed. He beheld the brands upon his chest, glowing with an inner fire, and marveled as the pain quickly faded. He felt changed, more than his former self somehow. The moment those brands touched his skin, the world moved beneath his feet, it shifted from its previous path, and onto the one it needed to be. He felt that if he'd not chosen this—that if he'd forsaken the Prophet and these men—the world would have been lost.

"Arise, Captain, and greet your fellow Warriors."

Dirge's eyes snapped to the Prophet. He'd heard Isaac's words clearly, but the man hadn't opened his mouth.

"Aye," Dirge heard the Prophet's voice in his mind. *"This gift and others the Lord God Ukase has bestowed upon you this day."*

The Prophet then spoke aloud. "Let it be known throughout the Righteous, that the day of reckoning is soon at hand! God's judgment will befall the disciples of Chaos and smite them!"

Chapter 15
Permission
(505 -R.C.-)

Dirge lay on his bed, staring at the ceiling, his eyes following its painted swirling patterns. He'd been living in the Malik house for nearly a year and still wasn't used to it. Everything felt far too big. His room—at least twice the size of the one at the Angelic—had three overstuffed chairs large enough to swallow anyone who sat in them. A polished dark-oak writing desk took up nearly an entire wall, and his wardrobe stretched to the ceiling, looking nearly bare with the meager amount of clothing he owned. Even his bed was so large and comfortable he found it somehow unsettling.

He shook off the thoughts to get back to the task at hand—trying to sleep. He rolled over onto his side, his eyes taking the failing light of the day. Tomorrow was to be a momentous day, and he needed all the sleep he could get. Yet sleep eluded him. His mind kept skittering from one thought to the next—he was to be in charge and had a lot on his plate. He didn't know if he was up to the task though. They trained every day and he still didn't feel ready.

With a sigh, he heaved himself out of bed, made his way to his washstand, and turned up one of the two lamps affixed to the wall on either side of a gold-framed mirror. The room had nine lamps. Nine! He'd only one at the Angelic. Also, his mirror there was simple polished tin. The very idea of having one of glass, and in a gold frame, embarrassed him with its opulence.

He quickly splashed water on his face from the porcelain washbasin. He peered at himself in the mirror. The dripping water from his ebony skin looked like tears, which he found funny. He didn't feel like crying, yet he wondered if he should. There was a very good chance he would die in the morning, and the thought of his death pained him. Not that he feared death—everyone faced it at some point—but it would devastate Lynette.

Lynette. Yes, she was the chief reason for his sleeplessness. She lingered in his thoughts night and day. They'd spent as much time together as possible over the past months, yet it wasn't enough. He wanted to spend every moment of his life with her. Her very presence put him at ease—when it wasn't driving him to distraction, anyway.

Jacob had asked him once if they'd been intimate yet. Well, that wasn't quite the term he used but Dirge knew what he meant all the same. The answer, of course, was no, but it was not for a lack of desire, and that thought shamed him. He did want her. Her scent intoxicated him, her soft, sweet voice pleased him to his core and her touch made him tingle and grow stiff—which then made him blush and curse himself. Even thinking about it at that moment hardened his member.

He turned away from the mirror in disgust. "I've no right to think of her that way!"

Yet he did. He couldn't help it.

"You must make it right in the eyes of the Lord," he heard the Prophet say into his head.

His cheeks burned all the hotter. "What must I do, Prophet? How do I make this right in the eyes of the Lord?"

"By the ancient ritual of marriage."

"Marriage?"

"It is God's term for pair-bonding. A man and a woman are made one, in the eyes of the Lord. And in so doing, their offspring will be one with the Lord as well. A proper birth, from a proper pairing. As it should be."

Dirge smiled as the Prophet continued to explain everything marriage entailed, for it was truly a blessing on to the Lord, and the answer to his prayers.

He wiped his face, dressed, and dashed out his door. He first needed permission from Lynette's father, according to the Prophet, so he raced down the hallway and skidded to a halt at the door to Duncan Malik's room. Steadying himself, he took several deep breathes before knocking.

"Dirge," Mister Malik said upon answering. "I thought you'd gone to bed some time ago. Having trouble getting to sleep, eh? Well, can't say as I blame you. With the day you have ahead of you, I don't think I'd sleep a wink, myself. Have you tried warm milk?"

"Oh, do stop prattling on and let the boy in," Dirge heard Lynette's mother say from within the room.

"Oh, yes, of course. Come in, lad, come in." He waved for Dirge to enter. "What can I do for you?"

"Yes, dear, come and have a seat. What can we help you with?" Lynette's mother, Elli, was nearly a mirror image of her daughter, except the streaks of gray in her long brown hair, and the wrinkles about her eyes. "You know we'd do anything in our power to aid you or the Prophet."

"Thank you for the offer of the seat, ma'am, but for this I feel I must stand."

He turned to Mr. Malik. "I've come to ask…" He cleared his throat. "I've come to ask your permission to marry your daughter, Lynette."

Duncan Malik scrunched his eyes. "My permission? You want to do what to my daughter?"

"According to the Prophet, marriage is an ancient rite where two people swear themselves to each other in the eyes of the Lord. It is a permanent pair-bonding. Something quite common in the days before the cursed Edis stole control over the world."

"You wish to pair-bond with my daughter?" Malik's frown concerned Dirge.

Elli, on the other hand, wore a grin that nearly split her face. "Oh don't go putting on airs, Duncan."

She turned to Dirge, a tilted smile upon her face. "The truth is we both thought you two had mated long before this."

Dirge took a step back. "No, ma'am. It would be wrong for me to do such a thing." His cheeks heating once again. His eyes darted about the room as he found he couldn't look them in the eye.

The eldest Malik chuckled. "I don't believe I've ever seen a man your age act bashful. Why would you think it would be wrong to lie with my daughter?"

"It didn't feel right." Dirge looked at his feet. "I've felt something holding me back for some time. And it wasn't until the Prophet told me… that is, until I found out about… well…"

He took a deep breath and raised his head to look Mr. Malik in the eye. "I love Lynette. I would do anything for her. What I do tomorrow, I do for everyone, but mostly I do it for her. This world has no future under the continued reign of Chaos. I want Lynette to live in a world of the Lord God, Ukase."

Duncan smiled. "Of course you can marry our daughter. We would consider it a great honor to be as a father and mother to you."

He turned and gazed at Elli. "Marriage, a ritual pair-bonding. I like the sound of that. You and I should do so as well."

"Thank you." Dirge bowed to the both of them and left them to their conversation.

Dirge rushed to the stairs and down to the second floor. Lynette's room was at the end of the hall, directly below her parents. He needed to knock on her door a couple of times before she answered.

She answered the door with a yawn. "Dirge, my sweet. What is something the matter?" Concern filled her face.

Dirge's eyes went wide and his jaw became slack. She stood in the open doorway, her hair an auburn cascade falling about her shoulders and fanning across her nightshirt— her thin nightshirt. The light from her bedside lamp silhouetting the curves of her waist and hips, along with her bare supple legs, washed all thought from his mind.

She glanced down at herself and blushed before taking hold of herself. She looked back up at Dirge, and with the sweetest smile, reached out to caress his cheek. "What is it, my love?"

Dirge shook himself. He cleared his throat, knelt before her, and took her hand in his. "Lynette Malik, would you do me the great honor of becoming my wife?"

She tilted her head. "Your what?"

"I have spoken with the Prophet. It means that I would take you for my own, to be my one and only pair-bond for life. It means I would promise myself to you and no other, and that I would give my life to see you safe."

Her eyes lit up, and she flung herself at him, wrapping her arms about him. "Oh, yes. Yes, my sweet, yes. It is all I've ever wish for and more." She kissed him fiercely. "We shall do it after the battle. We shall—"

Dirge gently placed a finger on her lips. "No. Now. I would have you this very night. I may not live to the next morning. Tonight may be our only night."

"Yes, my sweet." She kissed him again. "Just tell me what you need me to do."

He explained the ritual as put to him by the Prophet. "We must each have a witness, he said. Someone to stand at our side. I want Jacob to be that man."

Lynette wrinkled her nose.

"I know you two have your differences–"

"Differences?! The man is a lecher and a braggart," she huffed and crosser her arms. "For the life of me I still don't see why you still abide him. Wouldn't you rather have someone at your side who could fight if needs be?"

"Jacob simply doesn't understand the idea of order. He says he finds it be too confining. He may yet come to see the truth." Dirge placed his hand upon her shoulder. "You are right, though, regarding his fighting. For all of Jacob's bravado he's nearly worthless in a fight. His only real weapons were his mind and his mouth. He'd stick someone with his dagger, but only if they weren't paying attention." He hesitated a moment. "That being said, I want him as my witness because he's my truest friend. My only friend." He gently placed his hand under her chin and lifted her head to look her in the eyes. "He's also the only family I have."

Lynette slowly smiled. "Well, you won't have to worry about that anymore."

"So is that a yes?" Dirge asked.

She went up on her tiptoes and kissed him. "Yes, my love. Yes."

Dirge slept very little that night, and he couldn't help but smile over it. As awkwardly as it started, by the end they got it right—much to the delight of them both.

Chapter 16
Judgment
(505 -R.C.-)

Dirge stood in the middle of a busy intersection. A cold wind, flowing from gray turbulent clouds that filled the sky, tugged at his coat. The intersection was the busiest in the entire city. The road ahead of him led to the city Square, the one behind to the Slaag, the right went toward the wharf, and the left to the city gate. With the rest of the Warriors of the Righteous spread throughout the city, each at major intersections.

The black iron rod felt heavy in his hand, far heavier than its base materials. Each of the Warriors had one in their possession. Dirge observed their creation. The Prophet had placed his hand upon the blacksmith as the man cast each one out of raw iron. The Prophet called them the "Rods of Divinity," with the seven-pointed star sigil capping each end of the seven-foot rods, and four more sigils jutting out of the center, one for each major direction of the compass.

"It is noon," the voice of The Prophet said in his head. *"The time of Judgment is at hand. Raise your rod up on high and repeat after me."*

Dirge did as bade, raising the rod above his head, heedless of the traffic moving about him. "By the word of Ukase, Lord God of Order, I hereby banish the darkness!" Dirge felt the fire of God burning in his mind. "I hereby bring you into his righteous eye!"

The power of God flooded his body and into the rod, causing it to glow red.

"By the word of Ukase, Lord God of Order, I hereby cleanse this land!"

He slammed the rod into the street, the seven-pointed star sinking deep into the pavement. The ground quaked, and the air blasted away from him in all directions as wave upon wave of the Lord's will expanded outward. The shock wave sped away from Dirge. The surrounding buildings shook, causing several of them to crumble, and threw people and animals to the ground. The dust from the collapsing structures blew away, leaving the air pure and clean.

The people, those that had lived through the blast, stood and beheld the wonder about them. The buildings that hadn't fallen seemed stronger, the air smelled fresher, and the sky above was a pure blue. Ukase had consecrated the ground about Dirge. The six other Warriors of the Righteous throughout the city were performing the same rite.

"That ought to stir the hornet's nest," he said.

Soon, every remaining Chaos priest in the city would come flooding out of their temple with as many fighters they could muster. They would descend upon Dirge and his fellow Warriors around the city.

At least that was the plan.

Dirge unconsciously touched his seven-pointed star pendant hanging about his neck, the same one he'd found as a child. A matching pendant now hung around Lynette's, who lay safe in the basement of the Malik house. He smiled. "I still can't believe she said yes."

His reminiscing snapped at the echo of stomping boots, and the din of a mob, coming from the bend in the street ahead of him. He drew his sword and set his feet next to the Rod of Divinity. He drew a deep breath and went through his mental exercises to calm and align himself.

This is the time. This is the place. I am the spike driven into the heart of Chaos.

A mass of leather clad men and women rounded the corner. These weren't the usual chaotic mob; these were armored soldiers wielding swords, maces, and spears. And at the center of their front line was a priest in multihued robes.

The civilians who survived his planting of the Rod scattered. They knew what was coming and wanted nothing to do with the coming violence. Dirge gave them little thought, his entire focus was on the multihued woman.

The priest of Chaos stopped less than a hundred feet away, multicolored strands of hair hanging before her face, and raised her hand. The soldiers halted. The priest lifted her head and swung it from side to side as though smelling the air. She then smiled, and spoke quietly, "Kill him."

With a roar the soldiers raced forward, their boots hammering the stone like a stampede of bulls, their weapons flailing above their heads glinted in the sunlight, and their eyes filled with maniacal bloodlust while their throats screamed murderously.

They charged into the intersection and slammed into the invisible barrier surrounding Dirge. Ten feet from Dirge's face, they parted and flowed by, like a wave around a massive pillar of stone. Most had flooded by him before they could bring themselves to a halt. Once stopped, those nearest Dirge hammered at the barrier with weapons and fists to no avail, their screams filling the air as spittle flew from their mouths.

Dirge paid them no mind; they were nothing. The real threat lay behind them—a vile pus filled cyst spat up from the bowels of hell—slowly approaching from the back of the soldiers. The priest walked through the mass of men, shoving them aside with her powers until she reached the barrier.

The woman snarled. "What filth is this?" Her voice grated on Dirge's ears. "The Great Lord is forgiving with cults from the past, but he will not suffer this blasphemy."

She placed a hand upon the barrier and Dirge felt it flux. The stars upon his chest burned white-hot and the barrier solidified. The priest drew her hand back as though burned. She cursed and slammed her fist down to no avail. The woman's snarl became a wicked grin as her right hand filled with a glowing, multicolored globule. She pressed the glob-filled hand upon the shield and Dirge felt it warble.

"Extend the barrier," the Prophet said. *"Draw her in and deal with her."*

Dirge concentrated upon the shield and gave it a shove. In an instant, the barrier expanded another five feet. It passed through the priest, but sent her men and women flying in all directions. They smashed into one another, many tumbling to the ground in heaps of bruised bodies and broken bones.

"Now," Dirge screamed.

With a roar, the warriors of Ukase under his command flooded out of the alleyways of the surrounding streets and smashed into the bewildered and battered soldiers. Swords slashed at exposed backs, axes chopped into limbs, maces crushed bones, and iron clad clubs smashed skulls.

Dirge raced toward the momentarily bewildered priest, slashing at her neck. She quickly recovered and caught his sword with her globule-covered hand, sending a shock through the sword and up his arm causing his shoulder to spasm. His sword vibrated so strongly he nearly lost his grip.

He yanked it back.

The priest smiled triumphantly, pointed her hand at Dirge, and unleashed a bolt of Chaos.

Dirge pivoted at the waist, back on one leg, causing the blast of Chaotic power to flow over his head. He then drove forward and kicked her square in the sternum. She flew back into the shield, slammed into it, and rebounded toward Dirge. In a flowing move, he sidestepped her and slashed at her back. Dirge heard her back snap as she shrieked and fell.

The woman flailed on the ground, unable to move her legs. Undaunted she turned and pointed her hand at Dirge. He spun to the side and hacked her hand off at the wrist. Blood poured from the wound as his next strike took her in the throat. Bones snapped and blood vomited out of her neck as her head tumbled away.

Dirge regarded the woman's body for a moment and realized he felt nothing. "I guess I've gotten used to killing women." He turned and helped his men kill the rest of the soldiers.

Once they'd finished, the group's second in command – the Prophet called him a "Lieutenant" – turned to Dirge. "Captain, what next?"

"Next, Henson, we–"

"Next," the Prophet said into his mind, *"we punish those guilty for their participation of the atrocity that was the Cleansing."*

"How will I know who to punish?" Dirge asked.

"You will know." The Prophet said nothing more.

With a shake of his head, Dirge gathered his men. Of the twenty-five men he'd started with, twenty survived their ambush. He wasn't sure if that was a good ratio. The Prophet had named him Captain, yet he had no practical experience in this type of thing. With a deep breath, Dirge shook off his doubt – after all, who was he to question the Prophet of God?

"What news from the Prophet, sir?" asked Henson.

"Next, we seize the nearest city gate. Along the way when we see anyone guilty of atrocities we are to deal with them." He saw Henson frown. "What's wrong?"

Henson hesitated a moment and looked down before bringing his eyes back to Dirge. "That is my gate."

Henson had been a former member of the city guard.

"Is this going to be a problem?"

"No, sir."

Henson turned to the rest of the men. "Form up!"

Dirge smiled as the men lined up in formation. None of them were soldiers, not even Henson, but with the influence of the Lord they'd gained discipline. With a nod to his second, he turned and marched down the road to the nearest city gate.

The streets were empty as they made their way—hawker's carts lay abandoned and random objects littered the streets as though dropped. Dirge watched the buildings as they marched. He could see people peering at them through shuttered windows, but no one confronted them. News had spread as to what was happening.

Halfway to the gate, Dirge heard a woman wailing down the road to his left. She lay cowering in an alley, grasping her right ankle. Blood covered her long blonde hair and face, and her flowered dress was torn in several places. She was quite beautiful, yet he found her disgusting. He saw an ugly "aura" about her. There was no other way to describe it.

"Please, help me," she cried, reaching out to him. "People started running and screaming. I fell, and they trampled me. I think I broke my ankle."

He knew this woman. He didn't know how or why, but he knew her.

"Please, you must help me," she implored.

"You'll have to—" A picture of the woman bloomed in Dirge's mind. He knew her. He'd seen her years before—four years, to be precise.

"I remember you," he growled. "I watched from the rooftop as you walked into the street with an infant dangling in your hand. It was your own child, wasn't it? You slit your child's throat and bathed in its blood!"

She snatched her hand back, and cringed, nearly curling into a ball.

Dirge realized what the aura was; it denoted someone who participated in the Cleansing. Her hair and face weren't actually covered in blood; he was seeing her crime.

He drew his dagger with his right hand, stepped forward, and grabbed her hair with his left. She screamed as he yanked her toward him, exposing her neck. "I find you guilty for your heinous crime, and I sentence you in the name of Ukase."

He slashed her throat, the dagger digging deep, from one side of her neck to the other. Blood gushed from the wound. He stared into her eyes while she gurgled, flailed her arms, and thrashed in his grasp. When she finally fell silent, and the light faded in her eyes, he let her fall to the ground.

"Judgment has been passed," the Prophet said into his mind.

Dirge bent and cleaned the blood off his dagger with her dress, then returned to the head of his column—he ignored her blood on his gauntlets and armor. His men eyed him grimly, but they understood. The guilty must be punished in accordance to their crime.

Chaos driven mobs attacked them multiple times on their way to the city gate. They slaughtered them all to a man. No one was allowed to escape God's judgment. Dirge lost only one of his men in the attacks—a former clockmaker named Krasner.

He bent over Krasner's body and prayed to Ukase. Once finished, he addressed Henson. "We shall bring him with us. He was a valiant man of God and I'll not see him desiccated by Chaos."

"What of the others we left behind?" Henson asked.

"They lie on Holy ground. No minion of Chaos would dare step foot there." Dirge did his best to sound certain, but he had doubts, along with a good deal of guilt. He realized he'd not prayed over the others. He would need to remedy that.

"No need to worry, my son," the Prophet said on to him. *"They have already been recovered and now lay before me. I shall give them last rites, and they will be with Ukase ever after."*

"How goes the fight about the city, oh Great One?" Dirge asked him.

"Everything is proceeding as planned."

Dirge sighed in relief.

They traversed the city's winding roads and finally came in sight of the gate. A lone guardsman stood his post in boiled leather armor. The man shifted his feet as they approached, his gaze shifting between Dirge and his men. He hastily drew his sword and set his feet.

Dirge couldn't help but be impressed. The man knew he was severely outnumbered, yet he still kept his post. "This one has promise."

"That he does, Captain," Henson said at his side.

"Will he join us?"

"I've been best friends with Jim Ozmun my entire life, Captain." He paused. "But I honestly don't know."

"Go and speak with him, Frank. Do your best. But if he refuses to join, you know what needs be done."

"Yes, sir." Henson nodded and slowly approached the lone city guard, removing his helmet on the way.

"Frank, is that you?" The guardsman lowered his sword and heaved a sigh of relief. "What in all the hells is going on? People been storming by me like they's bein' chased by a grunkin."

His eyes shot to Dirge and his men and then back to Henson. "Wait; *is* there a grunkin in the city?"

"Not so as I know," Henson replied.

"Then what's goin' on? Why do we need all these people to man the gate with us?" The guardsman sheathed his sword.

Henson slowly advanced on his friend until they were face to face. "The time of Chaos is at an end, Jim." Henson held his head high. "The Day of Judgment is at hand."

"What are you talkin' about, Frank?" Ozmun shook his head. "Is this about that cult of yours?"

"In the name of the Lord God, Ukase, we, the Righteous, are taking over the city. The guilty are being judged for their crimes during the Cleansing. By the end of the day, this city shall be held in the hand of God." Henson placed his hands on the pommels of both his sword and dagger hanging from his belt.

"Look, Frank," Ozmun said, raising his left hand toward his friend. "You know I've no truck with Chaos. As for what happened back then, well, what's done is done. But you're talkin' crazy. How the hells are you going to take the city with twenty men? The priests will rip you apart."

"The priests are all dead, as are their soldiers. We are but a fraction of the Righteous that have flooded the city. We must now hold the gates lest any more of the guilty escape their fate."

"They're dead? All of them?" Ozmun shook his head, his eyes looking back into the city. "How?"

"We are the Fist of God. None can withstand us." Henson lowered his head a little, as well as his voice. "Will you join us? Please, say yes."

The guardsman looked at Henson, his eyes hooded. "Look, I told you, I don't care about Chaos. But I do have to answer to the City Masters."

"The City Masters will bow to the will of the Lord or they will die."

Ozmun licked his lips and held out both hands. "Tell ya what, I'll just go lie low. Okay? If you're right and you win the city, then I'm with you. But if you lose, you know what they'll—"

Henson yanked out his dagger, stepped forward, and plunged it into the crease of his friend's leather breastplate. Ozmun grunted, grasped at Henson—his lifelong friend— and blood spat up out of his mouth as Henson eased him to the ground.

"I am sorry, my friend. But you are either with us or against us. There is no other way in the eyes of the Lord." He pulled his dagger from the side of his dead friend and wiped it on a cloth at his belt before sheathing it. He then reached out and gently closed his friend's eyes. "You're a good man. The Lord will judge you fairly. I will see you at his side when I join you in the afterlife."

"You have done well, my Captain," the Prophet said into Dirge's mind. *"You need to praise your second for his righteous decision and leave him in charge of the gate. No one is to leave. If anyone who fled returns, they are to be apprehended. I require you and five of the Lord's warriors under your command to return to me. Once I have all of my Warriors of the Righteous with me, we will go to the City Masters and inform them of the miracle that we've bestowed onto the city."*

"Yes, Prophet."

His eyes went to Henson. In his estimation, the man didn't look like he wanted any kind of congratulation as he knelt, head down, over Ozmun's body. The hand he placed upon his friend's head trembled slightly.

Jacob flashed through Dirge's mind and he violently shook it off. No, there was no way he could even consider "congratulating" Henson. Nevertheless, he still had a job to do.

He walked over to Henson and gently clasped him on the shoulder. "The Prophet bids me to return to him. You are in charge." He gave his second the details from the Prophet, gathered up five men, and headed back at a run.

An hour later, he, along with the six other Warriors of the Righteous and their men, stood with the Prophet in the center of the City Square. Behind them over a hundred supporters of the Prophet from the Slaag quickly set up a scaffold to support another Rod of Divinity, three times larger than the one he'd used earlier. The Malik family was at the heart of the group with Duncan coordinating the assembly. Lynette stood next to her father, her eyes beaming at Dirge. He was proud and happy to see her at the heart of their movement, but he didn't like her being so exposed.

"This is war and we are all at risk, Dirge," the Prophet said next to him. "Everyone has their part to play, and no one can stand aside. You know this."

"Yes, Prophet."

Doing his best to put Lynette out of his mind, Dirge marched his men to the base of the House of the Masters. They mounted the stairs, with Dirge at the lead. The rest of the Warriors of the Righteous followed behind him in two columns while their men fanned out on either side in wedge formation. Every step up to the broad stone landing was measured, their pace, precise. It was a momentous occasion; Order was replacing Chaos. The Prophet demanded a majestic moment, and he was getting one.

Dirge motioned for two of his men to get the massive double doors before turning to speak to Eric, who was acting as his second. "As soon as we're inside, I want everyone to spread–"

The sound of his men opening the doors was quickly followed by several loud thumps. Something slammed hard into the side of his head as well as his chest, sending him tumbling down the steps. He blacked out before reaching the bottom.

He awoke to a roaring in his ears. He shook his head to clear his blurred vision. Pain blossomed in his head, but he fought through it. When his sight finally cleared his eyes fell upon Eric, lying next to him at the bottom of the stairs with a crossbow bolt lodged in his face.

Dirge looked about, his hearing going from a high-pitched whine to one of clarity. The clash of steel and the screams of dying men filled the air. One other Warriors of the Righteous, along with half of their men, lay dead on the steps—riddled with bolts. He tried to stand but fell back to the ground, his side erupting in pain. A bolt protruded from his armor, with several inches lodged in his right side. He put a hand to his head and felt the large dent in his helmet.

"Well, at least that did its job," he croaked.

"It won't really matter," came a menacing voice from behind and above him. "In a moment you'll be joining the rest."

Fighting through the pain, Dirge turned. Two steps above him stood a tall, gaunt man, with black eyes and hair. His clothing was black as well. His right hand rested on the pommel of a long sword at his belt while his left held the head of a woman by her long gray hair. Dirge recognized her as the Master of the Coin.

"You must be the Master at Arms," Dirge said through clenched teeth.

The man smiled, but it didn't reach his eyes, those stared malevolently at Dirge as he continued down the steps. He tossed the head to the side and stepped on Dirge's chest.

Dirge grunted and squeezed his eyes shut to stave off the pain.

The singing sound of a sword escaping its scabbard rang as the man spoke again, "Open your eyes, blasphemer. I want you to watch your people die before you join them."

Dirge didn't want to comply yet he felt compelled. He opened his eyes and turned his gaze toward the center of the square. He feared that he'd see a slaughter, but it appeared as though the rest of his men had quickly retreated and now defended the civilians. Yet even from his vantage point, he knew it wouldn't last long. They were out numbers three to one. The only thing that held the Chaotic fighters at bay was the discipline of his men.

Dirge searched the crowd, desperate to find Lynette, but there were simply too many fighters in the way. His vision thinned, the edges growing dark. The screaming mob of fighters pressed ever inward on his people—on Lynette. He saw movement above the heads of the combatants, next to the massive Rod of Divinity. The Prophet stood atop the scaffolding and placed his hands upon the Rod. Dirge wanted to cry when he saw several of the Chaos fighters raise their crossbows and fire. Through his failing vision, he saw those bolts fly true.

He could take no more. He closed his eyes and awaited the end.

The ground shook, and a single harmonious tone filled the air. It was as though a massive bell had been struck; its glorious tone, like the voice of God, filled his entire universe. His pain faded, and his vision filled with light.

He opened his eyes expecting to view paradise. Instead, he regarded the Master at Arms, still standing above him, his eyes filled with horror as though witnessing the ending of the world. The man stumbled backwards and fell onto the steps, his hands to his ears to hold out that marvelous tone, and his mouth agape in a silent scream.

Dirge didn't hesitate. He drew his sword and hacked at the man's head. It split the Master's skull down the middle with the sound of a cracked melon and sunk into his chest.

Dirge wrenched his sword free and stood. To his amazement, he felt no pain. He looked down, surprised to see the bolt still lodged in his side. He pulled it out, again feeling nothing, and threw it aside. He turned to the Square and smiled.

The Prophet still stood atop the scaffolding, his right hand upon the Rod. The Chaos fighters all lay upon the ground, their hands to their ears, writhing in pain. The sun shone down from the blue sky above, bathing everyone in the glorious light of God. His Holy Warriors quickly gathered themselves and slaughtered every man and woman of Chaos.

He saw all this but ignored it as he slowly walked toward them. He searched for only one thing, the most important thing in his world, until he found her. Lynette stood at the base of the Rod with a bloody sword in her hands, her eyes beaming with glory.

She dropped the sword and dashed to his side, elegantly picking her way through the carnage—seeming to dance in the process—and threw herself into his arms. She grunted as he wrapped his metal clad arms about her. He worried about hurting her and tried to ease up, but she clung all the tighter.

"Don't you dare let me go," she said.

He reached up and pulled off his dented helm, dropping it to the ground. He kissed the side of her head and squeezed her all the tighter. "Thank you, God. Thank you for keeping her alive."

She pulled her head back and kissed him fiercely. Tears streamed down her face. "I saw you go down. I saw you and Eric get shot and fall and I feared the worst." She kissed him again and buried her face in his chest.

"Eric is—"

"I know. I saw." She sniffled and wiped her hand across her face. She gazed deeply into his eyes. "But I didn't lose you. The Lord took Eric away, but He spared you. And I thank Him for that." She kissed him again. "Besides, Eric's at the Lord's side now. He sacrificed himself so that we would live in a world of the Lord."

Dirge marveled at his wonderful wife.

The ground trembled and the air split with the sound of cracking stone. They all gazed in wonder as the monstrosity that was the temple of Chaos crumbled. Brick by brick and stone by stone, the massive temple collapsed in on itself, filling the air with dust before being swept away by a pulsing wind that emanated from the center of the Square—from the Rod of Divinity. That pulsing wind spread throughout the city, blessing it in the name of Ukase, enthralling the pure people with his glory, and cleansing it of the demon Edis, the Lord of Chaos.

"Go now, my Holy Warriors. Gather all the remaining City Masters and bring them to the center of the Square," the Prophet declared, his voice carrying throughout the city by the will of the Lord. "Then bring forth all those that did heresy on to the innocents on the day of the Cleansing. What they wrought shall be done onto them. They are to be made an example of."

As the day progressed, those sinners who had bashed the children upon the ground were thrown from the tops of the city walls. Their bodies left to rot. The monsters who'd cut their children's throats were taken to the city square and put to the sword. And the fiends that burned the children of God were taken to the square and put to the torch—their screams a crescendo of glory on to God.

For days, the city reeked of blood, feculence, and burned flesh... but it was *clean*.

Chapter 17
Fireside
(505 -R.C.-)

Dirge tried to lounge in a large padded chair near a crackling fire in the living room of the Talic house. Reaching for his ale cup sitting on the table with his right hand, he winced. Lynette clasped his other hand as she perched on a stool on his left. After taking a sip and replacing the cup, he did his best not to scratch at the bandages wrapped around his midsection.

"Don't scratch it, my love." Lynette raised his left hand and kissed it. "It needs to heal."

He suppressed a sigh and smiled. It had been less than a week and the wound still hurt. The Lord's gift of feeling no pain had faded as the Day of Judgment passed, and by its end, he found himself bedridden.

Dirge—along with the Prophet, the rest of the Warriors of the Righteous, and several members of the Talic household—sat at a low, round table discussion what was to come next. They lost three Warriors of the Righteous that day, including Eric, but God blessed them with replacements.

"Are you sure you don't want to see the Brotherhood healer?" Dennis asked.

On Dirge's second day in bed, Dennis came to him, pledging himself to the Lord of Order. He took the oath that night and became the new second in command of the Warriors.

Dirge shook his head. "No. We are no longer members. I think a clean break is best."

"Your Captain is correct," the Prophet said, sitting in the chair opposite Dirge. "You have moved beyond them, and the domain of Aza'zel. The Brotherhood is the past. Ukase, and the battle with the enemy, is all that matters now."

Dennis nodded. "Yes, Isaac."

At informal meetings such as these, the Prophet insisted that his Warriors address him by name.

"Do we know how many escaped Judgment?" Dirge asked.

"Not many," Dennis replied. "We have a list posted at all gates along with their descriptions."

"Anyone of note?"

"Only one. Matrum Kent."

Dirge's eyes furrowed, fury boiling in his stomach.

"Honey, you're tensing. Who is this, Matrum Kent?"

Dirge tried to relax. "Matrum Kent was a member of the city guard. I saw him feed children to the fire. Talic and I were on the rooftops. I saw Kent throw children into the flames. He didn't even bother killing them first; he just laughed as they screamed and writhed." Dirge lowered his eyes. "There're times I still hear those screams when I lie awake at night."

"That's terrible." Lynette gave his hand a squeeze. "Why didn't you tell me this before?"

"I didn't want to burden you with it. It's bad enough that I remember."

"Those that have escaped will still know Judgment one day. Rest assured, my Captain," the Prophet said.

Lynette lifted Dirge's hand and kissed it again, then turned to the Prophet. "How did we so lucky to have God grace us with your presence?" she asked.

The Prophet bestowed a rare smile. "I was a fisherman, born and bred, far to the south—well beyond the horizon—in a place called the Lost Isles."

"I've not heard of it." Lynette shook her head.

"I'd be surprised if you had," the Prophet replied. "It's a string of islands in The Shallow Sea, out in the middle of the ocean. Most of the world has forgotten it exists. Beyond the boundary of The Shallow, the ocean water runs deep for over a thousand miles in all directions. Few dare to cross that water other than the occasional trading vessel."

"Why is that?"

"Chaos Storms. As rampant as they are on land, they are doubly so out in the deep water." His eyes took on a distant look. "I dearly love the sea…"

With the smell of the salt water in his nose, Isaac looked out over the great expanse of clear water. The sunlight shimmered on its surface like a million glittering jewels, and gulls screeched high overhead. Many of those birds nested in the God's Tooth, a tall jagged island just to his south. Birds were the only things that lived there. Many thought it cursed, saying the deep water separating The Shallow, and the Tooth was the gaping mouth of a long-forgotten god that died and sank beneath the waves. They claimed only a single tooth remained above the waves as a warning to those that would dare confront the God of Chaos.

Isaac chuckled. How could an area devoid of Chaos Storms be cursed? If anything, it was blessed. The only people to call it cursed were the priests, and those who held Edis in their heart. Isaac couldn't bring himself to trust anyone like that. You don't trust Chaos, pure and simple.

The wind picked up, making the water choppy, so he pulled in the lines to try elsewhere—perhaps next to the Tooth. He'd be more sheltered from the wind that way.

He smiled. *Besides, I've always wanted a better look at it.*

Pulling in line after line, he grew disgusted. No fish. "Where've they all gone?" The fishing was usually great anywhere near the Tooth. When he grasped the last line the wind stopped, and the water became as smooth as glass. The deathly quiet unnerved him—no whirling of the wind, no sloshing or clapping of the waves. Even the gulls had disappeared.

He tried to shake off the chill rushing up his spine as he hauled up the last line. It stopped dead as though snagged on something. He hadn't thought he'd gone that close to the Tooth to catch the sea floor. He considered abandoning it when the wind returned. It grew stronger and stronger by the second. His small boat rocked in the waves, pitching him back and forth. The sea became a bubbling cauldron.

He sweated. *Am I about to become soup?*

With a loud snap, the boom came loose of its lashing. It swung around, and caught him in the shoulder, knocking him into the icy sea. A born swimmer, he quickly regained the surface and shook the salt water from his eyes.

At least it didn't hit me in the head.

He dug into the water with his hands and kicked hard, making it back to the boat. As he pulled himself back aboard the wind died, and the sea stilled.

"That's what happens when you think about Chaos," he said as he shook himself off.

He saw that the last fish line had become slack, so he quickly pulled it in. Hook after hook lay barren, all except the last. Snagged on the very last hook was a silver chain with a silver, seven-pointed star pendant at the end. It wasn't ornate, just simple metal shining in the sun as he held up the line. It was pure and clean, neither tarnished nor encrusted.

"That's odd. Well, it'll fetch some coin," he said as he reached for it. "This trip won't be a complete—"

As he grasped the chain, something ripped his soul from his body and set adrift, engulfed in a vast emptiness, an ethereal place of perfection. It wasn't light, it wasn't dark, is simply… was.

A booming voice spoke, "*MORTAL, I AM UKASE. MY WORD IS LAW. EDIS, THE ENEMY, THE LORD OF CHAOS, HAS BROKEN THE COVENANT SET FORTH BY THE COUNCIL OF TANEER. HIS TIME OF DOMINION HAS EXPIRED AND HE HAS REFUSED TO ABDICATE. I HAVE CHOSEN YOU TO TAKE MY WORD TO THE WORLD. I HAVE CHOSEN YOU TO AID MY RETURN. WILL YOU ACCEPT THIS CHARGE THAT I HAVE SET BEFORE YOU?*"

The Prophet took a long pull from his ale and returned his eyes to his companions. "Lord Ukase bade me go north, giving me a vision of where I was to go. I sailed for five weeks, night and day without stopping. The Lord provided the wind, the sea provided my food, and the sky my drink. When I made it to the docks of this city, my boat sank as I stepped off. The Lord had provided, and I persevered."

"Ukase said you were to come here?" Lynette asked. Her hand trembled in Dirge's grasp.

Isaac pursed his lips and shook his head. "No, this is merely my first stop. The Lord said I was to gather up an army and march to war. He said the Righteous would go north to 'the land in shadow.'"

"A land in shadow?" Dirge asked.

The Prophet nodded. "It was only recently that I learned its true name."

A name popped into Dirge's mind. "The Lands of the Dead."

The Prophet nodded again.

Many around the fire fidgeted, including Lynette's father. "But, Prophet… the Lands of the Dead? Why would you have to go to such an accursed place a thousand miles away?"

The Prophet's eyes burned into Duncan's. "It is not something I want, but a mandate of the Lord. Do you fear such an arduous trek? The distance means nothing. It is something that must be done, so we shall do it."

He scanned the rest around the fire. "What we do is difficult, but we will do it. I have spoken with many of the former Trade Masters and they have given us maps of everything from here to Gate Hall."

He nodded to an attendant who had been refreshing their drinks. The man rushed into the other room and returned with a large map. He placed it on the table and unrolled it— using small paperweights to hold it in place. The map was vast, showing everything from the southern coast up to the edge of the Land of the Dead, with the great eastern and western mountain ranges on either side.

The Prophet leaned forward and pointed at the bottom of the map. "First, we will take the coastal cities, starting with Leria, then on to Glennen. That way we will secure everything from here to the Wilds in the far west. Then we turn back east and take everything to the Cunning River. Every city that falls before us will strengthen us." He stabbed his finger at a point of the map where the Cunning River flowed into the sea. "Once we reach Geous, we will burn it to the ground."

"Geous? But you said we needed to go north." Lynette said.

"We will, my dear. This is a reckoning, not a sprint. We must be thorough. Everyone's soul is at stake." He turned back to the map. "Once we control both sides of the Cunning, we'll turn north. The plains from here to the Reach are sparsely populated and will not prove a problem."

"Isn't that land full of grunkin and Chaos Storms?" asked Deckard, one of the newest members of the Warriors.

"The stronger we grow the weaker Edis' grasp will be. His storms will falter and his beasts will fall to our might."

"What of the Reach beyond the plains?" Duncan asked. "It has a large population; the greatest on the entire continent."

The Prophet nodded. "The Reach comprises the Westlands and the Eastern Hills. Few people live in the Eastern Hills, but the Westlands is indeed great. It is the breadbasket of the world and the heart of the economic might of Chaos. Yet, Chaos is weak there, and the people care not for Edis. They will join us with glee and revel in our might." He then pointed to a spot just south of the Lands of the Dead. "Then we take Gate Hall. It is the lynchpin of the world. Second only to Titan, it is the greatest stronghold of Chaos. Once Chaos falls there, nothing can stop us."

"And what of the Lands of the Dead?" Dirge asked. "Surely you don't mean for us all to go there?"

"No," Isaac replied, his face grim. "The Lord said that only a few are to go there. He said it's only there where you can awaken… Him."

Dirge sensed a moment of doubt in the Prophet, and it alarmed him. He asked Isaac with his mind, *Who is 'Him'? You're not speaking of Ukase, are you?*

"I know only what I was told," the Prophet replied.

Dirge didn't know what disturbed him more, the Prophet's answer, or the ambiguity. Uncertainty was something he'd never seen in the man before. Was it possible that the Prophet could be wrong?

He berated himself for his thoughts of doubt. "What does God ask of us next?"

"We must discuss that with the City Master," the Prophet replied.

"City Master?" Lynette asked, cocking her head slightly. "Only one? What of the others?"

"There is only one City Master now," the Prophet replied. "It is the way of Order, Miss Malik. Everyone has a place and must know it. A hierarchy is a necessity. For without that, one would fall under the sway of Edis. Chaos is seductive, and if you give it the slightest hold on you, you will be damned for it."

"When do you wish to visit the City Master?" Dirge asked.

"On the morrow," Isaac said with a nod. "You are well enough to be mobile now and we have little time. Chaos will not wait for us."

"I shall implore the armorer to have my breastplate ready by then." Taking the dent out of his helmet was easy, but patching a hole took far more time and effort.

"You won't require it," the Prophet said with a shake of his hand. "Only your presence as my Captain is. Besides, I've already set them on making you an entire new set that I will bless as he emblazons it with the mark of our Lord."

"I am honored, Isaac." Dirge bowed his head.

"It will be ready in time for our army to march, rest assured."

"So are *we* your army, Prophet?" Lynette asked.

The Prophet smiled. "Yes. All of those, willing will be a part of the army, but only the men will fight."

"And what of the unwilling?" Dirge asked.

The Prophet frowned.

The next morning, Dirge sat at a table in the common room of the Angelic. They were to go to the City Master within the hour, but this was something that Dirge needed to do before then. He felt uncomfortable. It was the first time he'd set foot in the Angelic since he'd left the Brotherhood.

"What are they doing with those that don't want to join his army?" Jacob asked, looking equally uncomfortable.

"The Prophet said that if they are not with us, they are against us."

Jacob's eyebrows rose. "Well, that's rather severe."

"This is war. There is no middle ground."

Jacob frowned, his eyes going to the table. "So what would happen to me if I refuse to join?"

Dirge dropped his gaze for a moment before returning it to Jacob's eyes. "Those that refuse to join will be thrown into the salt mines."

"The salt mines?" Jacob shook his head. "So who's all going to be in this army? Is he going to make the kids fight too?"

"No. Every man of appropriate age—" He held up his hand to forestall his friend interrupting him. "Everyman that can hold a weapon and not be a hindrance to himself and his comrades will be placed into the Righteous army of God."

He ignored Jacob's eye roll and continued. "Each will be blessed by the Prophet. It will grant them strength, courage, and most importantly, discipline; for it will be discipline that will win us the war."

"You said men. What about the women?"

"The women, also of appropriate age, will act as camp followers and support staff. They will tend to the injured, dispense food and water, and deliver messages. Some, like Lynette, will be the personal attendants to the Prophet. The crippled, the elderly, and the children will be left in the safety of the city. Even cripples and old men can hold the gates with crossbows, so there's no worry."

"I suppose I could throw myself down the stairs," Jacob said under his breath.

Dirge quickly looked across the room at Mistress Katlyn behind the bar, and then at Cal who stood in the corner. "There will be one exception. Due to their good standing with the Lord, and a thorn in the side of Edis, the Brotherhood has been allowed the courtesy of banishment."

Jacob looked about as well before shaking his head. "They like me well enough, but I seriously doubt they'd let me join them. I'm not exactly Brotherhood material. Is there any other chance?"

"No, I'm sorry. The Prophet has made it clear." Dirge pushed back his chair and stood. "I must go join the Prophet. We are going to inform the City Master of the edict. You will have until we return to decide." He paused a moment before heading toward the door. "If you leave before the edict is read you'll be allowed to go." His back straight, Dirge strode to the inn door.

"But where would I go?" Jacob said as the door closed behind Dirge.

Chapter 18
Glorious Thought
(505 -R.C.-)

Dirge stood atop the northern city wall, his new steel armor shining in the sun. Three months passed and Dirge could scarcely believe how well everything had transpired since the proclamation. Only a fifth of the adult population chose to remain heretics and were disposed of in the salt mines. Their children went to the homes of the most devout to be raised in the eyes of God.

Blessedly, Jacob was not one of heretics. He'd found the Lord at last—or so he said. Dirge knew his friend much too well to believe that. Jacob simply parroted what he thought the Prophet wanted to hear to save his life. Nevertheless, Dirge was confident that in time Jacob would find the Lord and be saved.

With a shake of his head, Dirge went back to examining his troops. At least that's what it was to look like. Dirge was more of a figurehead than an actual General—he knew nothing about armies, battles, or strategy. He left that all up to

Dennis who stood upon the parade ground, instructing everyone as to what to do. Actually, Dennis instructed the company commanders and they in turn passed that down to the squad leaders. Everything had to be by the chain of command. Discipline demanded it.

Shortly after the proclamation, Dennis showed Dirge some ancient manuscripts on war, battle tactics, and strategy. Apparently, the Brotherhood had many such manuscripts in anticipation of the day the reign of Chaos was to end. He claimed the hidden followers of all the factions that lost the Great War kept such items of lost knowledge.

"They are meant to help heal the world," Dennis told him as they perused the books. "Or so it's said. We… that is to say, *those* members of the Brotherhood only know that the time of Chaos *will* end, and we must all prepare for it."

According to the books, their army would be at something of a disadvantage, as they had no mounted units—not of any use beyond scouting, anyway. The best armies comprised heavy horse units—groups of horsemen in heavy plate armor much like Dirge's—heavy infantry, light infantry, and bowmen.

The Righteous Army of God had infantry in spades, both heavy and light, thanks to the members of the new merchants' guild. The heavy infantry consisted of men in plate armor with long pikes that marched about in units of one hundred, ten by ten, all packed tightly together. The light infantry comprised men in leather armor wielding either maces, or short spears with long blades at the end. They were to engage anyone that got through the front line of the heavy infantry, or those that tried to attack their sides.

Their bowmen were entirely crossbows. The book spoke of "long" and "short" bows. Dirge didn't know the difference between the two, the book simply stated that longbows were widely considered the best due to their accuracy and speed in reloading. Apparently there was something call a "horse bow" as well. He couldn't even fathom how a man could shoot a bow from the back of a moving horse, but it gave him the idea of arming their mounted scouts with light crossbows. They could only get off a single shot, but it still might save their lives in order for them to return with whatever information they'd gathered.

"They look glorious," Lynette said at his side.

Dirge nearly jumped when she spoke. He'd been so engrossed that he'd not heard her approach. "I do wish you wouldn't come up here. It's dangerous. You could fall."

"Is that an order, my dear husband?" she said with mirth.

"No, my dearest wife, it's not an order, merely a request. I don't want anything to happen to you."

"Honestly, Dirge. I'm not made of porcelain. I'll be fine. You needn't worry about me. I, on the other hand, have much to worry about. You're going to be at the front of our army, a prime target; whereas I will be at the Prophet's side, safely in the rear."

He looked away from the army and into her wondrous blue eyes. The pale skin of her face glowed in the light of the sun. She may not be porcelain, but she certainly looked it. "It'll hardly be safe, my dear. The Prophet will be a target. Any attack at him will endanger you."

"We'll have a heavy guard. Honestly, Dirge, you worry too much."

"I've much to worry about. My whole life, I've only dreamt of being a part of something, to belong. It was why leaving the Brotherhood was so torturous. I'd never thought—never wanted—to lead anyone. My life's hard enough. I'd no desire to take anyone down this road with me."

"And yet here you are, the Right Hand of God, ready to take down Chaos. You're meant for this. I know it." She caressed his cheek. "Anyway, I came to tell you that Father wishes to have a word with you."

He took her hand in his and kissed it. "As you say, my sweet. Lead the way."

They went to the City Master's building. Her father's influence had grown, having earned the position of Chief Aid for the City Master. Dirge knocked on the door to Duncan's office.

A young man he didn't recognize answered. "Yes? What business do you have for the Chief Aid?"

"The Chief Aid asked for me."

"And who may I say is calling on my Master?" The young man's voice was high but stern. It was obvious the young man recognized Dirge, but protocol must be upheld.

"My name is Dirge, Captain of the Warriors of the Righteous."

"Ah, yes. My master has told me to expect you and to welcome you in." He stepped aside and bowed his head.

Lynette's father sat behind a desk loaded with hearty stacks of paper. The look on his face was one of slight chagrin. "I told the boy he needn't be so formal with those that I know well."

"Don't be too hard on him. He is merely carrying out his charge. He's well disciplined. He'll do well in the army once he comes of age."

"Indeed." Duncan pointed to the chair opposite him. "Please, have a seat."

Dirge nodded and sat on the front edge of the chair. One could never truly get comfortable while wearing plate armor. "What did you wish to see me about?"

"I wanted to let you know that we're ready for your departure tomorrow. I will personally coordinate the manning of the gates." He looked perfectly calm, but there was a worry in his eyes.

"I've no doubt that you are doing a wonderful job. I know in my heart that the city will remain secure." Dirge tilted his head slightly to the side. "You did not bring me here to talk of this. What's wrong?"

"Nothing's wrong, I assure you."

"Then what is it?"

"Well," Duncan paused and eyed the table. "It's just that… you see…" He looked Dirge in the eye again. "Please don't make her go with you."

Dirge's eyes widened. "Me? I am not making her do anything. She offered herself to the Prophet as an aid and he accepted. I didn't even know she was going to do it."

"You can still stop her—"

"How!" Dirge's anger flared. "How can I do that? The Prophet has decreed it and it will be done. Do you think I *like* the idea of her being out there? I'm worried sick about it!"

He closed his eyes and took control of himself. "I am sorry. I shouldn't have raised my voice like that."

He opened his eyes to a perturbed Duncan. But instead of raising his own voice he slumped back into his chair. "No, you've no need to apologize. It was wrong of me to ask. It's just… she's my daughter. She's the only child I've left."

The man's last statement stung. "There's nothing I can do."

Dirge stood and bowed his head slightly to Duncan. "If you'll excuse me, I've preparations to see to." He quickly exited the office, ignoring Duncan's aid who bowed to him as he rushed by.

Glowering at everything, Dirge marched down the hall. He was angry with himself for letting his own frustrations get the better of him. Duncan deserved better. On the other hand, the man had no right to ask it of him in the first place—he was only a civilian. The Righteous army was the Fist of God, and only God had a say in its goings on.

The problem was Dirge's anxieties matched Duncan's. Lynette would be in danger staying that close to the Prophet's side throughout the war. He had all but begged the

Prophet to assign her to aid in managing supply lines, an important job with dangers of its own, but far less perilous than her current assignment.

"We all do our part that God has placed before us. Have patience, all will go as the Lord has foreseen."

Dirge missed a step. He'd not been expecting the Prophet's comment. It was still a bit disconcerting that his thoughts weren't his own. *"As you say, Prophet. The Lord's army is ready for tomorrow's march. I just need to check with the quartermaster regarding the preparations for loading the Rods of Divinity."*

"Excellent. You are doing wonderfully. You need not worry yourself about the rods though. I have already seen to it. We will have all we need for our journey."

"Yes, Prophet. I'll just check—"

"Everything is in readiness, Dirge. Go to your wife. She has need of you, and you, her. That is all I require of you tonight. Our war will be arduous. Take the time God has granted the two of you and make the most of it.

The Prophet's last words struck him as rather melancholy, but the man was right. At that moment, he wanted nothing more than to be with Lynette, to hold her in his arms. He marched to the command pavilion in the center of the square and removed his armor for an attendant to make ready for the morning.

When he arrived home, Lynette stood in the hall, directing the house staff. "No, those all need to come with us. It won't leave you much after we're gone but you'll just have to make do." Her voice was sweet but stern.

She turned to Dirge, a smile blooming on her face. "Hello, my love. What did Father—"

He rushed forward and kissed her, soundly. Her soft lips tasted like honey as usual. Her form melded into his as he held her in his strong arms.

She panted while looking down and away, her cheeks reddening. "Please, dear. Not in front of the others."

He swept her into his arms and carried her up the stairs.

She let out a squeak. "Must you be so incorrigible?" She did her best to frown but her lips kept twitching into a smile. Sighing, she laid her head upon his shoulder.

He carried her into their room and gently placed her upon the bed. He kicked off his boots, and quickly stripped off his shirt and pants, before kneeling down to help her with the small buttons on the front of her blouse. They both fumbled with them before she flung her hands away.

"Just rip it." Her breath was at a near rasp.

"Are you certain? This is your favorite," he said playfully.

"Yes, do it! I need you, please!"

Buttons flew in every direction.

She wailed, grunted, and moaned as they made love. She'd never been the quiet type, but that night he feared they might shatter the window glass. Afterward, he held her in his arms. He relished this time, possibly as much as when they made love. She'd the ability to soothe his heart and set his mind at ease when it felt most frazzled. She helped him with his doubts—of which he had many at that moment.

"There is nothing to worry about, my darling," she said as she nuzzled up against him, her arm draped across his broad chest. "Everything is going as God wills. Tomorrow we march to the glory of God and we shall drive the demon Chaos from the world. You'll see. They shall fall before us with ease."

"Are you sure?"

"Yes. Well, they'd better. Because something tells me that in a few months I'll be needing plenty of bed rest to recover from the glory we made tonight."

He smiled and patted her arm. "Yes, my love."

"I mean it this time. Before the year is out, I shall gift you with a son." She tried to snuggle up even closer to him and within moments let out a gentle snore.

A son, he thought as he drifted off. *Now that would be glorious.*

Chapter 19
Righteous Crusade
(505 -R.C.-)

They marched for two weeks before reaching the low rolling hills surrounding Leria. They'd kept to the road, as it was the easiest route, even though the large copse of thick trees often squeezed their groupings. The southern hills didn't look as though it would pose that problem being mostly high grasses and scrub brush—the trees were more scattered and a good deal smaller.

Dirge marched at the head of the Righteous Army of God, resplendent in his shining steel armor. His heavy infantry followed him in two columns of six, one hundred man groups—their spears and armor glinting in the light of the sun high overhead. Behind the heavy infantry marched the light skirmishers in ten rows of fifty each. Behind them came the Prophet in his wagon that carried his dais as well as the wagons filled with the women attendants. Four hundred crossbowmen marched at the army's rear all neatly arrayed.

Every step of his army was in perfect unison; over two thousand boots striking the ground with each step reverberating off their surroundings like the footsteps of God himself.

The forward scouts—of which Jacob was one—had yet to see any type of military force. They'd swept through several villages, absorbing all those willing to join, adding the men to the ranks of the skirmishers and scouts. Those that refused were driven north with nothing but the clothes on their backs. The Prophet didn't want them running to the enemy, and the army needed all the supplies they could get their hands on for the campaign.

"I can't help but feel sorry for those people," Dirge said to Lynette one night as they laid together beneath the stars, choosing to enjoy the perfect night instead of sleeping in his tent.

"The stars are just so beautiful. I can't remember a time that the weather has been so beautiful for so long," she replied

"Did you hear me?"

"Yes, my love, I heard you." She gave him a little kiss on the cheek. "But you can't let them bother you. They are heretics and the enemy."

"They weren't followers of Chaos—not all of them. I know they spurned the Lord, but they are likely to die out in the wilderness."

"It must be God. He's becoming so strong that Chaos can no longer even control the weather." She sighed after a moment. "I told you, you needn't worry about them. If they are truly not one with Chaos, they will come to their senses and beg to join our righteous mission. God will show them the way in time. And if not, he will judge them upon their deaths."

Dirge could not shake his unease by the time he drifted off to sleep.

Dirge ordered a halt three days into the hills when the scouts finally returned with news.

A young man galloped up, jumped off his horse, and saluted him with his fist to his heart. "Commander, a large force is approaching from the south. It is difficult to judge because of the terrain, but I'd put the number at around four thousand."

Dennis, who'd come running to join him when the scout crested the hill, heard the report. "It would appear that Chaos has not been idle."

"As expected," Dirge replied. "What do you suggest?"

"How far?" Dennis asked the scout.

"Fifteen miles at most, sir."

"Fetch the mappers, quickly!"

A third of their scouts were arrayed a short distance ahead of the army to explore the terrain and give that information to their mapmakers posted in the rear with the Prophet's entourage. There, he could relay any pertinent information to Dirge and the file leaders.

"There is a spot not far that looks like it would do well for us," the Prophet said into Dirge and Dennis' minds.

"Thank you, Prophet," Dennis replied out loud, "but I must see it for myself to be sure."

A short time later, a plump old man in the white uniform of the support staff—barely containing his girth—came huffing to the front of the army. He presented himself to Dirge, holding half a dozen scrolls in his left hand while trying to comb his long, scraggly white hair away from his bright red face with his right.

"Here you are, Master. I'm sorry, I meant Commander, yes, Commander. I did not mean to infer that you are a Master. I most humbly apologize. There is but one Master, one Prophet, and one God. Please, I do apologize."

"Calm yourself, Mister Therrin," Dirge said with a shake of his head.

They'd found the man deep in the bowels of the House of the Masters. Good mapmakers were scarce and the old Masters wouldn't let the man step foot out of the building for fear of losing him.

"Yes, Mas – I mean Commander. Here are the maps you requested." He rolled out three of the scrolls on the ground, using small lead weights he retrieved from a pouch to keep the wind from disturbing them. "I've made this from what I gather from the scouts. I must say they are very good at their job. You did remarkably well in choosing them although do wish I had a bit more information to make sure everything is right—"

"That's enough," Dirge intervened. "Just step aside a moment so Dennis can inspect them."

His second in command quickly looked over the maps and pointed to a location a short distance to their southwest. "Are the dimensions accurate?"

"Accurate, sir? Well that is difficult to say. As I said; if I had more information and more time to make sure—"

"Get on with it," Dennis said firmly.

"Yes, sir. Yes sir. Getting on with it. Yes sir, I do believe that map to be accurate. It is a shallow roughly a mile across, and there is very little in the way of scrub or tree."

"Fine," Dennis said before the man could go on. He then turned to Dirge. "This is the place, this dale. It will be perfect for your needs. We'll have plenty of room to maneuver. We can set up our skirmishers just out of sight past the rims on the east and west, and the bows, just behind this ridge on the north. We set the Heavy in the very center and use the scouts to draw them in. Once they engage the Heavy, our skirmishers can strike them from the flanks, and the bows can take out those late to the show, as well as those trying to leave early."

"If you say so." Dirge shook his head. He didn't know tactics of this size—it was nothing like his fights with the Chaos mobs. "I suppose it's best to pick the place you want to fight. But what if they don't want to engage us there, or they come at us from the wrong direction?"

"We will use the scouts and some of the skirmishers to make sure they do." Dennis pointed to a place just south of their intended position. "Think of their army as nothing more than a massive mob. They know no strategy and they'll likely attack the first thing they see."

"Prophet, would you please pass the word to the others," Dirge said aloud.

"Of course," the Prophet replied. *"How long will it take, do you think?"*

"No more than an hour," Dennis said.

To Dirge, that hour seemed an eternity. His mind flitted from one doubt to another: What if the enemy was closer than what the scouts thought? What if the enemy made it there first? What if Chaos took them in the side as they rushed to be in the place Dennis had chosen? The possible catastrophes seemed endless.

Thanks to the Lord's gift of discipline though, they made the fast march with no injuries, and were in position for the assault. Six, one hundred man squads made up the front line, with another six behind them. Gaps, the width of three men, separated each unit. They set the rest of the light infantry along both sides, with the bowmen in the middle. They set up the Prophet's dais at the rear, near the top of the rim, giving him an unobstructed view of the battlefield.

Everything looked perfect and Dirge cursed himself for his doubt and worry. Dennis knew his job, and he did it well. "He'd have been a far better choice as Commander."

"You are the heart of this army, Dirge," the Prophet said. *"Each has his part, and this is yours. You will do what must be done. The Lord has seen great things in you, my boy. Take*

heart and keep strong, no matter how troubled your road ahead may seem."

"You mean, our road," Dirge thought back.

The Prophet did not reply.

Before Dirge could repeat his question, a dozen of the scouts topped the ridge, their horses covered with froth. There should have been eighteen. While the scouts passed through the ranks of the heavy infantry, their captain rode up to Dirge.

He jumped from his horse and saluted with a fist to his heart and a bow of his head. "Commander, the enemy lies less than a mile away. They've engaged the skirmishers who broke off and are on their way."

"Where are the rest of your scouts?"

"I had them skirt the enemy force to see if more lay behind."

"You've done well, Captain. Go to the back and rest your horse. After we've engaged the enemy, I'll need you to take two squadrons of skirmishers around their back in case they decide to leave our little party too early."

"Yes sir," the captain replied with a slight smile. He saluted and quickly led his horse through the ranks of men.

Dirge followed him, taking his position at the rear of the heavy infantry, while the Prophet spread the news to the other Warriors of the Righteous—two of which were acting as column leaders.

Drawing his sword, Dirge addressed the bowmen. "Ready bows and wait for my order to fire! Remember, you are to target the rear of the enemy, we want to drive them into our spears, not scatter them!"

He gauged the time. The sun sat at its zenith, a brilliant ball of fire in a pure blue sky that warmed his skin in the cool air. A light wind blew from their backs, filling his nose with the fresh smells of grass and earth. It filled him with a sense of ease and rightness. It had been that way ever since the

Prophet consecrated the city—perfect weather for a perfect army.

The wind suddenly switched and began to blow from the south. A cloud-bank, dark and roiling, swept toward them. Carried upon that cold wind was a fetid smell of decay, along with the clattering of metal and the screams of thousands of men and women. The army of Chaos had arrived.

Dirge shot a look back toward the Prophet's dais where Lynette stood at its base. Try as he might he couldn't see her. Giving up, he turned back and caught the attention of Henson who was serving as a sergeant of the nearest heavy infantry squad. Dirge motioned the man to come to his side.

"Yes, sir." Henson saluted.

"The enemy's almost upon us. If things go awry and they break through our lines, or make it around our flanks, I want you to rally your squad and go protect the Prophet and his retinue. Do you understand me?"

They both knew it went against the initial battle plan, but the man smiled. "Yes, Sir. It would be my honor."

Dirge nodded and sent him back to his squad.

"They come," the Prophet said.

"Infantry, stand ready," Dennis shouted.

The skirmishers came sprinting over the ridgeline, their formation scattered and sloppy. Dirge frowned. Their discipline had slipped while away from the rest of the army—not a good sign. As they flowed through the openings in the front line, Chaos's army reached the edge of the hollow.

The shouts of the squad sergeants filled the air. "Shift, now! Move it, fill those gaps! Go! Go! Go!"

As their men fell into position, the army of Chaos poured into the shallow valley. They resembled the mobs he faced in the city in their crazed manner, but the similarities ended there. Those Chaos mobs, with their wild eyes and spittle-filled mouths, were simply citizens holding whatever weapons they could find. The army pouring over the lip of the valley, on the other hand, held real weapons—swords, axes, spears, and maces. To make matters worse, they were armored.

The mass of howling madness slammed into their front line. Screams filled the air along with the sounds of clashing steel. Dirge felt the "wrongness" at the front of the line; he felt the influence of Chaos taking place. He wanted to know what was happening, but saw nothing through the mass of men.

"The front line is wavering," the Prophet said.

Dirge raised his hand into the air and then threw it down in a chopping motion. "Archers, fire!"

The thump of four hundred crossbow strings reverberated behind him. The bolts sailed over their line and into the Chaos army.

"Most over shot," the Prophet said.

"Too far, damn you, too far! Reload!"

Dirge ran to the back of the bowmen where the ground was considerably higher. He didn't like what he saw. The front resembled the blade of a saw, jagged and uneven, rather than a straight line. Chaos's army hacked and flailed at the long spears, some actually throwing themselves into the spears, dragging them down to allow their comrades to draw closer.

A large portion of Chaos's army, roughly a thousand, broke off from the rear and made for the sides, trying to flank them. Dirge smiled as the light infantry protecting those flanks did not move, staying in perfect formation.

"Bows, divide aim, and fire at the flanks!"

As the frenzied men and women of that massive chaotic mob rounded the ends of their front line the bowmen fired. Two hundred bolts slammed into each group, causing the entire front of both flanking units to fall onto one another.

"Again! Reload and fire! Move, damn you, Move!"

The crossbows clattered as the men spun the cranks. They raised and fired, but many of the shots were too late, the enemy, having untangled themselves from their dead, were racing toward the light infantry. The shots were not a complete waste. At least one hundred more fell on each side. The remaining mobs slammed into the light infantry, but went no further.

"The front line is about to fall."

Dirge's eyes shot back to the front. The Prophet was right; the line was collapsing. The mob pressed forward, throwing themselves on his infantry, dragging them down however they could and crawled over them for their compatriots to chop into pieces.

His heart hammering in his chest, Dirge frantically scanned the field for Henson, but to no avail. "Damn it, man. Where are you?"

"You must do something now, or all is lost."

Dirge shot a look back at the Prophet sitting atop his dais. The man looked more at ease than at any other time he'd know him—the very portrait of serenity in living form.

Dirge sprinted toward the front line. He couldn't find Henson to give him the order to protect Lynette. Had to do something, and all he could think of was to attack. Dennis' plan had been to hold and let the mob break themselves on their spears. Dirge now saw that plan was wrong. You couldn't outlast Chaos, you had to attack and destroy it.

He made his way through his men who opened a way for him without even knowing. Calmly, he drew his sword as his men stepped aside, allowing the psychotic throng through.

The enemy came at him. Their swords, axes, and maces covered in blood, their eyes wide, their mouths frothing, screaming at the tops of their lungs.

And Dirge killed them.

He flowed into that swarm of insanity, his sword dancing in his hands. He slashed at faces, necks, arms, hands… and they never touched him. He drove a bloody, steady, swath into the army of Chaos, and his army followed him. The Righteous Army of God stepped forward as one into that sea of Chaos, thrusting their spears with each step. Thrust. Step. Thrust. Step. Thrust. Step. The ground shook beneath their feet.

The army of Chaos broke. The madness lifted from their eyes and their screams of insanity turned to ones of horror. They clawed at one another in their attempts to flee. That's when the skirmishers struck them from behind. The light infantry had pivoted around, as planned, and cut off the enemies escape. Within a matter of minutes, the whole of the army of Chaos lay dead on the field.

Dirge panted, staring up at the sky as his men cheered. The ominous cloud-bank escorting Chaos' army dispersed, replaced by a clear blue sky. The sun stood on high, a golden ball of joy, and smells of the earth filled the wind once more. His men clapped him on the back and chanted his name. His men. Dennis may know tactics and army organization, but these men truly followed him. He found it difficult to keep his emotions in check.

He raised his arm. "Thank you. You do me great honor, and I thank you. But the true honor goes to God. For without him, there is no honor."

"Ukase!" The cheer went up in unison. "Ukase!" They thrust their fists into the air. "Ukase!" Seven times, they chanted God's name, one for each point on his star.

Dirge waited for the chant to finish. "Now let us tend to the wounded and rest. You have earned it."

More cheers followed him as he strode through the valley to its far side. With every step, his eyes searched until he finally found what he yearned for most. There, still at the foot of the Prophet's dais, stood Lynette, her beautiful eyes moist with tears, her porcelain hands held up to her trembling lips.

He strode up, took off his helmet and gauntlets, tossing them at his feet, and gently touched her cheek. "Hello, wife." Oh, how he cherished calling her that.

She flung herself at him, wrapping her arms around his chest. He feared she might bruise herself on his armor, but she refused to let go. In truth, he didn't want her to. He gently held her in his arms as she cried.

"I was so worried," she said after a time. "The Prophet said I needn't. He told me that you would be victorious, and that you were safe in God's hands. But I worried anyway."

She gazed up at the Prophet. "Please, forgive me."

"You are forgiven, my dear."

"I must see to the men," Dirge said, stepping back but keeping hold of her arms. "Come."

"She must stay."

Dirge's head swung sharply to the Prophet.

"You must go. She cannot." Before Dirge could speak, the Prophet continued. "Everyone has their place. The women assigned to aiding the men are doing so, but she is to aid me."

"You would not even for this one moment—"

"It is not what I want. It is God's will."

Dirge closed his eyes, trembling while holding in his desire to explode in anger, until it passed. He sighed, opened his eyes, and kissed his wife. "Until we dine tonight, my love."

"Until tonight," she replied, giving his neck one last squeeze.

Dirge turned and marched to the center of the valley—to his men. He refused to look at Isaac.

Chapter 20
You are the Heart
(505 -R.C.-)

An hour passed as Dirge walked amongst his men. He simply nodded to them, encouraged them, and asked how they fared. There was little else he could do, but it was expected of him. The men were at ease upon the ground, yet still in formation. He marveled at how readily they took to organization.

"It's not a surprise, really."

Dirge had not heard Henson approach. Nor had he realized that he'd spoken aloud. "Why is that, Lieutenant?"

"We many have grown up in Chaos, but we have the Lord's heart," Henson said. "We now know what is right and what is wrong. We know our place."

"Speaking of which. What happened? During the battle, I couldn't find you or your men. You were not in position."

Henson dropped his gaze, his hand going to a red, blue, and gold braided cloth around his neck. "I beg forgiveness, but we were ordered to move to the flank by Major Davish."

Davish was the Warrior commanding Henson's column. Dirge frowned and shook his head. "Isaac."

"Pardon, sir?"

"Nothing." He then pointed at the braid Henson was fingering. "What is that? I don't recognize it?"

Henson stood tall. "It was given to me by my wife. She's back home seeing to our two little ones." He frowned, his cheeks reddening slightly. "She's a bad leg."

Dirge understood the man's embarrassment. A vast majority of the men's wives were with the army in one form or another—their little ones left with grandparents or elders. Henson felt shame that his wife didn't share the danger like the others' wives.

He placed a hand on Henson's shoulder. "Do not fret, my friend. It's as God wills."

A thought occurred to Dirge. "Where are they?" He lifted his eyes to the rim of the valley.

"What is it, Commander?"

"The scouts?"

"Sir?"

"Some of the scouts were sent to skirt the enemy and see what lay beyond them. They've not returned." Dirge felt a tingle run up his spine.

"I'm sure it's nothing, Sir—"

"I need to speak with Dennis." Dirge sprinted for the front of the right column.

"Prophet, has anyone reported the scout's return?"

The Prophet did not answer.

"Prophet," he said aloud. "Has anyone—"

Dirge felt a sudden wrongness. His stomach fluttered and his skin crawled as the air turned fetid. A flash of light appeared to the far edge of the rise to the south. The light grew to a sphere—a swirling mixture of every color imaginable, roughly the size of a man. Out of that demented ball stepped a man wearing black and gray robes and holding a long black staff in his right hand.

Dirge felt the hairs on the back of his neck rise and his stomach clenched. He bellowed the alarm, "Priest!"

Two more spheres appeared on either side of the first, and two more Chaos priests stepped onto the rise.

"Bowmen," Dirge shouted and pointed at the men on the rise. "Volley fire!"

The priests stood their ground as his bowmen cocked, raised their bows, and shot in unison. As the bolts arced high, the priests on the left and right thrust up their hands. Every bolt struck an invisible shield some twenty feet in front of the priests and fell to the ground.

"This is not good," Dirge muttered.

He pointed at the ridge. "Skirmishers, attack! Heavy, form up and charge!"

The priest in the middle stabbed his staff into the air. A dead black sphere, roughly the size of a man's head, shot out, and flew up into the brilliant blue sky. At two thousand feet, the black ball exploded, sending a shockwave that knocked most of the Righteous Army to the ground.

Dirge's ears rang as he picked himself up. He stared up into the sky as a large gray cloud spun and grew. The wind whipped up as the cloud quickly grew. The ringing in his ears turned into a whine, and the whine into a wail, sounding as though the air howled in anguish.

Dirge's heart sank. "Chaos storm."

The screams of men drew his attention away from the maelstrom. His light infantry had regained their feet and charged. He was proud of them, but he knew they didn't stand a chance. The central priest pointed his staff at his men and ragged arcs of lightning spewed forth killing whoever it touched. The lightning spread from man to man, creating a cascade of rippling death.

Dirge tore his eyes away and saw that his heavy infantry at the ready. He drew his sword and ran at the priests. "Charge!"

He wasn't even sure his men heard him over the sound of the shrieking air.

The cloud roiled and swirled, changing from dark gray, to black mottled with red. It blotted out the sun. Black lightning crackled from cloud to cloud before coalescing and stabbing into his bowmen, creating explosions that fountained dirt and men into the air. Long, thin, black funnels stretched out of the clouds like grotesque, gnarled fingers and tore the land asunder.

At a distance, he saw one of the storm's funnels draw in Henson's entire squad. When the cloud dissipated, only five things remained large enough to call a man. They hit the ground, and to Dirge's surprise, got up and ran. He thanked God that many men had somehow lived.

Motion behind the priests caught his attention. Over a thousand men and women, wearing everything from armor to rags, and wielding swords, maces, and staves, poured into the valley. They smashed into his surviving skirmishers, tearing them to pieces.

"We need the Rods," he thought to the Prophet.

"We have none."

"What?!" He stopped dead, letting his men flow by, and turned to stare at the Prophet's dais. "You said we have enough."

"I did."

Confusion and anger boiled within Dirge. "Why did you lie?"

"We hadn't enough time to make one large enough to handle this storm," Isaac replied. *"And the small ones simply would not have been strong enough. You would have died trying to plant them."*

"What do you mean 'would have?'" Dirge's mind reeled. "Are you saying you knew about this? You knew this would happen?"

"You must stay strong, Dirge. You are the future, the heart that will see Him to their goal." The Prophet's mental voice was filled with serenity. *"You must protect Him at all costs, for only he can awaken the Promised One."*

Dirge didn't understand a thing the man said. "You've lost your mind." He sprinted toward the dais. "Lynette!"

Dirge was only a few hundred feet away—his beautiful wife's eyes staring at him, her face filled with fear—when a half dozen massive bolts of black lightning stabbed into the earth around the dais. The ground exploded. Dirge hurtled through the air, his body twitching from the lightning. He didn't feel himself hit the ground, but he did feel the light of Ukase leave him as the Prophet died.

When he opened his eyes, the world felt dull. He struggled into a sitting position, pain wracking his entire body, and gently grasped his jaw tasting the slightly metallic tang of blood. His surroundings slowly came into focus. He lay alone on the ground at the lip of a shallow valley. People flailed at each other with swords, and axes, and spears. The sky roiled with gray and black clouds. The stink of burnt ozone mixed with charred flesh, offal, and shit, twisted his stomach.

The world sounded tinny and muffled, and his ears buzzed like a million bees in a bale of wool. Small bits of blackened metal lying all about him, and his clothing—along with a padded coat he was wearing for some reason—smoldered. He didn't know where he was, or even who he was. He only knew his mind hurt.

Soon the muffled buzzing gave way to the clashing of metal, and the screams of the dying. The sounds of the fighting became clearer, and he was happy to be so far away from it—he doubted he could lift his sword at that moment.

"Sword?" His words rang rough in his ears, and his throat felt stuffed with sand. "What sword?"

At his side, lie a twisted hunk of dross.

His eyes drifted back to the valley floor. Most of the fighting seemed to be dying down, except in a few locations where it looked wild and chaotic. At the nearest, men slashed and smashed at something in their midst, something that didn't seem to want to die. Whatever it was, it didn't take long for it to kill all the men. Only then did Dirge get a good look at it and wished he hadn't.

The thing, the monster, was larger than a man, with rough gray skin, and covered with coarse black hair. Using two arms, the ones that possessed hands, it picked dead people up from the ground while using a third, tipped with talons, to tear the bodies into pieces. It stomped along the ground searching for more men to kill. Boots shod two of its feet while a third simply dragged along the ground.

A chill ran up Dirge's spine when the thing turned toward him. Opening its gaping maw, it emitted a horrific shriek—blood and gore covered its razor-sharp teeth.

"Grunkin," Dirge croaked. He'd never seen one, yet he knew it to be true.

The grunkin threw its head back and screamed again—a blood-curdling screech of pain and rage—and charged, digging and tearing at the earth with its talon tipped hands to gain it speed. Dirge could do nothing but grab the useless hunk of metal that used to be a sword. It raced toward him covering two or three yards with every churning bound. Dirge hurled the remains of his sword at it, but it bounded off. Dirge threw up his hands as the thing leapt at him.

He was about to die.

A blur of movement came from his left, something large and black. It slammed into the grunkin's side, sending them both tumbling away. Dirge couldn't believe his eyes. It was another grunkin; jet-black, with no hair, and covered in tattered rags.

Shrieks, grunts, snarls, and howls filled the air as the two freaks fought one another. The black grunkin, its two legs, also boot shod, kicked at the earth to gain leverage in its assault on the gray. The black flailed with five arms, all tipped with claws or simple spikes. The spikes sank deep into the gray as its claws tore at the gray's flesh. The gray fought back with equal ferocity. Its talons dug at the black's midsection, sending flesh, blood, and tattered rags in all directions. Yet it was clear the gray was losing the fight. Its attacks slowed and finally stopped.

The black lifted its head into the air, howling in victory. A victory that was short lived. The gray lunged, one last time, and sunk its teeth into the black's neck. The black gurgled and thrashed until the gray's teeth snapped shut, severing the black's head form its body. With a hiss and a gurgle, the gray then died.

Shaking, Dirge got to his feet, keeping his eyes on the two monsters. Amazingly, with all the carnage, there was little blood. It oozed like black sludge. Both bodies decayed before his eyes, and the stench made him want to empty his stomach.

He shook his head and immediately regretted as it burst in pain once more. He closed his eyes, placing his hands on either side, and waited for the pain to subside. When he opened his eyes, he found a large chunk of flesh and cloth from the black monster. Something about the cloth looked familiar.

Ever so slowly, he bent and picked up the cloth. It was woven from three separate pieces: red, blue, and gold.

His eyes shot to the black creature. "Henson?"

Memories trickled back to him. He peered closer at them, at their boots. He recognized them. They were the type issued to the men of the heavy infantry. "They were men," he said, hushed.

His memories came flooding back. He looked at the blacked metal that had been lying about him. "My armor."

His eyes grew wide and his head snapped up. "Lynette!"

He took several wobbly steps, his eyes going to a large blacked hole in the ground—where the Prophet had died... where his wife had died. He sank to his knees.

"How?" he whispered, gazing into the ugly, muddy sky. "Why, God? Why did you let this happen?"

Not since the day he'd found his mother's corpse had he felt so... there were no words for it. It had all been for nothing—a huge celestial joke, seemingly on his behalf.

He buried his face in his hands. "What's the use in living?"

A sound behind him caught his attention. He slowly turned and his eyes went wide. "Jacob?"

There stood his oldest and truest friend in odd clothes—both pants and shirt were a hodgepodge mixture of brown and green. He smirked at Dirge with a rock in his right hand.

"Where've you—"

Jacob stepped forward and brought the rock down on Dirge's head.

Chapter 21
A Piece of Paper
(505 -R.C.-)

Dirge stared into the campfire without seeing the dancing flames. He peered beyond them, seeing nothing but oblivion and a life without meaning or hope, while Isaac's last words drifted in his mind.

"...Only He can awaken the Promised One..."

"Who the fuck is 'He'?" Dirge wondered aloud.

Jacob, sitting across the fire, cocked an eyebrow. "Who are you talking about?"

Dirge shook his head. "Nothing."

Shrugging, Jacob slurped a large spoonful of his stew, then pointed at the bowl sitting at Dirge's side. "What's the matter, you don't like my cooking?"

Dirge ignored the question and continued staring into the fire.

"Look," Jacob said. "You've got to eat. It's been two days."

The sway and swirl of the flames taunted Dirge. The fire had life, he didn't. The flames emitted warmth, unlike his heart. The blaze consumed its fuel, something for which he felt he had no more use.

"You need to snap out of this shit," Jacob said. When Dirge still refused to acknowledge him, he scowled. Picking out a piece of pork from his bowl, Jacob flung it at Dirge.

The sloppy chunk of meat splattered off Dirge's chest and bounded into the fire. Slowly raising his head, Dirge glared at his friend through hooded eyes.

"Oh, so you are still alive." Jacob grinned. "It's a good thing. I was 'bout to root through your body for any valuables before leaving you dead on the side of the road."

Dirge's eyes went back to the flames. "I should be dead."

"Oh, stop with that dung."

"No!" Dirge jumped to his feet. "I should be dead two days just like everyone else! Everyone else is dead: Lynette, Henson, Isaac… all of them! The entire army is…"

His eyes narrowed, and he glared at Jacob. "Where were you?"

"What?"

"You were assigned to the scouts. I never saw you once we made that field, and you can't ride a horse. So, where were you?"

"What do you mean, where was I?"

"Answer the question." Dirge's voice was like iron as his hands clenched into fists.

"I was doing my job."

"No." Dirge jabbed a finger at Jacob, his voice coming out as a growl. "Tell me."

"I was exactly where I was told to be." Jacob signed. "Your precious 'Prophet' told me to stay nearby, just outside the hollow, and to keep an eye on you."

"Why?" Jacob had always been a talented liar, but the answer made no sense.

"He told me…" Jacob licked his lips. "He told me what was going to happen: the battle, the priests, the storm; all of it. He said the only person who mattered was you. 'Whatever he does, don't let him throw his life away.' Those were his exact words."

"I don't believe you." Dirge lowered his hand and scowled. The last words of the Prophet went through his head once more. "Why would he say that? If he knew that we were to be wiped out why would he demand that Lynette come along?"

"You're not going to like the answer."

"Tell me," Dirge snarled.

Jacob looked both ways a moment and flexed his hands. "Fine, you asked for it. He said that your 'Lord' demanded a sacrifice, and that she was chief among them."

Dirge felt cold, like ice encased his heart.

"Are you hearing me?" Jacob asked. "He said that she had to die. A 'sacrifice' he said. What kind of god is that?"

Dirge shook his head. He took a step back and promptly fell over the log on which he'd been sitting. He lay there, staring up at the night's sky. Stars winked and twinkled through the intermittent clouds, mocking him with celestial glee.

God had demanded her sacrifice? He wanted to call Jacob a liar, but deep down he knew the words to be true. God wanted her dead. He wanted all of them dead, all but Jacob, and himself. It made no sense. *Why even go to war in the first place?*

"With gods, who knows," Jacob said.

Dirge hadn't realized he'd spoken aloud. "There's nothing left. Lynette is dead because of me, and God has forsaken me."

"Gods do as they want, or so the stories tell. They're strange. Who are we to judge?"

"No." Dirge waved his hand. "No more gods. No more death… except maybe my own."

Jacob stalked around the fire and loomed about Dirge. "Stop that!"

"It's the truth." Dirge pulled out his knife and placed it to his wrist, but Jacob kicked it from his hand. Dirge stared up at his friend, his eyes aflame.

"I said, stop. I gave you that for cutting wood, not yourself." Jacob pursed his lips. "What would Lynette think? Is this what she'd want from you? She sure as hell wouldn't like seeing you pout like this."

"I'm not pouting."

"Bull's balls."

"Fine." Dirge sighed, got up, and sat back down next to the fire.

He picked up his bowl and took a bite. After swallowing, he pursed his lips and glared at his friend. "Your cooking is terrible, by the way."

He had a dream that night, and for many nights thereafter. He was a child once more, standing at the opening of an alley in the Slaag, the fallen snow completely covering the body of his mother, all but her eyes.

They walked for ten days before finally reaching the outskirts of Tuilar—two men alone travel faster and longer than an army. They'd have arrived sooner, but they thought it best to skirt the towns along the road. The people they'd forced out would return once word got out about their army's destruction.

Dirge was adjusting his pack when a thought occurred to him. "Where did you get all the stuff, anyway?"

"What?"

"The packs, the food, the cooking supplies. Where d'you get it?"

"Well, your Prophet told me where it would all be. Apparently, he'd put it all aside for when I'd drag your sorry ass back here."

"He's not my prophet," Dirge grumbled.

Jacob laughed. "It's good to see you're finally coming to your senses. The man was a lunatic, you know that, right?"

Dirge ignored the statement.

Jacob continued. "What I don't get is, if he knew what was going to happen, why do it? I'm telling you, he was touched in the head."

They walked in silence for a while before Jacob piped up again. "I wonder if it was Edis who'd touched him. We all know that Chaos loves a good joke, and this would certainly rank up there with the best of them."

Dirge glanced at Jacob, then back to the road. The statement gave him pause. He found the idea of the Lord of Chaos touching him deeply disturbing.

"No. I know what I heard, and it wasn't Chaos. Chaos wouldn't have destroyed his own so gleefully."

The problem was when it came to Chaos you never knew. It was completely within the realm of that cursed god to do such a thing. Dirge shuddered, trying to shake the thought.

"I'll tell you this," Jacob said, giving no appearance that his statement had disturbed his friend. "I'm looking forward to sleeping in a bed tonight. Oh, and a nice meal. Mutton and potatoes would be great." He looked over at Dirge. "How about you? What are you going to eat?"

Food was the last thing on Dirge's mind. He was trying to figure out what to say to the people; their loved ones were dead and Chaos was likely to go on a rampage.

As though reading his mind, Jacob continued, "Look, Dirge, I know you're not looking forward to this, but it's not your fault. You didn't tell them to do this. You were bilked just like everyone else."

"I was their leader. It was my fault. I told them to trust me. I encouraged them to fight back. I told them to spit in the face of the Lord of Chaos." He straightened his back. "I will accept whatever punishment they wish to deal out. You may eat well tonight, but I will likely go to the gallows."

They rounded the last turn in the road and exited the woods that surrounded the city. Dirge stumbled to a halt, his eyes going wide. The walls surrounding the city, that gave them hope of holding off the world, were nothing but large piles of rubble.

"I don't think you have to worry about that anymore," Jacob said, weakly. "How did this happen?"

"Chaos Storm." Dirge strode forward.

"Where the hell are you going? If it's as you say then you know there's going to be grunkin about."

"I don't care."

"You don't care?!" Jacob rushed forward and grabbed Dirge by the shoulder. "There could be a hundred in there!"

"Not likely," Dirge replied. "There's no more than two or three at most. You saw how they went after each other during the battle. If there were that many to begin they'd have killed each other off my now." He started walking again.

"And you still want to go there?"

Dirge stopped and glanced back at his friend. "If grunkin were created in there, there's a good chance they didn't stay, especially if there was nothing left to kill. It's likely they left and are in the woods around here. Now, unless you have a sword or a crossbow hidden away, we have no way of fighting one." He pointed at the city. "But there is a good chance I can find a good weapon in there. I may even find a Rod in Lyne—" He cleared his throat. "In Mister Malik's basement. We may not have taken any with us," he growled.

"But I know for a fact that there were some there before we left."

As Dirge started for the city again, Jacob regarded the surrounding woods, his head swiveling about. "Wait for me."

They climbed the rubble that was once the city walls. When they crested the mound, Dirge's hopes for survivors evaporated. The inside of the city matched its walls, nothing but ruin.

"Even the Master's Hall is gone," Jacob said at his side.

Dirge didn't care about the Hall of the Masters, nor any other building in the affluent portion of the city. He looked only in one direction. He pointed toward where the Slaag should have been. "Does that look like a standing building to you?"

"I can't tell. You're not thinking of walking through all this, are you? It's got to be a quarter of a mile away."

Without answering, Dirge started down the slope, and into what remained of the city he'd spent his entire life.

"There's nothing alive here," Jacob said as they picked their way over a large pile of bricks that used to be someone's home. "I think even the rats are dead."

Dirge agreed with his friend. "I'm surprised we've seen so few bodies."

"Not whole bodies, anyway." Jacob nudged a lump of tattered cloth away with his foot. The cloth rolled down the brick pile and a portion of a head fell out – the top of the skull was missing as well as the jaw.

Jacob vomited.

Dirge refused to look. He'd learned to detach himself from these types of things while training with the Brotherhood. They were only things to him: not the remains of his friends, not the people he'd ensured they'd be safe within these walls; just things. He'd likely go insane if he thought otherwise.

It took over an hour to reach the Slaag.

"You're right," Jacob said. "It is a building."

"It's the Angelic." Dirge's eyes went to a large hole in the ground a short distance away.

"I'm guessing that's the Malic house." Jacob gently patted Dirge on the shoulder. "I'm sorry."

Dirge tore his eyes away from his last hope. Jacob was right; there was no way he'd find any weapons there, let alone any Rods of Divinity. He headed to the Angelic.

"Why do you think it's still standing?" Jacob asked as they reached the door.

"It's under the protection of Aza'zel. Ukase may be gone, but Death is ever-present."

"You think anyone's alive in there?" Jacob stood behind his friend, his eyes searching all around.

Dirge's hand hesitated a moment on the door handle. "I guess we'll find out."

The building was empty, for which Dirge held mixed feelings. As much as he wanted to find survivors, he didn't think he could have faced their accusing stares.

Jacob briskly rubbed his arms and wrinkled his nose. "It's like a tomb in here."

"As I said, we are now in the hand of Death." Dirge quickly made his way to the staircase.

"Where are you going?" Jacob asked as Dirge loped up the stairs.

"I have to check something," Dirge yelled back.

Dirge stopped at the second floor and slowly advanced down the hall, stopping before the door he knew oh so well. He reached out, reverently opened the door to his old room, and made his way to his old bed, knowing what he'd find. There, upon perfectly preserved sheets, lay a sword.

"Whose is that?" Jacob asked behind him.

Dirge jumped a little and cursed himself for doing so. He didn't think he'd been standing there that long. "It's Talic's."

A piece of paper lay folded beneath it. Dirge picked it up and read it, his hands slightly shaking:

Son,
You must stay strong. There is much in the world beyond our small lives, no matter how important they seem at the time. Just remember that small lives do still matter, yours more so than most. Do not give up hope. The day will come when you find the life that matters more than any other, far more than those you now hold dear. It will be a life you will gladly give your own to protect. Don't ask me how I know, I just do. Onto that, take my sword. Let it be a symbol to guide you, and a memory of what matters most.

Your father,
Talic
P.S. I'll want it back when next we meet.

Dirge stared at the words on the page. Each time he reread it he grew angrier. *'Your father'? What in all the hells does that mean? Father?!*

Dirge didn't have a father. His mother had been a whore. She had no idea who his father was. How dare he say that! His entire world had been ripped away from him. The last thing he needed was this man trying to lay this false claim just to placate him.

"What does it say?" Jacob asked behind him.

Dirge quickly folded and shoved it into his pouch. "It's from Talic. He wants me to have his sword."

"You don't seem too happy about it." Jacob's head cocked to the side. "How did he even know you'd need it? How did he even know we'd come back?"

Dirge didn't respond. He didn't know the answers and thought it best not to lie to his only living friend. "We should spend the night."

"Here?!" Jacob again rubbed his arms and looked around.

"We'll need to get as far away from here as we can while we still have daylight." He then peered over his shoulder at his friend. "Unless you want to face a grunkin in the dark."

Dirge read the note three more times that night as he lay in his bed. He found sleep elusive that night—and for many thereafter—but when he finally drifted off, two words kept echoing in his mind: *"Your Father."*

Chapter 22
A Man Remembered
(505 -R.C.-)

Upon waking, Dirge no longer felt the touch of Aza'zel within the Angelic, something Jacob found quite pleasing. Dirge understood his friend's apprehension. The touch of Death was cold and disconcerting, an ever-present reminder of one's own mortality.

The touch of Chaos was all about them: the floorboards creaked, the paint began to crack and fade, and dust covered everything. "Let's get out of here," Dirge said, "before this place crumbles around us."

They quickly headed toward the outskirts of the city. Flies assaulted them at every step and rats scurried about. Jacob spit and gagged. "One just went in my mouth! Where the hells did all these come from?"

"Edis is reclaiming the city." Dirge kicked at a rat. "Just another reason we need to get out as soon as we can."

They made the city's edge and climbed the wreckage that was once Tuilar's walls. As they topped it, Dirge scanned the forests' edge. Even with Talic's sword strapped to his side, he had doubts he could handle a grunkin, not without taking grievous injury in the process. Ukase was no longer with him. What chance did he have? Their best bet was to get as far away from Tuilar as possible.

Once he planted his feet firmly on the ground, he sighed in relief. The stones seemed far looser that morning than they had the previous day. More proof of Chaos clenching his fist.

"What next?" Dirge asked when Jacob stepped down next to him.

His friend cocked his head to the side. "Why ask me? I thought you were the born leader."

"Never again," Dirge said with a scowl. "I'm no leader."

"You could have fooled me."

Dirge refused to reply.

"Dirge—"

"No! Never again, do you hear me? I am not a leader." He looked to the ground. "Unless you wish to be lead to your death."

Jacob shook his head. "Fine, be that way. You do realize that means I'm in charge, right?" He cracked a smile.

Dirge grunted.

"Well," Jacob said, rubbing his hands. "What to do. What to do. Well, I'm much more of a city man than any kind of villager. Besides, villages are likely to give us short shrift. So, it's probably best to make for Dane Hook to the east. The last thing we want is to run into anyone that might know us. And who knows, maybe that's where those Brotherhood people went."

"It wouldn't matter," Dirge replied. "Even if Talic and the others did go there, they're likely to lie low for years after what I did here."

"What you did?"

"Yes, me!"

"How many times do I have to tell you it wasn't your fault? You were bilked by that prophet just like everyone else."

"That doesn't matter. I was the leader. I was the one they looked up to." He sighed. "I was the one who should have expected those priests to show up and do what they did. Everyone is dead because of me."

Jacob scowled. "How the mighty have fallen. Well if I'm in charge, I expect you to do what I say. You got me?"

Dirge merely nodded.

Jacob laughed. "I've got myself a snaggletooth puppy. Well, come along, Puppy, and keep that sword of yours handy. You wouldn't want anything to happen to me. You'd end up in charge again."

It took over two weeks to reach the coastal city of Dane Hook. Dirge felt an odd sense of familiarity upon entering the gates. Everything looked completely different from Tuilar, yet it was all the same. Like the city of his birth, the people were a multitude of races and colors—wearing many styles, from rich furs and silks, to simple rags—and they spoke a multitude of languages.

"It's almost like we never left home," Jacob said, echoing Dirge's thoughts. "That one, in the green silk, almost looks like Mary."

"Who?"

"Mary. You know, Mary, the redhead tavern wench at the Golden Trumpet."

Dirge simply shook his head.

"Mary? I brought her and her sister to our room that one night. Gods but those two could squeal. I can still picture the look on Mary's face when I talked her into touching her sister's—"

Dirge scowled and looked away.

"Really? Still, after all these years?" Jacob twisted his lips. "You need to get over that. Now more than ever. It's that kind of attitude that'll make you stand out. And the last thing we want is for someone to connect us with what happened back there."

Dirge sighed. "You're right."

"What?" Jacob's eyebrows shot up.

"You're right. Who am I to judge anyone for what they do, or who they want to lie with?" He then looked Jacob in the eyes. "Just don't expect me to follow suit."

Jacob barked a laugh. "Of course not. Hells, the very idea of you having sex is enough to make one's hair stand on end. What? Don't give me that look. I just mean imagining you having… sex. You know? I'm not saying that you didn't sleep with your woman, but I'm pretty sure that when you did you only had one arrow in your quiver. You lie on her, thrusting away, not making a sound, until the deed is done—simply going through the motions without really enjoying it."

Dirge turned and stalked away.

"Oh, don't be like that." Jacob ran after his friend.

"Where do we go from here?" Dirge asked, choosing to ignore the entire conversation.

"Well, if it's as much like home as it looks, we head to one of the inns nearby, the ones caravaners like to frequent."

They started for a large inn, a short way down the street. Half way, Dirge spoke up. "I did enjoy it."

"What?"

"Sex. I enjoyed it a great deal." He stopped and closed his eyes. "The heat, the passion. It was like… it was like we were touching souls."

"Touching souls?" Jacob scoffed.

Dirge glowered again and continued walking. "It doesn't matter. She's dead now so I'll likely never do it again."

Jacob grabbed his friend by the shoulder and spun him around. "What are you talking about? You're never going to have sex again?"

"I can't!" He lowered his eyes and his voice. "It would be a betrayal to her. I pledged myself to her and none other."

"You can't be serious." Jacob's eyebrows shot up. "You are serious. Dirge, she's gone. I know it hurts, but eventually you must move on. It's not a betrayal. Look, I liked her. I'm sure she didn't like me, but I liked her. She was good for you. And I think she would want you to be happy, not pining away for the rest of your life."

"Maybe," Dirge said. Jacob might be right, Lynette would want him to enjoy his life, but he still saw it as a betrayal.

"Come on." Jacob patted his friend on the back.

The sign over the inn had a crude carving of what looked like a man sitting atop a nude woman who was lying on her back with wagon wheels under her.

"Yup, this looks like a good place to start," Jacob said with a smile while pushing open the door and stepping in.

They stood near the doorway until their eyes adjusted to the dim. Dirge found it nothing like the Angelic. Unlike his friend, Dirge had frequented none of the other inns in Tuilar. This place was twice the size with less than a dozen smoky lamps along all the walls or hanging from the ceiling, making it difficult to make out anyone on the far side. The sounds of people yelling, shouting, and laughing filled the air just as it had in his former home, but it smelled horrible. The stink of years of unwashed bodies filled Dirge's nostrils. He wanted to gag from the stench.

"Let's ask the tapster," Jacob said over the crowd, pointing to a large, dirty man standing behind the bar. They made their way over and Jacob raised his hand to get the man's attention.

"What'll it be?" The man's voice was surprisingly high for his girth.

"Two ales," Jacob said.

The man pulled out two mugs from beneath the bar and filled them from one of the many casks behind him. "Six copper."

"That much?" Jacob asked.

"You wan' it be eight?"

"No, no, my good man," Jacob said, pulling out the coins from his pouch. "We only arrived from Selos, to the east. Didn't know ale was so precious here."

"I know where Selos is. Stinkin' place, if you ask me."

"Couldn't agree with you more." Jacob laughed.

Dirge grew tired of the banter. His old life was over and he wanted his new one to start as soon as possible. "We need to know—"

Jacob held up his hand. "I've got this. What, you in a big hurry to be in the lead again? I'm in charge now, remember?"

Jacob turned back to the barkeep and slid four more copper toward him. "As I said, we only just got here and we need some work. Any chance you could point us toward anyone who needs a couple of caravan guards?"

"You, a guard?" The barkeep laughed. He pointed to Dirge. "Him, I can see. But you?" He shook his head.

Jacob pushed across two more.

The barkeep shrugged and took the coins. "Talk to Kellen. He's the big black one in the back corner. I hear he just lost a couple of men. He might take you on."

"Much obliged," Jacob said with a smile. He turned and motioned Dirge to follow him.

They made their way through the crowd to the table the barkeep pointed out. There, a scarred, dark skinned man in a tan shirt lounged in a large chair. On either side of him sat two large men: one pale skinned with brown hair and one tan with black. Both men wore leather jerkins that seemed to strain at their girth.

Jacob nodded to the caravan owner. "Good day—"

"Piss off," the pale man said before taking a pull on his ale.

"Yes, but we have it from the bar—"

"He said, piss off," said the tan man, while standing and pulling a dagger from his belt.

"I understand you're short on guards," Jacob said, louder.

"And you'll be short a nose, if you don't fuck off," the first one said, also standing. He placed his hand upon the sword at his belt and sneered.

The man in the middle—Dirge assumed he was the caravan owner—said nothing while peering at Jacob and Dirge from over the rim of his mug. His eyes measured them, seeming to take it all in, before they suddenly shot to something on Dirge's left.

Dirge felt a hand on his shoulder, trying to pull him around. He placed his hand on his sword.

"It can't be him?" said the man trying to turn Dirge.

Slowly pivoting, Dirge peered into the man's cruel eyes, then at his short-cropped black hair, and then at the scar running across his face from his right ear to chin. Dirge knew that face, for as long as he lived, he'd never forget it: Matrum Kent, the former city guardsman who'd thrown living children into the flames.

"By the Great Lord, 'tis you." Kent turned to a man behind him and pointed at Dirge. "It's him—"

Dirge drew his sword with lighting speed sliced off Kent's hand at the wrist. He then slashed down at an angle, hacking into the man's shoulder. With the loud cracking of bones, the blade sunk deep. He stepped back and slashed sideways from the other side, sending the man's head tumbling to the floor. Blood fountained everywhere as the body collapsed.

"By the gods," muttered one of the guards.

Dirge calmly pulled one of the small pieces of cloth he kept in a pouch on his belt. He ran it down his blade, making sure it was completely free of blood before returning it to his sheath, and then tossed the blood-soaked cloth onto Kent's corpse.

Jacob pointed at the head as it came to rest. "I recognize him. Him and a couple of his friends tried to jump us on the road a while back." He smiled. "He was the only one that got away."

Dirge didn't care if anyone believed Jacob's story. He didn't care if the entire bar attacked him at that very moment. He would die with a smile on his face, knowing that he'd brought at least one more man to justice.

His smile melted. *Justice? What does that even mean anymore?*

A voice spoke behind him, one strong and sure. "You are hired. Please, have a seat."

Dirge turned and saw the dark caravan leader pointing to the chair across from him. Dirge nodded and sat down, leaving one leg out to give him clear access to his sword, just in case.

"I'm Kellen and I own three caravans. This is Dirk, and Scott," he said pointing to first the man on his left then his right.

"And what about you?" he said to Jacob. "This one's shown his worth. What do you possess that I would need?"

"Me? Well I've a sharp eye, a sharp mind, and a sharp blade." Jacob smiled, patting the short sword at his belt while rocking back and forth on his feet.

Kellen grinned. "I imagine you don't have many opportunities to dull that blade with him around."

Jacob threw his arms wide. "What can I say, I keep good company."

Chapter 23
Selos
(505 -R.C.-)

Dirge kept pace alongside the first of three wagons, keeping his eyes on the surroundings. Their job was to stay alert for bandits and grunkin, something his friend wasn't taking as seriously.

Jacob sat in the bench of the lead wagon. "I still say he should have given us more time to prepare. Hells, we were only in the city one night. I was so damned tired I didn't even have time to talk up a woman. What kind of man drags you off before you even get a chance to bed a lass or two? Not a good one, I'll tell you that. Are you even listening to me?"

Dirge sighed. "Unfortunately, yes."

"We can all hear you," said Trumbo, the driver and leader of the caravan at Jacob's side. "I'm sure the boss can hear you all the way from his room in the city. Hells, the gods above can!"

"You'll have plenty of opportunities to get your fill in Selos," Dirge said.

"Ah, but first I'd have to take the time to find where the best women are." Jacob nodded his head.

Trumbo cocked his head. "I thought yous two were from Selos?"

Dirge tensed but Jacob spoke quickly. "I said we were *in* Selos, not that we were *from* there. You need to open your ears, my friend. Besides, how did you hear that? From what I gather, you were up at the bar when we talked to the boss."

"As I said, your voice travels quite well." Trumbo frowned. "And don't look at me. You need to keep your eyes out there. You may be good with your mouth, but you sure as hells ain't no guard."

"Never said I was a guard. No sir. I'm a troubadour! And one of the finest you'll ever hear."

"Is that so? Well, mayhaps you'll prove it by the fire tonight. Any man who can carry a tune is worth his weight out here. If you're good, the boss'll likely up your pay. A good crooner can make a long trip short, and if they're real good, they can keep the raiders away."

"Why is that?" Dirge asked, still keeping his eyes on the tall grasses.

"Cause singers and dancers are blessed by the Great Lord. Everyone knows that, even the scum that rove about out here. The last thing a raider wants is to run afoul of Chaos."

"Truly?" Jacob pulled his head back. "Damn, why didn't I think of that? We should go back and tell him."

"We'll tell him when we get back," Trumbo said. "But that's only if you prove yourself. If you're a good enough singer, we can get you something to play in Selos. You a harp man?"

Jacob grinned. "No sir. I'm a lute man."

"Lute, eh? It's a bit cumbersome, ain't it?"

"Not when you've got fingers like mine."

Dirge shook his head. "How often do you have trouble with raiders out here?"

"No more than usual," Trumbo replied. "Which is to say, whenever they see a weakness."

Dirge didn't like that answer. He felt naked without his armor. Moreover, their little caravan had only four guards, including himself, along with another bowman on the rear wagon. To most, it would seem a fair number, but Dirge knew full well that if the raiders had men with bows, which they surely did, then half of the guards could be down in the blink of an eye.

Dirge swore he could feel the crossbow sight on his back at that very moment. "If what you say is true, perhaps Jacob should start singing now."

"Couldn't hurt none, I suppose," Trumbo said.

"Oh, I don't know." Jacob frowned. "I'm not sure these ruffians deserve to hear a voice as lovely as mine."

Dirge growled. "Just sing, Jacob."

"Fine." Jacob chuckled, and sang:

> *"Oh I dream of a girl with big blue eyes*
> *I dream of a girl with creamy thighs*
> *I dream of a girl with flowers in her hair*
> *I dream of a girl with a fine derriere*
> *I dream of a girl who'll bring me luck*
> *I dream of a girl I'd love to..."*

Dirge stopped listening. Oh, he heard every word; he just did his best not to pay attention to them.

A hundred feet ahead of them on the right side of the road, Dirge saw a large shrub rustle. In a flash his sword was in his hands, only to feel embarrassed when a deer came bounding out of the foliage. Filled with chagrin, he sheathed his sword, and looked up at Jacob to see if he'd noticed.

> *"I'd dandle the girl upon my knee*
> *So I'd have a chance to better see*

What wonderful treasures she kept in her top
I'd lick 'em and kiss 'em till she screams 'don't stop!'

The men laughed uproariously, clapping and hooting as Jacob sang. They didn't appear to be paying too much attention to their surroundings, not enough for Dirge, anyway. Yet time proved it didn't seem to matter. If there had been any bandits along that road, they didn't attack.

Perhaps there's something to it, after all, Dirge thought.

After three weeks on the road, stopping at villages for the night, and with Jacob singing the entire way, they reached Selos. Jacob went through every song he knew and picked up several more from their traveling companions and the folk at the village inns. When they came to Selos, they turned in at a corral outside the city walls.

"Here." Trumbo pulled out a pouch from the strongbox. "As agreed, four silver each." He then fished out two more and handed them to Jacob. "This is for the singing. As I said, Kellen pays more for folk who sing."

"Is that all?" Jacob asked. "I can get more than this at a good inn."

"You wasn't singin' to entertain us. You's doin' it to give any raiders pause." He re-tied the pouch and put it back into the strongbox. "If you can find an inn who don't already got a crooner and get them to give you an extra two silver a week, then more luck to yea."

Trumbo paused. "Tells you what. We're headin' on to Geous in four days. You get yourself a lute and want to sign back up for that trip then I'll get you another two on top of that. What say you?"

"You gonna get me the coin to get the lute?"

"You get your own outa what I gave you."

Jacob looked at Dirge. "What do you think?"

Dirge shrugged. "What else do we have to do?"

Jacob turned back to Trumbo. "You have a deal, my good man. We'll see you back here in four days."

"We're staying at the Pony Show, just inside the gates. If you're not joinin' us there, just know that we leave at dawn. Don't be late."

As they made their way through the city gate, Jacob turned to Dirge. "What's eatin' at you?"

"What do you mean?"

"I mean that you've been acting even more dour than usual. And that's sayin' something."

Dirge shook his head. "I've just been thinking a lot."

"Well, there's the problem."

Dirge glared at his grinning friend. "I'm saying that I've been thinking about what happened back at the bar where we met Kellen… about the man I killed."

"You mean the one that got us this job?"

"I had no right to take his life."

"Wait. What?" Jacob stopped, taking hold of his friend's arm, and pulling them out of the way of the traffic that funneled out the city gate.

"I had no right to kill him. After everything that's happened—" Dirge scowled. "I just didn't have the right. Besides, it put your life at risk."

"You do know what would have happened if he opened his mouth, right?"

"Yes."

"And the fact that everyone could see that we were there together?"

"You could have talked your way out of it. It's what you're good at."

Jacob laughed. "Well, I appreciate the compliment, but that's beside the point. He would have called you out, and they'd have been too fired up for me to do anything. You did the right thing to shut him up."

Dirge shook his head again. "You don't understand. I killed that man because of what he did during the Cleansing, not to shut him up. Justice demanded he die."

"And," Jacob said, throwing up his hands.

"The Prophet's dead," Dirge said, lowering his voice and looking around. "Ukase is gone. Who am I to decide who deserves justice?"

Jacob pursed his lips and eyed Dirge. "Every word you said is true, my friend. But, and I say but because you've got a big butt. Well okay, it's not that big, but it's sure-fire bigger than mine." With a smile, he raised his voice and a finger to keep Dirge from responding. "All I'm saying is that if you hadn't killed him, we both would have likely ended up dead after he'd opened his mouth. Look at it this way. You did it to save us, not to avenge some long forgotten kids."

Dirge sighed. "So be it." He turned and headed deeper into the city. He had to keep reminding himself that part of his life was in the past. He needed to keep his mind on the present and let the future take care of itself. No matter how bleak it may be.

They took much of the day to find someone who not only sold musical instruments but ones that lived up to Jacob's expectations. Once Jacob felt satisfied, they went back to the gate and took rooms at the Pony Show.

That evening they sat in the common room, taking in their surroundings. That is to say, Jacob was taking in the surrounds; Dirge simply didn't care.

"It's not as nice as the Angelic, but it's best we stay close to Trumbo," Jacob said. "We don't want to be left behind."

"I'm surprised you care." Dirge took a long pull on his ale.

"Hey, I know a good thing when I see it. They've got a fair amount of coin and we want to stay as close to that as we can."

Shrugging, Dirge downed the rest of his ale, and flagged down the tavern wench. "Two more."

"I just started mine," Jacob interjected.

"They're both for me."

"What? You gonna drink your troubles away?"

"I've never been drunk. I've been told it helps quiet the mind."

"So you only *plan* on becoming a drunk."

"Now's as good a time to start as any," Dirge said, sliding over his copper to the wench who returned with his ale. He took another long pull on the new mug and belched.

"Do I even know you?" Jacob grinned.

"My friend, I don't even know me." Dirge finished the mug.

The next morning, Dirge's head throbbed and his stomach roiled as he stared at the light pouring in through the window of their third story room. The warmth and brightness seemed to mock him. *How could I've ever liked sunny days?*

"It's the mornings that get you." Jacob chuckled. "So, you still want to be a drunk?"

Dirge belched and groaned.

"Did it help your deliberations?"

Squeezing his eyes shut, Dirge shook his head. The drink only seemed to make him think more, not less.

"Well, I'll leave you to your convalescence. I'm going to get something to eat, then go explore for a bit." He stood and strolled to the door. As he closed it, he added, "Seriously. Get some rest. You look like hell."

The closing of the door rang in his ears like an ominous chime from the pit of Chaos, and the mere thought of food turned his gills green. He drifted off.

Chapter 24
Green Eyes
(505 -R.C.-)

Dirge didn't know how long he'd slept by the time Jacob returned. From the darkness outside, he estimated it to be in the middle of the night. When Jacob lit a lamp, Dirge realized that his friend wasn't alone. At his side stood a beautiful girl, petite and delicate, with long blonde hair that shined like spun gold. Her green eyes smoldered as she looked him over with a ghosted smile.

"Have you been here all day?" Jacob asked.

Dirge groaned.

"Well, you really should go get something to eat."

"I'm not hungry," Dirge lied.

Jacob threw up his hands. "Alright, be that way."

He pulled off his shirt, pulled the girl close, and kissed her firmly. She squealed with delight. Peeling off her white blouse, she tossed it to the floor; her green skirt quickly followed. She stripped off her undergarments and the two of them hopped into Jacob's bed where they kissed and fondled one another.

Dirge considered leaving but refused. *That's something the old me would have done.*

Instead, he stared at the stunning young woman as though compelled. Her soft, delicate, alabaster skin glowed in the light of the lamp. Her small firm breasts heaved as she panted in ecstasy. Throwing her head back, her face contorted, and she bit her full pink lips as Jacob kissed his way down her body—her long, lithe legs kicking in delight.

It pained him to look on as they cavorted—thrashing about and crying in carnal pleasure. The only woman he'd ever seen naked had been his wife, and this girl looked nothing like her. Yet everything about the young woman made him think of Lynette. Oh, how he ached to touch his wife's supple form one last time, to hear her moan and gasp as they made love. Never again. Never again.

With a shake of the head, Dirge realized that Jacob had been right. Dirge only had "one arrow in his quiver."

"He certainly likes to watch," the young woman said, her voice like a crystal chime. "Is he going to join us?"

With a groan, Dirge hastily sat up and put on the pants and shirt, and stumbled to the door.

The girl laughed.

He expected Jacob to join her laughter, but to his dismay, Jacob said, "Hush, my sweet. Do not laugh at my friend. His dearest love died quite recently and I think he finds this a bit too much to take."

He then looked up at Dirge, "I'm sorry. I'll take her elsewhere next time."

Dirge shook his head. "No, that's not necessary. This is your room too." He softly closed the door behind him and headed downstairs.

Trudging down the steps, he decided he needed to eat after all—his legs felt weak and his stomach rumbled. Taking a seat in the common room closest to the stairs, he asked for stew and bread along with a watered wine—the very thought of ale churned his stomach. He stared out at the crowd without seeing anything until the wench brought his order.

She needed to shake him gently to get his attention. "Are you all right?"

"I'm sorry?" Dirge glanced up at the comely brunette.

"I asked if yous all right? I only ask cause I heard you came in with one of them caravans. I remember from last night. You put away a fair share of ale and your friend had to help you upstairs."

His attention fell away as she talked, his eyes drifting across the room.

She continued, "The last time I seen anything like that it was when a fella had a run-in with a grunkin."

His head snapped to her. "What?"

"I said, did you see a grunkin?"

He quickly looked away. "No, no. Please, just take this and go. I'll be fine." He fished out a few coins, not looking at them, and handed them to her. She thanked him profusely and hurried away.

He ate his stew woodenly while staring at nothing. He'd hoped eating would take his mind off things, but no. The mention of grunkin brought on thoughts of Henson, about the braided piece of cloth the man once wore about his neck—the very one Dirge now wore. He thought about his Righteous army, now decimated. He thought about the Prophet's last words. But mostly he thought about Lynette.

He also thought about a stunning blonde with green eyes and alabaster skin, and about how the very sight of her caused his blood to boil. Lust was not alien to him, he was still a man after all, but he was a *married* man, and shouldn't think of such things. Yet he lusted all the same and hated himself for it.

His head shaking, self-loathing filled him. *What have I become?*

After several hours—almost falling asleep twice—Dirge went back to bed. He quietly opened the door and saw, thankfully, that Jacob and the girl were fast asleep. He undressed and got into bed.

Reaching over to turn down the lamp, he froze. Those beautiful green eyes, the ones he couldn't stop thinking about, gazed at him through the dim. The girl winked, blew him a kiss, and closed her eyes, cuddling up tighter to a lightly snoring Jacob.

When Dirge woke, he saw that Jacob sat alone in his bed. Dirge sighed in relief. Something about that young woman bothered him, the look she gave him as the light went out…

His dreams had been shaming—dark and erotic, filled with pale flesh, golden hair, and green eyes.

"Morning, my friend," Jacob said. "You planning on sleeping this day away as well?"

Dirge groaned. He slept through the night, but it didn't feel like he had. "No."

"What's wrong? You not feelin well? You look like you hardly slept, but from the way you was snoring I know that can't be true."

Dirge heaved himself into a sitting position on the bed. "Just bad dreams. Nothing more."

"About what?"

"I don't remember." The lie was sharp on Dirge's tongue.

"Well, I'm going to go explore the city," Jacob said as he stood and got dressed. "You coming with me?"

Dirge shook his head. "I need to get back into my routine. I'll stay here and practice."

Jacob stopped at the door. "I am sorry about Dahlia last night. It won't happen again."

"Don't worry about it." Dirge shuddered a bit as Jacob shut the door. The last thing he wanted was to have a name put to those eyes.

As good as his word, Dirge spent the day in their room going through his ritual of stretches, exercises, and sword practice. By the time the sun began to set, he decided it was time to have a good meal. They were to leave in the morning and he wanted to have a good night's sleep with a full belly.

The common room was nearly full when he made his way there. He considered taking his supper in his room but dismissed the thought. He'd spent too much time alone recently. He ordered a slab of beef and a flagon of ale from the serving wench, thankfully a different one from the night before. As he enjoyed his meal, he took in the crowd. People laughed, and cursed, and ate, and drank, much as they had at the Angelic—simple people enjoying that they still lived.

"Everyone's the same," he said to himself.

"Oh, I wouldn't say that," a woman said over his shoulder.

Dirge turned and peered up into the deep brown eyes of the comely barmaid from the night before. She gazed at him as she twirled a finger through her long brown hair that partially covered an ample bosom that threatened to fall out of her open blouse. He didn't recall seeing that the night before. Nor had he seen the long dark legs her short skirt put on display.

He blinked. "I'm sorry, what?"

"I said that not everyone is the same." She took the seat next to him. "You're certainly different."

He held up his flagon. "I'm sorry, I've already been seen to, thank you."

"Like that. I don't recall hearing anyone as big and strong and beautiful as you, ever saying they were sorry for anything." Her voice was as velvety as the finger she ran up his arm.

His eyes dropped to the table and his cheeks burned. "Don't you have other tables to see to?"

"Oh, I'm not working tonight." With her soft hand, she placed it under his chin, turning and raising his head so she could gaze into his eyes. "I came here to see you."

He gently pulled his head away. "What do you want?"

"You."

"I'm sorry, what?"

"There you go again, being sorry. You have nothing to be sorry for, my sweet." She ran the back of her hand across his cheek.

He softly took her hand in his and pulled it away from his face. "Please, don't do that."

"Why? I just want to make you feel good." She stroked his palm with the tips of her fingers. "Dahlia told me you could use the attention."

"Who?" He yanked his hand back. "No. Please go, I'll have none of this."

He started to leave when he heard the barmaid cry. He turned back, his eyebrows rising at the tears running down her delicate cheeks.

"Please, don't go," she said with a sniffle. "She told me what happened to you, about your loss. I simply wanted to console you."

"I don't need consoling." He took a step away from the table.

"I've been where you are now."

He stopped, his head slowly swiveling back toward the woman.

"I know how you are feeling—lost and alone. I too lost my dearest love. My Henry died only three months ago. He was working on a house when he fell and broke his leg." She squeezed her eyes shut. "He didn't live a week."

She opened them once more, dark and large and filled with tears. "Please? I need this as much as you or more. Please, don't turn me away. I need to feel life, to know what it is to live and feel joy."

His mind flailed, one part told him to leave, and one urged him to stay. In the end, her eyes drew him back, large and dark and beautiful, and so filled with grief. He sat back down and took her hand. He needed this; he couldn't deny it. Drink hadn't been able to drown out his sorrows, perhaps the arms of a woman could.

She smiled, pulled his hand to her mouth, and kissed it. "Thank you."

They simply sat and gazed into each other's eyes for a while.

"What's your name?" he asked.

"Beth." Her eyes, tears now dried, burned with desire. Her breasts heaved, and her lips trembled as she gently squeezed and caressed his hand.

Dirge couldn't deny his hardness. He stood and pulled her to him. "Come. Let us go to my room."

His heart hammered in his chest with each stride. He hoped she couldn't feel his hand shaking in hers. Once they topped the steps, she clung to his side as they made their way down the hall. His hand hesitated at the door handle.

What if Jacob's here? Sighing, he decided he didn't care.

The room was empty. They made their way to his bed and perched on its edge. He couldn't help but twitch. It was the first time he sat in a bed with anyone that wasn't his wife. He shook his head to disperse the thought.

"Take me, please," her voice trembled as she reached up and kissed him.

He closed his eyes. Her lips were soft, oh so soft. He took hold of her arms—so smooth. He moved a hand to her head, her silken hair tangled in his fingers. It brought everything back. Love coursed through his veins and his heart was light and hot, like the noonday sun. It was as though she'd never left. Only when he opened his eyes did he remember this wasn't Lynette.

Breaking off the kiss, he pulled away. "I can't. I'm so sorry but I just can't. It's all too… too much, right now." Gently pulling her to her feet, he walked her to the door, and opened it. "Please understand. I do appreciate this, I just can't—"

The most beautiful green eyes he'd ever seen greeted him in the hallway. Dahlia's pure white robe hung on her shoulders, leaving her supple breasts, firm stomach, and silken blonde-haired womanhood completely exposed. Her lips, pink and full, held a smirk. "Going somewhere?"

"Dahlia?" Beth said, her breath quickened. "I'm sorry. I failed. Please, forgive me."

"Oh, hush. I told you he'd prove difficult. You did wonderfully just getting him here." Her hips shifting from side to side, she glided toward them.

Dirge felt dizzy, his eyes trying to take her all in. He stepped back into the room with every one Dahlia took forward. Barely aware of Beth at his side, Dahlia filled his mind, his senses. She smelled of rose petals and spice.

In one hand, Dahlia held a bottle, and in the other, she held a cup, and a small pipe. Without touching it, the door gently closed behind her. "Let us all have a seat, shall we?"

Dirge's legs bumped into his bed and he dropped onto it.

Not taking her emerald eyes off him, Dahlia set the bottle and pipe upon the bedside table. Then, with a shrug of her shoulders, she let her robe fall to the floor. "Ready these, would you darling," she purred to Beth.

Beth scampered to the table, opened the bottle with a corkscrew from her pouch, and poured wine into the cup. She then pulled out several small sticks from her pouch and set them next to the pipe before bringing the lamp closer and turning a small knob to lift the glass.

Dirge saw it all, yet none of it. He couldn't tear his gaze away from Dahlia. His eyes snapped to her lips when she pursed them. They were glued to her fingertip as she licked it. They tracked her hand as she brought her moistened finger to her breast.

He grunted.

"Let's get you out of these," Dahlia cooed.

She knelt before him, her delicate fingers going to the button of his shirt. He felt Beth tugging at it from behind, pulling it out of his pants, then over his head. Dahlia's eyes took in his muscular chest. "Very nice."

She reached over, picked up the cup, and took a sip. "Mmm, lovely."

She then brought the cup to his lips. He drank mechanically. The dark wine was strong but quite good. He swallowed it hungrily, burning his throat, and warming his stomach.

She handed the cup to Beth without taking her eyes from Dirge. "Ready the pipe, would you, my love?"

Dahlia gently picked up his right hand and placed it on her left breast. He tried to pull back, but she held it firmly in place. With her other hand, she softly ran two fingers up and down his chest.

He shuddered, his eyes fluttering.

Beth picked up one of the small sticks and lit it from the lamp. She handed the pipe and the lit stick to the green-eyed temptress. Dahlia put the pipe to her lips, touched the fire to its bowl, and drew in lightly.

"What is that?" Dirge's voice sounded coarse in his ears.

Dahlia ignored his question and handed the pipe to Beth, who took a long draw. Dirge tore his eyes off Dahlia and over to Beth. The beautiful ebony young woman—who at some point had completely disrobed—closed her eyes and drew in the smoke. Her lips stretched into a smile of sublime bliss as she slowly expelled the smoke.

His eyes snapped back to Dahlia as she took back the pipe. She touched the fire to it once more, and this time drew deep. She pulled the pipe away from her perfect pink lips and smiled. Holding the smoke, she leaned forward and kissed him. His kept his lips closed tight and tried to pull away, but she grasped his head with her left hand, holding him tight. With her right hand, she grasped and squeezed his chest.

He inhaled sharply from the shock.

Dahlia plunged her tongue into his mouth, along with the smoke. It filled him, harsh and acrid. She crushed herself to him, kissing him fiercely. Her supple breasts pressed into his chest as the smoke expanded in his lungs.

His mind raced. His heart hammered. The blood coursing through his veins made a whooshing sound in his ears. Coughing out the smoke, his skin tingled as stars danced before his closed eyes. "What was that," he croaked.

"Oh, just a little mixture of mine, opium paste mixed with a fair amount of coca leaf." Dahlia's voice rang in his ears. "Look at me, darling."

His eyes snapped open.

She knelt at his feet, an emerald-eyed goddess with hair that glowed with a golden fire. With a triumphant smile upon her succulent lips, she crawled up his body and sat on his stomach—the heat from her sex seemed to burn his skin. "What do you want?" Her voice seared into his brain.

He felt someone tugging off his boots, quickly followed by his pants and undergarments.

"You."

Beth appeared at Dahlia's side. The two of them shared a passionate kiss as Beth caressed Dahlia. "May I service you, mistress?" she hissed.

"Not yet, my pet. I want him first. He needs this more than you do. He may not admit it, but he needs this more than anything." Her smile turned wicked. "Then you may ravish me as he takes his turn at you."

His stomach twisted. His mind reeled. Seeing the two women kiss, knowing what they would do to each other…

He wanted it. He wanted it all! He would have them both and teach them who was master! He would relish the sights and sounds of the two women pleasuring one another as he dominated them! He became lost in a night of debauchery that seemed to stretch forever, one of sex, and smoke, and wine.

He didn't know when it ended. He only knew he felt more lost than ever.

Chapter 25
The Cost of Betrayal
(505 -R.C.-)

"Wake up, libertine," Jacob bellowed and kicked the bed.

Dirge's mind exploded in pain. He groaned as his head swam. His eyes cracked open. The sunlight pouring through the window scorched his mind until he thought he'd sick-up.

"What happened?" he croaked.

"You tell me." Jacob laughed. "It smells of sex and smoke in here."

Dirge rolled to the side of the bed and forced himself into a sitting position. As the night slowly came back to him, he nearly did sick-up. How could he have done that? He cracked open one eye and looked about. Only he and Jacob were in the room. "Where are they?"

"They?!" Jacob hooted. "I don't know about 'they' but I saw that dark piece of lovely come skittering out of here as I came up the stairs. Who was the other?"

"Dahlia." The word was out of his mouth before he realized it. "I didn't intend any of it. I swear. I would never covet your woman." The words sounded hollow to him.

"Mine? Dahlia?! Hardly. I was shocked when she picked me that night."

"What are you talking about?" Dirge prayed his would stop hurting soon.

"I saw her at the bazaar in front of the temple. She came out of it, carried in one of those fancy chairs with this little man walking at her side. I tell you, everyone in that square stopped to stare at her. Well, you've seen her so you understand why. I swear to you. I could actually feel when her eyes fell on me. She whispered to the little man who came to fetch me."

As Jacob spoke, the hairs on the back of Dirge's neck stood up.

"She said something along the ways of, 'I love the feel of the taverns over that of my chamber.' Did you hear me, Dirge? The woman is a Highborn."

Dirge doubled over and wretched.

"Hey!" Jacob jumped back. "At least use the chamber pot! Look, you need to get your shit together. The caravan is heading out within the hour."

"I'm not going." Dirge didn't want to go on any caravan, now or ever. He wanted to just lay back down and die.

Jacob scoffed. "Bullocks."

More memories of the previous night came rushing back to Dirge: the feel of Dahlia's body, the taste of her flesh, her moans of ecstasy, Beth calling her "mistress"... the door closing behind her without touching it.

He shook. "Dear God!"

The woman had been a priestess—a wicked minion of the enemy, and he had lain with her! How could he have done such a thing? How could he have ever wanted such a creature, let her bewitch him so easily?

Why could he not rid himself of the desire to have her again?

He staggered to his feet. "We need to leave, now!"

"Hold on. We'll be on your way soon. As I said, the caravan is leaving within the hour."

"I don't care about any damned caravan," he shouted, then grasped his head in pain.

"What's wrong?" Jacob placed his hand upon Dirge's shoulder. "You know you can trust me."

Dirge hesitated and then cursed himself for doing so. Of course he trusted his friend, he trusted him with his life.

He told Jacob his thoughts on Dahlia, and that they needed to be away before she returned. "If she in any way finds out who we are, we're dead men. I could have told her anything last night. We need to go, now."

"A priestess of Chaos?" Jacob whistled. "That would explain a lot. Okay, we'll head out now, with a quickness, and wait for the caravan to catch us up."

"I told you, I care not one wit about caravans," Dirge said as he struggled to get dressed.

"Look, we still need to work. I'll have a quick word with Trumbo, make up something about a gambling debt, the man will understand. We can leave quickly; making sure everyone sees us leaving without the caravan, then meet up with them later. It'll work, believe me."

Dirge stumbled down the steps and out the inn's door behind his friend. They hurried to the caravan lot. Dirge continued to the gate and waited while Jacob talked to Trumbo near the office. He couldn't hear what the two said, but it was heated. Afterward, Jacob strode up to Dirge, grabbed him by the arm, and pulled him along.

"Fuck him," Jacob said, loud enough for everyone to hear. "We don't need him."

They ran down the road leading to Geos—well Jacob ran. Dirge mostly staggered. The run quickly slowed to a walk once the city walls were out of sight, to which Dirge was eminently grateful. They walked for another hour before Jacob found a nice place to rest by the side of the road—a large clump of trees provided the shade and a small stream their water.

"This will be as good a place as any," Jacob said. "The caravan should be here in a couple of hours. You get some rest."

Dirge slumped to the ground under the tree and stared off into the middle distance. "I couldn't feel her."

"What?"

He stared up at Jacob. "I couldn't feel her. The priestess, I should have been able to feel her, the Chaos within her. Priests have always given me a sense of unease. But not with her, with her I felt nothing."

Well, not exactly nothing.

Jacob paused a moment. "Maybe she could hide it."

Dirge shook his head. "No, if they touched Chaos I knew it."

Jacob shrugged. "Well, you did say you lost your—whatever it was—connection, when that prophet fellow died."

"Yes, but I could feel them before that. My f—" He grimed. "Talic, he showed me how to feel them."

"But that's when you were with the Brotherhood."

Dirge's head dropped to his chest. "That's my point. I've lost it, I've lost it all. The Brotherhood, Ukase… Lynette. I've lost everything."

He looked back up at Jacob, his eyes bleak. "And now I've lain with one." His eyes went back to staring at nothing. "I've lain with a minion of the beast. I partook in acts of depravity and I'm forever soiled by it."

"Just get some sleep," Jacob said softly.

"I don't know what to do…"

Jacob knelt next to Dirge. "What would Lynette want you to do?"

The thought of his beloved made him cringe. He looked up at his one and only friend and sighed. "I'll try," he said before lying down next to the road. He doubted he'd ever sleep again.

Dirge woke to the squeaks and squeals of axles. He lifted his head off the ground to see four wagons headed their way with Trumbo at the reins of the lead wagon. Jacob stood, waiving them down.

With a grunt, Dirge rolled into a sitting position. "Time to get going."

Three days later, Dirge walked next to the lead wagon, doing his best to keep his mind on the job. It wasn't easy. Jacob sat next to the driver of the second wagon, playing and singing his heart out, every song or story bawdier than the last. Dirge didn't know why the vulgarity still got to him after the things he'd done with that green-eyed devil. Perhaps it was a steady reminder of how low he'd sunk. Whatever the reason, he needed not to dwell on it. He had a job to do, and he intended to do it to the best of his abilities.

As the sun neared the horizon, Trumbo pointed to a rock-walled clearing by the side of the road. "We'll stop here for the night. There's plenty of water at a nearby creek and the rocks will give us some shelter. Tom, Case, you two go scout out the area. I don't want to be taken while we're setting up for the night."

He pointed at Dirge. "You, I want out front twirling your sword like you do when you practice. It's damned intimidating, so if anyone is watching, I'll want them thinking twice."

The entire time the group set up camp, Dirge stood at the edge of the road going through his exercises. He did his best to center himself, to put his mind at ease. With each stroke, with every shift, with every pose, he battled with his past until it all drifted away in the perfection of the moment.

As the sun set, the drivers, a pair of guards, Jacob, and Trumbo sat about the campfire while Dirge stood watch at the head of the wagons next to another guard, a man named Clark who favored a crossbow. The last two guards stood at the back of the wagons, their backs illuminated by the light of the flames.

Dirge knew he should also search the darkness for any threats, but instead he watched Jacob, who stood playing his lute. Jacob sang a song about a green-eyed temptress who would steal men's souls. Dirge wanted to look away but forced himself to keep his eyes on his friend. If Jacob was singing it to taunt him, he wanted to show his friend it wasn't effecting him.

Once the song ended, Jacob bowed to the laughter and claps of his fellow caravan workers. "I have something new I want to try," he said, setting his lute aside.

He walked to the center of the camp and held up his empty hands. He showed them his palms, then the backs of his hands, and then with a flick of his wrists he held a pair of daggers. He flicked one dagger in the air, pulled a third from his belt, and juggled them.

"Huzzah, huzzah!" The men clapped and hooted. "Well done, young man!"

"You'll be a Traveler one of these days," Trumbo said. "I've seen many a show from one group of Travelers or another in my days, and I'm here to tell you, you're a natural."

"If you like that, you'll love my next trick." With another flourish, Jacob snatched one of the daggers out of the air and threw it.

The dagger whirled past Dirge's face... and sunk into Clark's throat. The man gurgled, dropped his crossbow, and put his hands to his neck. Dirge watched the light go out of his eyes as he crumpled.

Jacob wasn't finished. Like the first, he threw his remaining daggers: one sank into the chest of Cyril, one of the drivers, and the other into Trumbo's eye.

Jacob dashed for Dirge as bedlam erupted. He stopped, picked up the crossbow Clark had dropped, and yelled at Dirge, "Now, damn it! You know the plan!" He then dashed by him into the darkness.

Dirge, bewildered, watched Jacob disappear. He turned back to the camp at a complete loss. He had no idea what was going on. That didn't matter though as the remaining eight men charged him with whatever weapon they could find. He ducked to the side, dodging a piece of firewood a driver had hurled, and his instincts kicked in.

Thomas, one of the other guards, came at him with a sword thrust. Dirge drew his own and slashed off Thomas's hand, sending the man screaming to the ground, grasping at his stump. Dirge whirled to the left as the two remaining guards charged him, weapons in hand. He blocked the first's sword stroke and followed up with a thrust at the second's throat. With a snap, it sunk deep. He pulled his sword out of the man's throat, blood spewing. He then stepped forward and removed the first guardsman's head.

Another driver was on him by then, trying to tackle him. Dirge sidestepped and gave the man a shove, sending him tumbling into the darkness. Dirge charged the remaining four who stood in an uneasy line, only one of which was holding a proper weapon—a spear. He knocked the spear aside using a crossing strike, then dodged to his right, and with a backhanded slash, sunk his blade into the side of the man's chest.

Dirge didn't stop. His only thoughts were those of attack. He spun around, kicked the next man in line in the back, and hacked at the one next to him. His sword sliced the man in the leg, sending him screaming to the dirt. The last man simply ran. He made it to the edge of the camp when Dirge heard a thump from out in the darkness. The man tumbled away with a bolt in his chest.

With no more assailants coming, Dirge stared at the camp. "What have I done?"

"You did wonderfully, that's what." Jacob sauntered out of the darkness, smiling, with a crossbow in one hand and a dagger in the other. "Hell, I couldn't have done it without you!"

"What did you do?" Dirge implored. "Why?"

"Why?" Jacob's asked, puzzled. "Because–"

With a flick of his wrist, Jacob threw his dagger. Dirge dodged to the side and is sailed wide left… and into the chest of the man he'd kicked to the ground earlier.

"Because," Jacob continued unfazed, "this is who we are now."

He threw his hands up onto the air in dramatic fashion. "Seriously, six measly silver?"

"It was eight," Dirge mumbled.

"Whatever," Jacob said with a wave of his hands. "Point is I could make more than that in just two nights at a decent inn."

"Then why didn't you do that?!"

"Because this is more fun."

Jacob's smile floored Dirge. He slumped, his eyes taking in the carnage he'd just unleashed on people he knew, people he'd broke bread with that very night. He threw up.

"Again with the puking," Jacob quipped.

As Dirge ran the back of his hand across his mouth, Jacob knelt next to him. "Do you have any idea how much coin we just earned? I saw that lockbox of Trumbo's. There's gold enough in there to last us a month living on high in the finest establishment we could find." He then stood and flung his arms wide. "Not to mention what we'll get from the best of the ware we was hauling, and everyone's personal affects."

Dirge could hear no more. He threw his sword aside and laid down. He just wanted to die, right then and there. "I won't do it."

"You will do it. You hear me? You don't have to like it, but you'll do it." He stood over Dirge and pointed a finger at him. "You owe me that."

"What in all the hells are you talking about? I owe you nothing of the sort."

Jacob sneered. "You owe me because you killed my family. You killed my brothers, you killed my sister… you killed my *Mother*."

Dirge stared up at Jacob in disbelief, guilt roiling in his stomach. "How did you know? How long have you known?"

Jacob shook his head. "I'm not a fool, Dirge. I've known for years. All I needed to do was ask a few questions and put things together."

Jacob was right. He'd taken away Jacob's family, and he owed him a debt he could never repay in full. He felt his soul wither into a black pit.

"Come on." Jacob held out a hand. "We need to get everything together and get out of here before morning. We'll throw it all into one wagon and make for Geous as hard as possible. A fellow back in Selos told me who to go to there."

"You've been planning this the entire time?"

Jacob chuckled and cocked his head. "Of course."

Dirge woodenly helped Jacob gather everything into the secondary wagon. "The lead is Trumbo's," Jacob explained. "It's likely to be recognized. Best not take a chance."

They didn't sleep at all that night as they made their way down the road. By dawn, Jacob said, "You get some rest in back. I'll drive for a while."

Dirge lay down, yet sleep eluded him. Jacob sang a light witty tune about a fool who'd fallen and couldn't get up. Dirge knew it was about him. He'd lost himself to Chaos.

Instead of fighting it, he'd become one with the monster that engulfed the world.

When he closed his eyes, he saw the body of his mother lying in the filth of the alley, her eyes staring up at him.

"You did this to me," her voice whispered from the emptiness.

Chapter 26
A Matter of Spirit
(505 -R.C.-)

Dahlia's thoughts whirled as she strolled down the halls of the temple. Why couldn't she stop thinking about this gloriously beautiful man with the sorrowful heart? It was more than just his physical assets—which were glorious. Something about his spirit called to her. So, she sought out the only person who could help her in matters of Spirit, her mother, Celeste.

She opened the door and glided into her mother's laboratory. Carcasses, lying on a multitude of tables and slabs, produced an appalling stink. Dahlia looked at her mother sitting at a writing table at the back of the room. *How does she stand it?*

The powerful priestess raised her head, her bright green eyes shining in delight. "Ah, my darling. How are you today?"

"Glowing, Mother," Dahlia said as she took the comfy chair next to the writing table. "I've had the most marvelous time these last two nights."

"Oh, is that so," Celeste replied with a knowing grin. She shook her head slightly causing her long cascading dark hair to undulate. "Do they still live?"

"Yes, Mother." Dahlia sighed. "That's only happened a couple of times."

"It could be more. Your fiddling around with that opiate concoction of yours will lead you to trouble. Don't let it to get too strong of a hold on you."

"I have it well under control, Mother. Besides, I only ingested a little. Most goes to my subjects." She grinned. "Though it does make the sex that much more enjoyable."

Her mother shook her head. "What can I do for you?"

"Well…" Dahlia bit her lip. "It's about a man."

"Truly? What a surprise." Her mother's eyes sparkled. "I take it this is about more than sex."

"Yes," Dahlia said looking down while fondling the tri-colored braided cloth. She'd taken from him as a memento. "There's something different about him."

"Different how?" Her mother's eyebrows rose. "Are you saying you've fallen love with him?"

"No, I wouldn't say that. It's much too soon for that. No, he was just… different."

"My dear, we live in the world of our Great Lord. Different is always good."

"Yes, I know. It's just that he was very different. He was dark and sullen."

"Oh, that type is always fun." Her mother chuckled.

"But there's more. He had a rigidity to him." She sighed at her mother's guffaw. "Not like that. Well yes, he had that—and it was amazing. No, I mean his entire manner was stiff, even alien. It was almost… otherworldly."

Her mother frowned. "And what would you have of me?"

"Well, you're the best at matters of Spirit. I was hoping you'd help me find out if there was more to it."

"Is he still here?"

"No, unfortunately." Dahlia sighed. "He and his friend left in a hurry this morning. I talked to several people at the inn where he stayed. Apparently, the two of them were caravan guards. Only, they left a couple of hours before the caravan did."

"Any idea why?"

"Well, they said it had something to do with debts, but I know that's not so. They'd arrived only a few days ago. Jacob, the other young man, didn't seem the type to acquire that kind of debt that quickly. And as for Dirge, he barely set foot out of his room."

"Dirge?" Celeste said. "What a wonderful name. How do you know this?"

"From a tavern wench."

"And how would she know?"

"Well, she'd seen him the day they arrived. I've played with her in the past, so I had her try to seduce him."

"What?" her mother asked.

She told her mother about first seeing Jacob and finding him delicious. "And when we went to his room, Dirge was lying in his bed. He looked so sad, yet strong. It's hard to explain. The entire time Jacob and I played, he just lay there and watched."

"So he was a voyeur?"

"No." Dahlia shook her head. "He wasn't watching out of titillation. It was more out of… pain. I saw in his eyes, how it hurt him, but he refused to look away. It was only when I asked if he'd like to join us that he left. Apparently he'd just lost his dearest love."

"Oh, the poor dear," her mother said with a frown.

"Yes, my heart truly went out to him."

"I'm sure it did, my sweet."

Dahlia dropped her eyes, her cheeks reddening.

"What's this? You, blushing?" Her mother reached out and took her daughters hand. "You truly feel for him, don't you?"

"I suppose I do," Dahlia replied. "I had to have him, Mother. But I knew that if I approached him, he would spurn me."

Celeste's head cocked to the side, slightly. "Spurn you? My dear, you have a true talent at making people do as you wish. And you're telling me you thought he'd spurn you?"

"I did try, Mother."

Celeste's eyebrows shot up.

"I tried to compel him with the Lord's Breath, but he resisted. The best I could do was to get him to notice my eyes. Once I did that, I knew I had a chance, but it was a thin grasp. So, I had the tavern girl, Beth, try to seduce him with a story of losing her own love.

Dahlia smiled. "You should have seen me, Mother. I sat across the room and tweaked him from afar. A nudge here, a gentle pull there, and yet he still fought me, all the same, without even knowing it. It was only when she'd gotten into his room that I felt I'd won. Yet even then, he refused her. So, I had to take matters into my own hands. I honestly don't think I'd have succeeded without the concoction."

Celeste said nothing for some time. Dahlia was about to add something before her mother finally spoke up. "Do you have anything of his?"

Dahlia smiled and placed her hand upon her belly. "You mean other than his seed?"

Her mother signed. "Truly? You are barley seventeen, my dear. Do you really think you are ready to carry a child? How do you even know it will ripen?"

"The timing is right, so I'm sure to come with child. As to my age, why should that matter? You were my age when you had me."

"Yes, well, your father is quite a pathetic dear at times, especially when I tease him. I couldn't bear the look in his eyes when I told him I'd thought of removing you."

"How is Father?" Dahlia asked. She wasn't fazed about what her mother said about aborting her. She'd done the same on more than one occasion.

"Insufferable as ever. He wants me to attend another of his stuffy dinner parties."

"Has he had any luck with any of the children?"

"Please, darling. Your father may be talented at manipulating creatures, but with those pathetic children he's been an utter failure." Her mother sighed.

"Does he really think that he can give the gift of the Lord's Breath to a mundane?"

"Yes," Celeste replied. "He's utterly obsessed with the notion."

"Are you going to stay the night with him?"

"Perhaps," Celeste said with a wave of her hand. "It is fun giving him hope."

"You're such a tease, Mother."

Celeste smiled. "Watching Ruddick twitch is an irresistible joy, but I'm afraid that he's as big a fool now as the day I met him.

She shook her head. "As I was saying, are you sure you want to go through with this? The pain of giving birth is tremendous. Why do you think I've had no other children?"

Dahlia frowned but she wanted to smile. "I know Mother, but Dirge is so beautiful and strong, and not just physically. He seems to possess a will that could move mountains. Just imagine what our child would be like."

"Beauty is just a façade, my dear. Now I'm not saying it hurts," Celeste said with the smile of a woman who knew many thought her the most beautiful in a thousand miles. "But to have inner strength? That is a rare thing indeed. Especially these days."

"So you approve?" Dahlia couldn't help but feel giddy.

"Perhaps. Let us find out more about this man of yours, first. Do you have anything else of his?"

Dahlia handed her mother the braided cloth. "He had this about his neck. It had such a strong resonance that I felt I had to have it."

Her mother inspected the cord. Grasping the Lord's Breath, the very essence of the Lord of Chaos, she send it into the cord. Celeste's eyebrows quickly shot up. "I should say you felt a resonance. This was once in close contact with a grunkin. I think the person may have even been wearing it when they changed."

"But that makes no sense, Mother. Dirge certainly wasn't a grunkin."

"No, but he had a run-in with one, that's for certain. I am sensing the residue of a man as well as a woman. Neither seems particularly special…" Her mother's eyes grew wide. "This must be him. It's faint, but I feel him. Strong, powerful, and tortured, a man of conviction, a man who—"

Her eyes snapped to Dahlia, burning with an intensity she'd never seen. "Where did you say this man was last?"

"What is it Mother?"

"Where is he?!"

"I don't know, Mother. I swear."

Celeste looked back at the cord. "This man has had contact with Ukase."

"That can't be." Dahlia gasped. "The Lord of Order?"

"It's too weak a sample to be sure how much." Celeste's eyes went to her daughter's belly.

Dahlia put her hands to her tummy. "Must you, Mother? It will be truly exceptional, I just know it."

"That may be true," her mother said, her eyes forlorn. "But I will need more than this. I can send this to Geous, to the High Priest Hannibal himself. He is sure to know one who can delve something so small. But in the meantime we must know for certain while this man is still nearby." Her eyes drifted to Dahlia's stomach. "I must have something of his flesh. There is no other—"

"Beth," Dahlia shouted. "The barmaid. I allowed her to share him with me. He planted some into her as well."

"Wonderful!" Celeste clapped her hands together. "We must bring her here right away so I can open her up. If she does indeed have his seed in her, I'll not want to take the chance of it being damaged by my merely scraping it out."

Dahlia felt a bit crestfallen. She liked Beth. She was such a gracious and giving lover. Of course, simple lovers were easy to come by. This man, on the other hand, he was special.

She again put her hands to her belly. *And our child will be special as well.*

Chapter 27
A Long Memory
(Year 507 -R.C.-)

Dirge lay in a comfortable bed in the finest brothel in the westernmost city of Glennen. A lovely harlot rode his member, her dark brown eyes locked onto his. On the rare occasions he fulfilled his carnal needs, the woman had to be of dark hair and eyes, and he demanded that they always face him.

Jacob had asked him once, "Why do you always pick that type. There are a thousand different kinds of women. Why so picky?"

"I don't trust green eyes," he'd replied.

Jacob had shrugged. "Alright, I get that. But why have them face you?"

"Because if their eyes change color I want to see it."

"Oh, please. You can't honestly think that after all this time she's still looking for you?"

"I know she is."

Jacob asked with his arms held wide. "How?"

Dirge shook his head. "I just know."

That priestess was still after him. It was a truth that haunted him, always lurking in the back of his mind. He was afraid that one day the woman he was lying with would change into a stunning girl with brilliant green eyes and blonde hair. Dahlia was the personification of Chaos, and she wanted his soul. What haunted him most, though, was the part of him, deep down, that hoped she'd catch him.

Their foray into depravity two years earlier had not started out as fruitful as his friend had hoped. Jacob's contact in Geous wasn't there—the man having died several months earlier. They tried to sell the goods from the wagon but received only a tenth of what it was worth. And to make matters worse, one buyer recognized a gold painted vase as one he ordered from Kellen. Dirge had to kill two of the would-be buyer's guards in order for them to make their escape.

They still had a good deal of coin in their purses but they couldn't spend it, not in Geous anyway. It turned out that Kellen was highly respected among the merchants. Once word spread that the two of them had brought in merchandise from a caravan that never showed up, they had to flee the city.

"Nice plan," Dirge mumbled as they ran west along the road.

"How the hells was I supposed to know?" Jacob shouted back.

"Looks like we're going sleeping under a tree or hedge to-night," Dirge said. "We don't even have the cooking gear anymore." That, along with most of their other gear, had been in the wagon they'd abandoned in their escape.

Jacob huffed at his side. "Don't remind me. We'll just have to spend our nights at some village inns."

"I'll not trust any place days from here. News travels fast, and it appears that Kellen has a lot of friends."

It wasn't until they were halfway back to Selos before they could get a good night's rest in a bed in a village called Highpoint. The inn, the Reveler's Rest, was large, warm, and comfortable. A layover for many caravan teams, they knew how to treat travelers well. The ale was good, the food was wonderful, and the wenches were more than accommodating if you were willing to compensate them.

As they finished their meal of roast pheasant, the proprietor approached Jacob. "I see you have a fine lute there. Might I implore you to play a few tunes for us?"

Jacob smiled. "Yes, it is indeed a fine lute, and it cost a good deal too. That being the case, I must demand compensation. I have to make my coin back somehow after all."

The bargaining didn't last long: food and lodging for the night for them both, plus a silver piece on top. For a time, Dirge could forget as he sat and watched his friend play and sing. It was almost like being back at the Angelic.

> *"Oh, when the night is dark and full of fright*
> *There is nothin' like spendin' the night*
> *In the arms of a filly fair*
> *With great big teats and long black hair"*

Of course, Mistress Katlyn would never approve of a song with such language, but the spirit was there all the same. The crowd laughed and cheered, and sang along, if they knew the tune, which wasn't always the case.

After spending two nights at the Reveler's Rest they moved on, walking from town to town. Each night was much the same as the last with Jacob singing for a nice meal and a comfy bed with a coin or two on top. They skirted both Selos, and Danes Hook, and went straight on to Leria where they hired on as caravan guards once more.

As they waited for the caravan to move out, Dirge felt a great deal of unease. "Someone might recognize us from the war."

"How could they?" Jacob asked quietly. "Every man who saw your face at that battle died."

"The priests didn't," Dirge said, his eyes casting all about. He was sure that at any moment someone would decry him as a heretic.

Jacob scoffed. "What are the chances that one of them is hanging out in this hole? Look, you can spend the rest of the night in the room if you want. As for me? I'm going to find myself a woman to bed."

They worked as actual guards that trip, and for several more after. In time he, as well as Jacob, learned how to ride a horse. Some jobs were with fast traveling caravans, those with light but precious contents, and it required them to travel fast. That meant traveling by horseback.

Jacob didn't care too much for it, but Dirge loved the feel of a horse beneath him, how he could control it with the reins as well as his legs. It felt as natural as breathing in no time.

"You are a man born to ride," the guard leader told him on his first time.

After a while, Jacob gained contacts he could trust—people who didn't care where things came from and knew how to keep their mouths shut. Only then did they rob from within again. Every third of fourth job they took, Jacob decided it was time to plunder. And with every betrayal, with every ounce of blood Dirge spilled in those robberies, he grew darker and darker. Taking the life of an innocent hardly mattered after a while. One life or a thousand, what difference did it make? What was done was done. His only duty now was to protect and aid Jacob.

His mind returned to the present. He stared into the dark brown eyes of a woman, dreading they'd turn green. They didn't, of course. They merely stared at him lustfully as she writhed atop him, her grunts and pants filling the air. Dirge didn't make a sound as usual. He refused to enjoy it to its fullest. He simply lay there waiting to fulfill his carnal urge.

The door burst open and Jacob ran in. "She tried to kill me!"

The woman atop Dirge smiled wide and pulled a dagger from behind her back. He had no idea where it came from, not that it mattered at that moment. "Kellen sends his regards," she said and slashed down at him.

Dirge threw her off and rolled to the side, her dagger scoring his left arm. She hit the floor with a scream, jumped up and lunged at him. Dirge grabbed his sword lying next to the bed, yanked off its sheath, and took off her hand. Hand and dagger fell to the bed as the woman's scream of rage turned to one of pain. Dirge slashed one more time, taking off her head. Her head landed atop the bed next to her hand while her body fell to the floor, flopping for a bit before quieting.

He stared at the corpse. "I killed her," he mumbled.

Her dead eyes glared up at him, accusingly. He'd thought he was over this type of feeling. *One death or a thousand, what difference does it make, right? Right?!*

Jacob shook his head. "What?"

"I killed another woman."

"So!" Jacob threw up his hands. "She was going to kill you."

Dirge's head whipped to Jacob, his eyes smoldering. "Do I not deserve death?" he bellowed.

"We all deserve death! That doesn't mean I want to meet him anytime soon. Now get dressed," Jacob said as he went to the window. "Damn. It's nailed shut. Shit!" He dove to the side as a bolt smashed through the window and lodged into the ceiling.

"We won't be getting out that way," Dirge said as he calmly pulled his boots on.

"Any suggestions?"

"Grab our packs." Dirge pulled on his shirt quickly followed by his coat. "They likely have bowmen in the halls waiting for us as well."

"Why the hells would Kellen still care after all this time?"

"It would appear that he has as long a memory as he does a reach. It would also appear that he's not a true devote of Edis."

"Fuck, Chaos. I just want to live."

"If that's your decision," Dirge said. "When I give the word, I want you to open the door."

"But what about the bows? Unless you're hiding a shield, they'll pincushion you. And I need you alive if we intend to keep going."

"Then it's a good thing we got a room at the end of the hall."

He picked up the dead woman by both arms, doing his best not to think how much colder she felt then when she'd been on top of him. Walking to the door, he motioned Jacob to follow. Jacob, trying to juggle both their packs and his lute, reached out and clasped the door handle. When Dirge gave the nod, he yanked it open.

Dirge sprinted out, holding the woman's corpse in front of him. He heard the thumps of crossbows. One bolt sailed past, grazing his arm, while two more sank into the makeshift shield. He sprinted down the hall and hurled the corpse at the three bowman standing at the top of the stairs at the hall's end. The body crashed into them, sending one tumbling down the steps. Before they could reload their bows, Dirge drew his sword and slashed the other two in the throat with one swing. They gurgled and fell to the floor.

He picked up the smaller of the two by the shirt and turned to Jacob. "Let's go!"

With Jacob on his tail, Dirge marched down the steps and into the common room where three more men awaited them. Thankfully, none of them had bows. The few remaining customers gawked at Dirge—covered in blood, with a corpse in one hand and a sword in the other, the very visage of a demon spat out of hell. They ran screaming, buffeting the remaining swordsmen.

Dirge charged, bellowing at the tops of his lungs. He was quite happy to see one swordsman follow the crowd out the door. He dropped the corpse—it was more of a hindrance than a help at that point—and quickly dispatched the remaining would-be killers. Dirge and Jacob ran out on the heels of the crowd, staying low. The hunters remaining outside didn't hinder them as they made for the city gates.

264

Chapter 28

Redemption
(Year 507 -R.C.-)

Dirge shrugged the water off his cloak from the sudden, yet short, rain that had engulfed them. He left his hood up to block the glare of the now blaring sun from his eyes. His boots squelched in the mud as he trudged down the road next to Jacob—they were forced to leave their horses behind in Glennen three days prior. Since fleeing the city, they'd come across only one village, and it had been their only chance to sleep in an actual bed. The rest of the time they slept under whatever cover, they could find. With the amount of rain that had fallen, Dirge didn't look forward to having to sleep on the wet ground.

"You know, I still can't believe you did that," Jacob said.

"I don't want to talk about it," Dirge replied.

"No, seriously. What even made you think of that? Especially you, considering how squeamish you are about women." Jacob pulled his lute from its case, checking if it had gotten wet, and strummed it. He looked a proper fool that day, but he always said he liked to dress to impress.

Dirge glowered. "I said I don't want to talk about it."

"Oh, come now. I want to write a ballad about it and I need to know your mindset."

Dirge ignored him and trudged on.

After a time, Jacob piped up again, spinning his lute to his back without casing it. "Well, at least we won't have to worry about Kellen out here. This road goes straight north into the Wilds. Nothing out here but flyspeck villages for months if not further. And those are days apart. Hells, it's probably like that all the way to the Reach."

Dirge continued to ignore him, keeping his eyes on the road ahead.

"Not that there's anything there either," Jacob continued. "Can you imagine an entire region with nothing but farms and pastures—not a single city in sight? Not a place I'd like to go. Especially not with the Lands of the Dead, lurking on the other side."

Dirge eyed his friend with a sideways glance.

The Lands of the Dead. Isaac's words popped back into his head, *"...it is only there where we can awaken, Him."... "You are the heart that will see Him to their goal."... "Only He can awaken the Promised One."*

Dirge squeezed his eyes shut, trying to rid himself of that loathsome voice.

"You know," Jacob droned on, "I'll bet there are places out here that don't even know about the Cleansing yet."

"Please stop," Dirge implored. Thoughts of that day only brought on the rest. He had to shake his head once more.

"What's the matter? You got a head ache?" Jacob shrugged when he got no response. "You know what, though. I bet that the Travelers do mighty fine there. Now that would be a thing to see, an entire group of fools singing and dancing and doin' as they please. You know, I never got a chance to see any that got to Tuilar. Of course they say none of the good ones go anywhere near the cities. I wonder why that is?"

"You can ask them, yourself." Dirge pointed down the road. Coming at them was a large caravan of wagons, all brightly colored and looking like little houses on wheels, rather than the typical trader wagons.

A hundred yards away, the driver the lead wagon gave a sharp whistle and pulled to a stop. He reached behind him and pulled out a crossbow before saying something to a man on horseback. The horseman quickly rode back to the other wagons while the lead driver urged his horses on once more, keeping the bow low as though trying to hide it.

"Well I'll be. Ain't that a sight?" Jacob squinted. "They look a bit nervous. Wonder why?"

Shortly before the wagons came abreast of them, Jacob tossed back his hood, doing his best to impress, letting his hair flow in the breeze. He spread his arms wide. "Ho friend, we mean you no harm."

The man pulled his horses to a stop once more. "What can I help you gentlemen with?"

Jacob laughed and threw back his cloak, exposing bright red pantaloons and a flowered white silken shirt. He swung his lute about to the front and played. "I am Jacob the minstrel, and I mean you no harm. Merely a weary traveler on the road of life, seeking to bring a bit of entertainment to all that I can." His playing picked up its speed and he sang:

> *"Oh the road is a very weary place to be*
> *Going 'bout a world full of hostility.*
> *With death and strife both near and far*
> *Surely it's safer to stay where you are.*
> *Ah but this I must confess*
> *It's a life I dearly love best.*
> *For all the world I would dearly love to see—"*

The driver spoke up. "You can stop now. You can clearly see we are Travelers, so you are either singing to stall for time, or you're auditioning." He brought up the crossbow and laid it across his lap, pointing it their general direction. "Which is it?"

Dirge scanned the surroundings for other bowmen. He wondered if this might be some elaborate ruse by Keller. He doubted it, but one never knew.

Jacob simply laughed. "Why an audition, of course." He slung his lute back across his back and slowly approached the wagon. "I meant what I said about it being a dangerous world, and as I see it, it's better to travel with like-minded friends in some form of safety than to trek the world alone."

"You are hardly alone. Jacob, was it?" The man continued after Jacob nodded. "Who is your friend with his face still covered and lacking any kind of instrument? He hardly looks the type to bring the crowd to their feet in applause."

"Hardly," Jacob said. "This is my dear friend, Dirge."

Jacob looked back. "Come now, old friend. No need to be uncivil. Throwback your hood and show these good people we mean no harm. We've no need to hide our faces from them."

Dirge slowly lowered his hood, he didn't want to give the man any impression he might go for his blade.

"Why have you need to hide your faces?" the man asked.

"Ah, well, you see," Jacob said with flair. "My friend and I are not well liked by the people of a certain city-state on the coast. There was quite a bit of disagreement some years ago and Dirge and I were on the losing side of it. So we mostly keep them hidden out of habit."

Dirge couldn't believe his ears. *Why the hells did he just admit that?*

Jacob's eyes turned to several troupes' guards as they approached on horseback before continuing. "So I ask you, good man. Will you let me perform for your troupe, to prove that my skill is not only worthy, but would be a good addition to your group?"

The man nodded his head back to the wagon train. "You can walk with us until we reach good ground to camp upon. Once we're set, you can show us your skills."

"Wonderful," Jacob said with aplomb. "I know of a perfect place, we passed it not but an hour from here." He made to climb aboard the lead wagon but stopped short when the driver raised the crossbow.

"Ah, yes, of course. You did say 'walk' didn't you." He waved to Dirge. "Come Dirge, it would appear that you give our good troupe master a case of the jitters." He then laughed again. "Not that I blame him one bit."

Dirge wanted to smack him.

As they walked back into the wagon train, the driver gave the reins a shake and got the team moving again. Jacob patted Dirge on the shoulder. "Dirge, my friend, you must learn to smile more if you are to make more friends."

Dirge gave serious thought to doing more than smacking Jacob. He considered asking what his plan was regarding these Travelers, but decided against it. It didn't matter what Jacob's plan was. Dirge would go along with it as he always had. It did give him a moment of pause when he discovered they had eight guards. Having any was surprise enough, but eight? *What are they so afraid of? Travelers are supposed to fear nothing.*

None of the performers would let them aboard their wagons, so they had to walk alongside. Dirge didn't care one whit; in fact, he preferred it. Walking gave him a sense of purpose and allowed him to set a rhythm. It centered him in a way he couldn't quite understand.

Jacob on the other hand… The fact that their walk was only about two hours didn't matter. Jacob hated walking. He considered it beneath him. "Walking is for animals, soldiers, and fools," he'd once said. "Give me a comfy wagon seat, and I'm a happy man."

Jacob chatted with the Travelers, walking alongside each wagon for a time, and then letting them pass him up so he could do the same with the next. He gave no outward appearance of any kind of slight, but Dirge knew his friend seethed inside. Through Jacob's body language and the way he spoke to these people, Dirge knew his friend was simply placating them.

Once they reached the spot, they parked their twelve wagons in a rough circle and built up a large fire in its center. They didn't use the fire for cooking; that was done in the small ovens built in to each wagon. No, for the Travelers the fire appeared communal, a place to talk and sing and play.

One after another, different members of the troupe placed themselves in front of Jacob and Dirge and performed. Singers, either alone or as a group, sang. Jugglers twirled their batons or balls – one even used axes and swords. They had japes, minstrels, tumblers, and actors. Each one put on a show as though they were the ones auditioning.

Dirge had never seen the like. Every one of them seemed beautiful, and talented. Their very mannerism was one of joy. He understood how people fell in love with them. They basked in the glory of life. It even showed in the way they walked, each step light as though ready to dance at any moment. It was like they didn't have a care in the world.

All accept their leader. The man's name was Cord, and he was not the sort one expected to be among a group of Travelers, let alone leading them. As each member performed, Cord observed Dirge and Jacob. His eyes never wavered, seeming to see everything, as he looked them up and down.

As night fell, Cord finally spoke up. "So my friends, you have seen our wares, let us see yours."

Jacob stood and bowed to the troupe leader before stepping before the fire. The members of the troupe sitting on the other side of the fire moved to get a better view. Jacob bowed to the group, pulled out his lute and played. Shockingly, it was a song Dirge never heard before, one soft and sweet. He never knew that Jacob was capable of such tenderness.

Jacob then moved on to a ballad, one of valor, of marching forth to war and to all the wondrous things victory would bring—as well as the pain and loss that came with it. He sang songs of gallantry and courage, and songs of sorrow and lament. Dirge had never seen Jacob perform so well. He captivated the audience and made them see the world through his eyes.

Near the end, Jacob pulled out a pipe and had everyone's feet stomping and dancing. Once done, Jacob bowed to raucous applause. He sat at Dirge's side once more and accepted a large mug of ale from one of the performers.

"You did wonderfully," the young blonde lady said with a wink before slowly walking away, her hips undulating with each step.

"Where did you get a pipe?" Dirge asked quietly.

After taking a long pull, Jacob replied, "This thing? I've had it forever."

Dirge's brows furrowed, and he tilted his head slightly.

"No, I mean it," Jacob said. "I never played it at the inn because Katlyn didn't like the pipes. She said that pipes were for children. Truth is I always thought she was right since it was my mum who gave it to me and taught me to play." He then took out a tobacco-pipe and smiled at Dirge.

Dirge knew that Jacob was playing one of his games, only this time Dirge was the brunt of it. The comment about his mother was meant as a barb, a particularly sharp one.

With a frown, Dirge stood and walked to a wagon where one of their men-at-arms stood at his leisure. "May I ask you something?"

"Certainly," the man replied.

"I've always heard that Travelers have no fear of the wilds, be it from bandits or grunkin. Why the need for protection?"

The man laughed. "It is true that we are favored by Chaos, but that doesn't mean we are immune to his more wicked side. It is a dangerous world out here in the wilds. You of all people should know that," he added, pointing to Dirge's sword.

"Aye, I think I may know it more than most."

"Caravan guard?"

Dirge simply nodded.

"Name's Lem. I've done a fair share of that myself in my time." He cast his gaze about the camp before nodding toward them and adding, "They pay well, but truth be told, I'd do it for free. These are wonderful people, and I would do anything to keep them hale. You'll see. In time, you'll feel the same. It can all be a bit much at first, I know, but you'll get to love them as much as the rest of us do."

"Only if your master lets us join," Dirge said softly.

"Oh, he'll ask you. I saw the look in Cord's eye when your friend performed. He's impressed. And believe me, that's no easy feat."

"But I'm no performer," Dirge said as he regarded the people of the troupe.

"You've no problems there," Lem replied. "Cord can see it in you, as well as the rest of us guards. You are a fighter, born and bred." He then tilted his head and smiled. "And I can already see by the look in your eyes that you'd do anything to protect them too."

Dirge closed his eyes, refusing to admit such a thing. They were beautiful and talented, it was true, but beauty is only on the surface, and it could hide a great many wicked things. These people were the epitome of Chaos, and being as such, Edis loved them. How could he care for something the Lord of Chaos found so precious?

Cord was different though. He did not fit in with these people. He had a commanding presence, and the will of a giant with a sharp eye. He had none of the frivolity of the rest of the troupe. Quite the contrary, he had a severity about him. Dirge looked back at the Travelers leader and frowned. The man reminded Dirge of his father.

He shook his head. Still, after all that time, he couldn't believe that his former master had been his father. "If I see him again, I'll have words with him," he mumbled.

"Pardon?" Lem said.

"Nothing" Dirge replied. "Cord just reminds me of someone."

His eyes moved on to other members of the troupe until they landed on a pair of men sitting rather close to one another with a familiarity that put him on edge. When they leaned into each other's arms and kissed he grunted and looked away, sharply.

"What is it?" Lem asked.

"It's wrong; men showing such displays." Dirge was shocked he'd answered honestly. The last thing they needed was for him to bring attention to his... different attitudes.

Lem cocked his head to the side. "But they're in love. How can that be wrong? Love is love, my friend. No matter the form. Look at them. Can you not see the love there? Is it not a thing of beauty? Love, my friend, is a gift, to be forever cherished. No matter the form."

Dirge looked back at the two men, at the way they held each other, the way they gazed into each other's eyes. The tenderness they displayed. It was no different from the way he used to hold Lynette.

Could I have been wrong all this time?

Shaking his head, Dirge cast his gaze to the other men leaning against different wagons. Most looked to be no more than horse handlers, but one was obviously another guard.

The others were not in sight. "So you keep six out on watch through the night?"

"Aye, we cycle two every two hours. I'm about to head out myself. Care to join me?"

"It wouldn't be right," Dirge said. "Not until your master gives the word that we can join."

Lem looked at him sideways and smiled. "I wouldn't worry about that. I'm the Guard Leader, and Cord left hiring up to me. You are a man of honor, something plain for everyone to see, and it would be my honor if you'd join us."

Dirge dropped his gaze. The statement stung. *A man of honor? Not anymore.*

His eyes went back at Lem. "Give me the night to think on it."

"As you wish." He stuck out his hand for Dirge to shake. "I take my leave of you. If you change your mind, come and join me. If not, we'll talk on the morrow." After Dirge shook his hand, Lem walked through a gap in the wagons—as did the other guard across the fire—and two men came in, lying down under the wagons to sleep.

Dirge regarded his friend in front of the fire. Jacob sat on the ground, leaning against a log, deep in conversation with one of the lovelier members of the troupe. Dirge didn't know what Jacob had in mind; he just hoped it wasn't what he was thinking. Lem was right about one thing, he was taking a liking to these people, something he was sure to regret.

His attention turned to Cord when the man spoke up.

"So tell us, Jacob," Cord said around the stem of his pipe. "Where did you and Dirge meet? Was it in an army? It's more than apparent that you were a piper, as well as a common-room bard."

"Ah, very true, my good friend." Jacob said around his own pipe. He nodded toward Dirge. "Dirge and I go way back. Why I've known him my whole life. We grew up together in Tuilar, a city on the coast. Do you know it?"

"No," Cord replied. "We've never been this far south."

"Ah, the coast is wonderful, so long as you like the smell of salt and dead fish." Jacob then sat up and looked over Cord's shoulder to a small child clutching the wheel of Cord's wagon. "And who is this now?"

Cord looked back at the child standing just out of the light of the fire. The boy was staring at Jacob with his head down, his body turned slightly, and a large frown upon his face.

Why is he afraid of Jacob? Dirge wondered.

Cord spoke up and waved the child to his side. "Ah, this is my boy, Dennis. Come here boy, you've nothing to fear."

The boy didn't move.

Dennis? Dirge stared at the boy. He had more than just the same name as his departed friend and fellow Warrior, he had the same bright blond hair and blue eyes.

Dirge frowned. *Just a coincidence.*

Jacob shook his head ever so slightly. "How old is he, if you don't mind my asking?"

"He's eight," Cord replied. "He's a little small for his age, I know. He just hasn't hit his growth spurt yet."

As Dirge continued to stare at the boy, all else seemed to fall away—the fire, the wagons, the people—he saw only the child, ambling toward the fire. The boy passed his father and walked around the fire. His eyes were glued to Jacob, his brows furrowed and the frown firm, until he passed. His gaze then shifted to Dirge and his eyes grew wide. Smiling, with a tilt of his head, he trotted across the circle until he stood before Dirge. He then reached out and gently patted Dirge on the leg.

"It's all right," the boy said in a piping voice, full of reassurance. "I understand. It will be all right." The boy's eyes beamed brightly. He then yawned, rubbed his eyes, and walked back to the wagon he came from without another word.

Dirge felt a jolt the moment that boy touched him. A voice from the past flashed in his mind. *"You are the heart that will see Him to their goal... You must protect Him at all costs. For only He can awaken the Promised One."*

Dirge violently shook his head. *No! No more! Damn you, Chaos. Leave me be!*

He needed to get out of there.

"It's time for my watch," he said, and headed through the wagons.

Walking ten feet into the darkness, he then fell to his knees as faces flashed in his mind: Talic, Isaac, Dennis… Lynette. It took all his effort not to scream.

He could no long see the people about the fire, but he couldn't hold out their voices as he crouched upon the ground.

"What was that all about?" a man asked.

"I have no idea," Cord replied. "That boy is always a wonder as well you know."

"Your friend is a man of few words," a woman quipped.

"Aye, he's a quiet one all right." Jacob said with a laugh. "Why that man will go days and not say a word to anyone, not even me. But then some say that I talk enough for the two of us. And I suppose it's true."

"Perhaps you talk so much that he can never get a word in," another man said with a laugh.

Jacob laughingly replied, "Very true, my good man, very true. But then what I have to say is often far more interesting."

"So tell us, what news have you from the south?" someone asked.

"Oh, nothing other than the war," Jacob replied nonchalantly.

The troupe erupted with shouts. "War!" "We are headed into a warzone?" "We could always turn back?" "We cannot, they will still have nothing for us at the villages." "What are we to do, Cord?"

"Calm yourselves, my friends," Cord said in a raised voice. "By the look on Jacob's face he has more to say on the matter. Come now Jacob, I see your smile. Stop trying to play us and speak the rest."

"Very true, Cord, very true. I'm sorry I just couldn't help myself. My nature sometimes gets the better of me. There was a war between Tuilar and Leria a couple of years ago, but it is long over. Leria was the victor and Tuilar is now a smoldering ruin."

Dirge lived it all again: the blood, the screams, the Storm… Lynette. No matter how hard he tried to push it out, the memories enveloped him.

"Didn't you say you were from Tuilar?" a man asked.

Cord added, "And that is why you two have kept your heads down. Do you fear reprisals?"

"No, not at all," Jacob said. "You've nothing to fear. As I said, it's mostly out of habit. We did not desert our army as there was no army left to desert."

A strange statement coming from Jacob. Desertion in the Righteous Army was a hanging offense, but in a world of Chaos, the word "desertion" held no meaning. Why would he say that? Dirge wondered. He tried to think, hoping it would hold his emotions at bay.

"So why did the two cities go to war?" a woman asked.

"It was the Cleansing," Jacob replied.

As Jacob described the Cleansing, Judgment Day, and the day of their destruction, Dirge banged his head on the ground, trying to hold out the sights flooding in, but nothing could hold back that tide. Dirge lived it all over again. He cursed himself, thinking he was past all this. What did reliving the past do other than cause more pain and remind you of your failures?

Dirge heard Chaos laughing at him in Jacob's retelling.

Three days later, as the troupe made camp for the night by the side of the road, Dirge brooded. Things were not going as he'd expected. He'd thought that being around these people would drive him mad, and perhaps they had in a way, for he found them growing on him more and more. He'd seen no cracks in their beautiful veneer. They'd been pleasant, kind, and thoughtful with him; giving him space when he needed it, and solace when he'd least expected.

Could they truly be as simple as they seem? He wondered.

"There's something wrong with these people," Jacob said softly as he saddled up to Dirge.

Dirge glanced sideways at him, raising an eyebrow.

"Come now. Don't tell me you don't see it."

Dirge shook his head.

"These people are off. Have you ever seen a bunch of Travelers as tight lipped with their secrets as these? All right, I've never actually seen Travelers before, but I've heard enough about them to tell me they're up to something. Cord, especially. I got a quick look in their moneybox when he was putting away the coins they got from the villagers yesterday. It's loaded. What's a bunch of Travelers doing with that much coin?"

Dirge shrugged. "How else would they get paid?"

"You really don't know anything, do you? They get paid in food and wine. Most villages don't have a lot of coin so they pay in whatever food they can afford. That's the real reason they're not hit by raiders, not some farce about being 'favored by Chaos.'"

"Then why are we with them?"

"Because I figured it'd be a good place to lie low for a while, that and Traveler girls are supposed to be great in the sack. So I figured we'd have fun for a while."

"And now?"

Jacob smiled wickedly. "I say we take the money box and get as far away from them as we can."

Dirge frowned and dropped his gaze.

"What, you disapprove? Don't tell me you believe that tripe about Chaos cursing anyone who molests them?"

"I don't give one fuck about Chaos," Dirge growled, his eyes burning into his friend's.

"Then what—" He blinked. "Wait, you're falling for these people, aren't you?"

Dirge looked down once more. That Jacob saw it was proof enough. Dirge was falling under the Travelers spell and hated himself for it.

"Well I'll be," Jacob snorted with a shake of his head. "It don't matter. We're doing it. We hit it tonight, head back to that village to steal us some horses, and get out of here." He shuddered a moment. "I want to be as far away from these people as I can. Especially that boy."

"Dennis?"

"Yea, him. Every time that kid looks at me, it gives me the shakes. It's like he's looking into my soul," he finished with a mumble.

Cord's wife, Tasha, approached them. Wife, not partner or lover, but wife. It was yet another thing that Dirge admired about Cord. He nodded to her as she came close.

"Good afternoon, my good new friends." The woman's smile was infectious, and it never appeared false, for it even showed in her bright blue eyes. Her blonde hair shined as she cast her gaze into the sky. "It is such a wonderful day, is it not? Though something tells me it may cool off in the evening."

"Oh I'm sure we'll keep warm enough under the wagon, thanks to the blankets you so graciously gave us," Jacob said with a laugh.

"Did you not try to get a tent whilst in town?" she asked, her head tilting slightly. "I'm sure they had some in their shop. People come through there all the time from the Wilds, so they should do a great deal of trading in such things."

"Alas, it slipped my mind," Jacob replied, throwing his hands wide. "It was our first opportunity to see you all perform, and we were quite taken. What you showed us that first night was but a pittance I now see."

"Oh, you flattering devil, you." She laughed. "You performed beautifully, yourself. I'll have some of the seamstresses see if they can't come up with something for you until we reach the next town. You two do deserve some private time together, after all."

"Pardon, Mistress?" Dirge asked.

"I never would have thought it so at first," she said with a smile, "but you two do make quite a cute couple."

Dirge stared at her as she sauntered away. "Couple?"

Jacob laughed uproariously. "I told you they'd see," he said loudly.

Dirge stared daggers at his friend.

"Oh calm yourself." Jacob waved his hand. "This works in our favor. We can talk as close and quietly as we wish with no one the wiser." He then winked. "Lover."

"You dare call me that one more time…" Dirge growled.

"Oh don't get in such a snit. I told you before I only like you as a friend."

Dirge knew that Jacob loved this.

"So," Jacob continued, "I'll bed down tonight under the wagon belonging to that dulcian player—"

"Duncan," Dirge interrupted.

"His name does not matter. The only thing that does is that he parks next to Cord's." Jacob continued to lie out his plan…

As instructed, Dirge took the late-night watch post nearest to the Travelers lead wagon. The moon was waning, so he could barely make out either of the guards to his left and right as they surrounded the camp. He crouched and slowly made his way to Duncan's wagon. As he came abreast of it, Jacob rolled out from underneath.

They quietly made their way to Cord's wagon. Jacob approached, put his foot upon the bottom step, and quietly pulled his short sword from his sheath at his side.

Dirge reached out and grabbed Jacob's arm.

"What?" his friend hissed.

"No killing tonight," Dirge replied, just as quiet.

Jacob shook his head, his snarl barely visible in the low light of the moon. "Whatever happens will happen. If they awaken, they'll not just let us walk away with their gold. You know that. Now stop fucking around and keep an eye out."

Movement beyond Jacob drew Dirge's eyes. Barely illumined by the moon, Dennis stood with his arms crossed only a few feet away.

No, Lord. Please, not the child.

His thoughts surprised him. What did he care about some sniveling brat? A brat that could somehow, as Jacob put it, look into his soul—a soul beyond redemption.

Jacob spun around to see what Dirge stared at.

"What are you doing?" the boy asked. His high, piping voice sounded deafening in the quiet night.

"I should ask the same of you, little man," Jacob replied quietly. "What are you doing up at this late hour?"

"I had to pee," the boy replied matter-of-factly. "You're a bad man. You should go away."

Jacob crept close to the boy, keeping the sword low. "Now why would you say such a thing as that?"

The boy's eyes swung to Dirge, eyes that seemed all encompassing, that did not judge him, but accepted and loved him.

Dirge saw his future in those eyes and finally knew the truth: his soul was not beyond reclamation. He saw some of himself in the boy. Through the child, his soul could be cleansed, his faith, renewed. His sole mission in life crystallized—just as the Prophet said it would.

"I'm sorry," the child said somberly but assuredly. "But it has to be done."

Jacob lunged for the boy, grabbed him by the arm and yanking him closer. With his other hand, he raised his sword and started to slash at the child.

Time slowed for Dirge. Jacob's arm moved as though through honey and the air became deathly still as Dirge's father's voice flashed in his mind.

"You must fulfill the contract."

Dirge drew his sword and hacked off Jacob's hand.

Jacob screamed, raising his stump to his face.

Dirge drew back and plunged the blade into his best friend's back.

The scream became a gurgle, then a whimper. Jacob clasped at the sword protruding from his chest with his remaining hand before he slid off and landed on the ground with a grunt. He curled into a fetal position and stared up at Dirge, his eyes begging the question that he could no longer bring to his lips.

"I am sorry, my friend." Dirge said. "But it has to end. No more needless death and destruction. This world must change. Chaos must end, and this boy can bring that about."

He knelt and closed Jacob's eyes forever. "I am sorry, my friend. I will see you on the other side one day."

To be continued...

Acknowledgments:

I wish to thank everyone at the Writing at the Ledges group; Randy, Colleen, Rosalie, Lori, and well, the list goes on and on. Thank you all.

I wish to thank my many friends at the Meet up - Lansing Writers & Readers Guild for their help in the proofreading.

I wish to thank Colleen Nye for taking a chance on me, and giving me the opportunity to publish this novel.

I also wish to thank my folks, Jerry and Barb for your years of love and support.

I especially want to thank my Angel Eyes, Sarah. I couldn't have done it without you, my love.

About the author:

G. S. Scott works at a civil engineering firm in Lansing, Michigan. He enjoys writing all types of fantasy stories and poetry. He is active in local writing groups and is an avid gamer. He enjoys local theater with his playwright wife. They share their new home with her wonderful cat and their overenthusiastic dog.

Also by G.S. Scott:

Sorrow's Heart

A True Tree Chronicles Story

Keep watch for more on Dirge in…

The True Tree Chronicles:

Chaos Reigns:

The Hand of God